This book is to be returned on or before
the last date stamped below.

ATC

LEARNING FOR LIFE
LONDON BOROUGH OF SUTTON LIBRARIES

John Burnside has written five works of fiction and eleven collections of poetry, including *The Asylum Dance*, which won the 2000 Whitbread Poetry Award.

THE DEVIL'S FOOTPRINTS

Michael Gardiner has always lived in Coldhaven — as an outsider. Now living in self-imposed exile out on the point, Michael feels at one with the landscape, yet more distant from the village community. But that is about to change. When Moira Birnie decides that her abusive husband is the devil and kills herself and her two young sons, a terrible chain of events begins. Michael's infatuation with fourteen-year-old Hazel, Moira's only surviving child, leads him on a journey where he must face his present and his past. Walking in penitence, he must be reborn into the world where he was always a stranger.

JOHN BURNSIDE

THE DEVIL'S FOOTPRINTS

Complete and Unabridged

ULVERSCROFT
Leicester

First published in Great Britain in 2007 by
Jonathan Cape
The Random House Group Limited
London

First Large Print Edition
published 2008
by arrangement with
The Random House Group Limited
London

British Library CIP Data

Burnside, John, *1955 –*
    The devil's footprints: a romance.—Large print ed.—
Ulverscroft large print series: general fiction
1. Social isolation—Fiction 2. Fishing ports—Scotland
—Fiction 3. Abused wives—Fiction
4. Suicide victims—Fiction 5. Psychological fiction
6. Large type books
I. Title
823.9'14 [F]

ISBN 978–1–84782–056–3

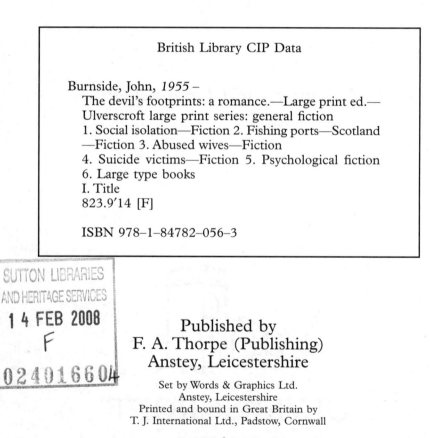

Published by
F. A. Thorpe (Publishing)
Anstey, Leicestershire

Set by Words & Graphics Ltd.
Anstey, Leicestershire
Printed and bound in Great Britain by
T. J. International Ltd., Padstow, Cornwall

This book is printed on acid-free paper

Better the devil you know
than the devil you don't.

old saying

The Devil's Footprints

Long ago, in Coldhaven, a small fishing town on the east coast of Scotland, the people woke in the darkness of a mid-December morning to find, not only that their homes were buried in one of those deep, dreamlike snowfalls that only happen once or twice in a generation, but also that something strange had happened while they slept, something they could only account for in rumours and stories that, being good, church-going folk, they were ashamed to repeat, stories that mentioned the devil, or spirits, stories that grudgingly allowed for some unseen force in the world that, most of the time, they preferred to ignore. In those days, Coldhaven was much as it is now, a confused jumble of houses and gardens and cramped boatyards running down to the sea on tight, rain-coloured streets and narrow cobbled wynds. The people of that time were ancestors of the neighbours I have lived with these past thirty-odd years: obdurate, seagoing folk with their own superstitions and terrors, their own logic, their own memories of sandbanks and tides and the treachery of water — and

1

though their children's children have all but lost that kinship with the sea, a kinship part-love, part-dread, like any other, I allow myself to imagine that I know them, if only a little and from a considerable distance. It may well be pure fantasy, as rare as that is, but I imagine I can see, in their slow-witted, clannish descendants, the ghosts of those old seafarers, men who were obliged, on too many occasions, to find their way home in thick fog or pitiless storms, women whose gaze did not stop at the horizon, but travelled out into the beyond, to the banks and troughs they only knew from maps and shipping forecasts, transforming them into seers, oracles, harpies. It must have been a terrible burden to them, a terrible and commonplace affliction, this way of looking they had evolved for a handful of critical moments, extended into a lifetime, twisting and gnarling into a rictus of foresight and premonition. I have seen that gaze in the eyes of the postmistress, a gift she cannot use, but cannot set aside. I have seen its last, fleeting traces in the eyes of schoolgirls and young wives as they go about their business, waiting for a disaster.

On that long-ago winter's morning, those who were first out of their beds, the bakers and chandlers, the women stepping out to fetch coal, the men who were not at the fishing that day but were up out of habit or restlessness, were the first to witness the phenomenon that, later, the whole town decided to call the De'il's Footprints, a name that not only stuck but was also, for reasons they never acknowledged, even to themselves, a fanciful-sounding description that, for outsiders and for their posterity, would always be shrouded in disbelief or irony. *The Devil's Footprints*: a title, like the title of a hymn, or a book borrowed from the library on a wet afternoon and dismissed later as a *queer old lot of nonsense*; a phrase only ever spoken as a quote, when it was spoken at all, as if the name they had chosen for what they had seen had been delivered to them from the wrong side of beyond, just as those marks in the snow had been, neat, inky marks laid down by some cloven-footed thing, some creature that had not only walked on two legs through the streets and wynds from one end of the town to the other, but had also ascended their walls and crossed their high, crowstepped roofs in the pursuit of an undeviating straight path through their sleeping domain. Later, they would examine the phenomenon, looking for an explanation that might allow them to return, untroubled and blessed, to their ovens and nets and kitchen sinks, and they would find that the marks began on the shore, just beyond the little graveyard at the west end of town, as if the creature had walked up out of the sea, crossed the narrow, tidewashed beach where the snow had not settled, then strode silently and purposefully up James Street, along Shore Street, across the roof of the church and then down again, hopping over the trickle of a burn that ran between Coldhaven Wester and Coldhaven Easter, along Cockburn Street and up and down the houses on Toll Wynd, before it stole away, into the fields beyond, into the interior, where nobody cared to follow. They would never know how far that line of neat black prints continued, but they could all be sure, or they could all agree later, when the snow had melted and there was no evidence to the contrary, as to the nature of the beast that had made them. Those were not human footprints, they said, neither were they the marks of any animal, of land or sea, that had ever been observed in those parts. They were sharp and cloven and dark, the prints of some sure-footed thing that had moved quickly — the impression they had of swift movement was undeniable, if entirely unproven — through their narrow seaside settlement as if in flight from, or in pursuit of, some terrible, unearthly resolution. There were those who insisted that there must be some rational explanation for this phenomenon, those who declared that everything under the sky could be explained, because only God was beyond understanding, but most of the townsfolk were content to say it was the devil who had passed by, a being they had never quite accepted as real, but had nevertheless kept in reserve for just such an occasion, like the bogeyman, or elves or, for that matter, God.

This is all hearsay, of course. I was told this story as a child; or rather, I overheard it. I caught a fragment here, a glimpse there, and I put it together piecemeal, adding details and amendments of my own, making it richer, making it bright and mythical and sure. Making it up. I imagined that line of footprints running through a narrow, snow-covered garden, or dancing across a smokehouse roof, and I followed them on, up the hill and away, past old Mrs Collings' cottage, past the broken ruins of Ceres House, past the old limeroom. I imagined a child at his bedroom window, a boy like the boy I was when we still lived on Cockburn Street, gazing at the miraculous fall of snow in the first light and making out the deep black prints in its crisp, glittering crust. I imagined the devil striding across the chimneys: not a man, as such, but a living creature nonetheless, somewhere between angel and beast, between Ariel and Caliban. I knew, in my mind, that he was no more real than Santa Claus, or the white-faced seraphim in my *Children's Illustrated Bible*, but in my heart I believed in them all. When I asked about it, the teachers at school would be embarrassed, or they would laugh it off but, on one occasion, Mrs Heinz, my class teacher in third year, took the trouble to explain it away. The story, she said, was an old myth that had been in the land long before it was Christian. Some said the devil was an old pagan god, one of the Pictish spirits who dwelt in these parts, and that it was rare to hear such stories told on the coast, because they belonged properly to the old farming communities and to the dark woods of the interior. Here, beside the water, the typical myths had to do with sea-trows and kelpies and strange beasts caught in the nets, half fish, half human. There was no harm in those old stories, she said, as long as you remembered that they were just stories. Then she lent me a book called *Myths and Legends of the Greeks and Romans*, and told me I should read it. I did, but it wasn't what I had in mind.

The Evening Herald

A year ago, almost to the day, a woman called Moira Birnie and her two sons, Malcolm, aged four, and Jimmie, three, were found dead in a burnt-out car seven miles from Coldhaven. Moira was thirty-two, and was married to a man called Tom Birnie, a local tough, with whom she shared a ground floor flat at the dank, lower end of Marshall's Wynd. A flat that I happen to know she rented from Henry Hunter, now also deceased but, in his day, a notoriously mean landlord and entrepreneur whose reputation for shady dealing went back thirty years or more to when he bought his first house, next to the chip shop on Sandhaven Road and rented it out — faulty wiring, bad ventilation and all — to a bunch of students from the fisheries college. I don't imagine Tom and Moira Birnie were paying a high rent for their accommodation, but whatever it was, it was too much. Henry Hunter was better known for his greed than his conscientiousness.

The local press reported the fire, treating it as a freak accident to begin with, but as more details emerged and the full story of what

Moira had done became clear, the national papers got involved. As it happened, I didn't read about the events leading up to the tragedy, and the gruesome details of the fire itself, until the Saturday after it happened, when Amanda was over at her mum's. I like to get all the Saturday papers and scatter them about the kitchen table, doing the crosswords, reading the odd story at random, catching up on the week's news, clipping puzzles and reviews and human interest pieces that I want to keep for later. I might have missed this particular item, had it not been for the fact that, two days before, the police had released a statement to the effect that the fire in the car had been started deliberately and they were treating the case as suspicious. By the time the nationals got hold of it, the story had become a major event, a tale of tragic, or vicious, proportions: Moira Birnie had drugged her young sons, driven them to a quiet, sandy road near a local tourist spot, and torched her car, with herself and the boys inside. Nobody seemed to know why she had done this, but the powers-that-be had no doubts about where the guilt lay. The only question in anybody's mind was: how could a woman, a *mother*, do this terrible thing? And why had she only killed the boys and not her fourteen-year-old daughter, who had been abandoned in remote farmland, alone and terrified?

I read the story between the *Scotsman* crossword and the *Guardian* review pages. Naturally I thought it ghastly, and I was intrigued by the fact that it had happened so close to home, but it took me a minute or two to realise that I knew the main protagonist, Moira Birnie; or rather, I had known her once, when she was Moira Kennedy, eighteen years old and almost pretty, with a bright, slightly nervy smile and — it seems irreverent to say it now, but it was the first thing I noticed when I met her, and it was the first thing I remembered, reading about her tragic death — legs of a kind you usually only ever see in advertisements for silk stockings. When I say I had known her, I mean I went out with her for a while, thinking, partly because of her legs but also because she was intriguing in any number of ways, that I might even be in love with her. I was at college then and she wasn't, which may have been why it ended fairly soon, but I imagine the real reason for the brevity of the affair was Tom Birnie, whom I never really knew, but remembered as a forceful and crudely handsome boy, manufactured, as our house cleaner, Mrs K would say, on one of God's off-days.

As it happens, Moira Kennedy was my first

real girlfriend. My first lover, in other words and, for a few months, it was a fairly intense affair. Even then, I think I knew that it was going to end, so it didn't surprise me when she wrote, halfway through the summer term of my first year, to say it was over. I think I may even have been relieved because, though I loved Moira's legs and her pretty smile and the excitement of the sex, I could see that we had little in common and, when the sex was over, nothing much to talk about. We had begun the affair by accident, more or less, and it had always been tainted by a secret I had kept from her, a secret that — had I been in my right mind — should have prevented me from forming any association with Moira in the first place. For the fact was that I felt guilty, and drawn in, transfixed by a kind of morbid fascination, if that's the right word for it, because, even though Moira didn't know it, even if nobody knew it but me, I was the one who had killed her brother, when I was thirteen and he was fifteen, killed him and left him to rot in the old limeroom on a weekday afternoon, when we should have been in school doing Maths or PE, in out of the cold and the rain, thinking about Christmas, or birds' eggs, or the pretty girl with black eyes and shoulder-length pigtails in 4C. That was what really drew my attention, that Saturday

10

afternoon: not Moira's unspeakable act, or the image of her dead children. It was the memory of something I had never told, something I had managed to shift to the back of my mind and leave there but still relived in my dreams from time to time: the story of a simple lie; the compelling logic of a child's fear and a surprised boy falling away into the blackness of shadows and water.

When she got home that day, Amanda was annoyed about something. She often was when she came back from her mum's, and usually it was with me — or rather, with the idea of me, the man she had intended to do a better job on, the man who so mystified her mother, a kindly woman, who had wanted to like her only daughter's husband. Amanda was, and no doubt still is, pretty, alert, sensible, hard-working, and *fun to be with*. If she were placing an ad in the lonely hearts columns, she would get plenty of offers. She liked spending time with friends, enjoyed good food and fine wines and, though she didn't read much, she kept up with current affairs and the arts. She deserved better than me. 'Do you have to make such a mess?' she said, as she came into the room. She said it so quickly, before she even had time to register the mess, that I wondered if she prepared these entrances, knowing exactly what she would find and tailoring her opening gambit accordingly.

I looked up and smiled. 'Nope.' I tore a page out of the *Telegraph* that I thought I might want to read again later. 'It's entirely voluntary.'

'It's chaos in here,' she muttered, heading for the kettle. 'God, I need a coffee!' Amanda always said she needed a coffee when she'd had a hard day at work, or some kind of run-in with her mother. It was a formula; she always used the exact same phrase; it was intended to evoke sympathy, concern, interest.

I ignored it. 'I like chaos,' I said. 'Anyway, Mrs K will be here on Monday.'

'I swear to God,' Amanda said. 'You make all this mess on purpose, to give the poor cow more to do.'

'What's wrong with that?'

'What do you mean, *what's wrong with that?* It's obvious what's wrong with it.' I enjoyed it when Amanda mimicked me. It was one of the few things that I still found charming about her.

'Mrs K cleans,' I said. 'That's what she does. She cleans.'

'She probably gets enough of that at home, don't you think? Without you giving her more to do here.'

I shook my head. Sighed. 'You don't understand her at all, do you?' I waited for a response, though I didn't expect one. Amanda was far too dignified for that level of banter. In fact, Amanda was far too dignified to be married to me, full stop. She tolerated Mrs K — just — but she didn't care about the workings of her heart, or of her mind. '*She can't* clean at home,' I said. 'There's *no point* cleaning at home. If she cleaned at home, it would just be a mess again five minutes later. Here, she gets to see a result.' I considered this for a moment. I hadn't thought about it before — though it was obvious — but now that I was thinking about it, I realised that I *did* give her more to do, I *did* go about the place making little islands of chaos for her to attend to, and I rather suspected the real reason for it all was so she could see the result of her labours. Or was it so I could see it? 'Come to think of it,' I said.

Amanda wasn't listening. Her coffee was made, and she was on the way out again, heading for the sitting room to keep up with current affairs and the arts on the telly. Work, Mum, telly. Mum, coffee, work. Telly, telly, telly. Not that I cared. I was thinking about Mrs K. I had hired her, originally, because she had married into one of the Coldhaven family clans who had made my parents' time on Cockburn Street so miserable.

Now she was miserable herself, as anybody could have predicted the day she married Alec. I suppose, back then, it gave me some kind of perverse satisfaction, having her as a cleaner — not that I had anything against her personally. She was a decent woman who had made a fatal mistake in life and was determined, according to the custom of the place, to spend the next several decades paying for it. Amanda only tolerated Mrs K, but I enjoyed seeing her about the place, making things neat and tidy, restoring order. She enjoyed her work, and I enjoyed letting her do it. Sometimes I even suspected that I enjoyed having her around, not just because she had been as ill-treated by the Kings and the Gillespies and their ilk as my parents were, but because she had the added disadvantage of being a local. She was born at the western end of Coldhaven, just where the devil is supposed to have emerged from the sea, that winter's morning, long ago; now, she lived in the house on Cockburn Street, opposite my parents' old place, surrounded by her children and the other members of the interminable King clan, a people dark and remote as beasts of the field. When I tried to imagine what her life was like, the life she lived when she wasn't clearing up after me, I

14

envisioned something like hell: big Alec sitting with his paper, licking his dry little piggy lips and muttering to himself; the dog coiled and twisted like a contortionist, licking its balls in front of the coal-effect fire; the wee ones squatting around the television set, covered in dirt and spaghetti hoops, like Japanese game show contestants.

Perhaps I was being unfair but, even if I was, I knew that Mrs K didn't really belong among the Kings. At first sight, she wasn't particularly out of the ordinary: a roundish woman of around forty with surprisingly fine skin and undecided hair. After a few weeks of seeing her at close quarters, however, I noticed something remarkable about her, which was that she was an almost carbon copy of Ingrid Bergman in her face and in her manner, except that she lacked even the smallest trace of Bergman's beauty. It really was remarkable. It wasn't always easy to see, but every now and then, turning to glance at this woman with whom I could spend whole afternoons, I would see the faded ghost of the great movie star passing across her features. It was eerie, and I couldn't get enough of it. Yet, in spite of all that, the main reason I employed Mrs K was for the gossip. She was my only link to the town, a human lifeline to the squalor and indignity of Coldhaven life.

15

I live out on the point, at Whitland. It's a lonely spot, I suppose: if you come by car, driving out along the high road, past Seahouses, skirting Sandhaven, then Cold-haven, you come to an odd configuration of telegraph poles, nothing else there but sky and the rise of the hill and, occasionally, the huge flocks of birds that gather, waving and turning in the air like a single fabric of awareness. When you get to the turn-off for Whitland — population today, 1 — there's nothing; you drive a short distance and all you can see is the cold, grey water of the firth. This is as far east as you can go and still be on the mainland; beyond here there's nothing but sheep and buzzards and, out on the point, the great colonies of sea and wading birds that my father photographed incessantly during his last years. So there are those who would say that this house is isolated — yet it's not far from Coldhaven, if you go on foot. In the house, it feels as if you are high up, especially on the top floor, but it takes only a couple of minutes to follow the little track from our side gate down to Shore Road, and then it's just a few yards to the first houses, on Toll Wynd. Still, it feels comfortably remote, in this era of the car, and it's not visible from anywhere in the town, or from the road for that matter, so it can seem as if I

16

am cut off sometimes. A solitary. A recluse.

My father chose this house. He wanted to be alone, to concentrate on his work. He had come to a point at which he had chosen to live apart; there was a saying he had, a quote from a poem he had read: 'To be separate, to be apart, is to be whole again.' He had also chosen our first house, on Cockburn Street, but he'd always wanted to be further out, away from people, closer to the birds. He loved the birds here, that was why he came; he loved them more than anything else he knew. They weren't like other life-forms to him, they were more an extension of his own mind, his own way of being in the world. He would go out every day with his binoculars and his camera bag and sit out on the rocks for hours, but he wasn't really a birdwatcher in the conventional sense; he wasn't a human being observing the gulls and cormorants and wading birds that live around this coast, he was one of them, one of their kind, in his own head, or rather, in his soul. He was always trying to get me to go with him, and I'm sorry, now, that I didn't. I was a child, and I was afraid of being seen — afraid, perhaps, of seeing myself — as a birdwatcher, for birdwatching was a hobby that was as bad, or even worse, than stamp collecting or trainspotting. It was fine to collect the cards

17

with pictures of footballers or television stars that came inside those packs of chewing gum they used to sell in the tuck shop, it was almost forgivable to collect stamps as a hobby, because you could always say that they were valuable and you were really doing it for the money, but there was no excuse for birdwatching. Not for a boy.

My father had chosen the house on Cockburn Street and then, later, he had chosen this isolated old Georgian-style villa on the point. To begin with, my mother had probably agreed with those choices, but after the first few years, when we were still living in Coldhaven, I think she would have been glad to go back to London for good. London, or maybe Paris. She had lived in Paris for years before she knew my father: Paris was where they had met, when he was on an assignment, not long before he finally gave up working for magazines and started making the austere, even stark landscape photographs for which he is now almost famous. I believe that, when they first met, he was already on that path: he had used the Paris trip to make some time for a private assignment in the west of France, where he had already begun making a series of marshland photographs, in La Brière and elsewhere, for what eventually became his first book. He met my mother at a party and, according to family folklore, it was love at first sight. My mother had come to Paris from Massachusetts in her early twenties, to study art and to live off the trust fund that her grandmother had set up for her: a young woman of independent means, she had worked hard to become, not the amateur, art-for-art's-sake painter she could easily have chosen to be, but an artisan who earned her keep, someone who could turn her hand to magazine work or commissions as well as selling her paintings at exhibition. She didn't want to be one of *those* Americans, all money and talk, sitting around in cafés discussing their fellow expatriates and moaning about how philistine people were back home. She wanted to work; she wanted to be a professional. She spoke perfect French, with only the hint of an accent, and most of her friends were French, people she knew through galleries and journals. So she must have been happy in Paris, independent, caught up in her work: a free spirit, with enough money to live as she chose. Then she met my father, and she knew from the first that he would be her husband — which is only to say, perhaps, that he fulfilled some darker, more or less subconscious function in her life, something

19

to do with history and conditioning and need. Family is a self-perpetuating mechanism, like a virus. Nobody escapes. My mother was happy living alone in Paris but, in her happiness, she was missing something that only my father could provide, a set of echoes, a theatre of shadows that she had been trained to inhabit from the day she was born. Meanwhile, my father, a natural solitary if ever there was one, had fallen in love with an idea of womanhood that he had cradled in his soul from childhood, and once the possibility of that love occurred to him, he had to make it last. In other words, theirs was a romance. Not a true story: a romance. I suppose I could say the same thing for myself, more or less. After all, I probably married Amanda for similar reasons. I must have done. I think there was even a part of me that married her because of her name, because I had never met anyone called Amanda before, and it made her special, it made her seem worthy of something. If not love, then something close to love.

So it was the house, and my isolation from Coldhaven, that had first prompted me to hire Mrs K as our cleaner, because Mrs K, like many internal exiles, was an expert in gossip and it wasn't long before she became my main source of information. What made her special is that, unlike so many in the gossip trade, she never repeated a word of a story until she was sure of her facts. Like Miss Marple in the Agatha Christie books, she waited till her knowledge was complete, then she revealed everything, in all its subtle and ironic detail. How she knew what she knew, she would never tell; but she always came through. She was the one who told me about the abused children, the beaten wives, the real reason for Janet Carruth's suicide out on Ceres farm. She was the one who knew who was having an affair with whom, who had been tricked out of money by his brother, who was being treated for depression when they were supposed to be away looking after a sick relative — and she was the one who, eventually, filled in the blanks in the case of the Birnie killings. To the best of my awareness, she knew everything there was to know about everyone in Coldhaven. Everyone except me, of course. To the best of my awareness, I was the only person of her acquaintance whose secret was still intact. Of course, she may have known all along that I was involved in the death of Moira's brother, but I cannot imagine her knowing that and still being so complicit with me, as the Birnie case unfolded. It's not that I believed she would have felt any sympathy for Malcolm Kennedy, or attached any blame to me for my actions, but surely she would have been more thrilled and, at the same time, a little more distant, if she had even suspected anything untoward had happened, twenty years before.

I almost wanted to tell her the story, just to see how she would react, but it wasn't an easy story to tell. For example, my first encounter with Malcolm Kennedy was a depressingly predictable affair. I was walking home from school, on a damp, rather wintry afternoon not long after the Easter holidays. I disliked school, just as I had expected to do, though with a good deal less of the intensity with which I had hated it to begin with. After a while, I think, most children get numbed by school — which is why it's such a good preparation for work — and they sleepwalk through it, learning tables and fragments of grammar by rote. They play games and eat and argue with people they neither like nor dislike, people who could fall down dead at any minute without causing much of a stir — then they go home to do spelling exercises and quadratic equations in little notebooks full of inconsequential comments in red ink from whoever last marked them. That was my experience of the place, anyhow. I minded going; but not enough to take any form of action. Even when Malcolm Kennedy chose me as his special friend, I never once thought of simply staying at home. School was what children did. Adults took photographs and wrote articles, they painted, they chopped up meat and caught fish, they taught mathematics and religious studies. Children went to school so that, one day, they could do the same.

I always walked to and from school alone. I didn't have a best friend, I didn't really have friends at all and, now that we had moved to Whitland, there were no neighbour children to stumble upon by chance along the way. In wet weather I enjoyed this walk, because my being alone didn't attract attention. When it was dry, however, people would study me as I passed them on the street, trying to remember who I was and giving a half-hearted little scowl, or a knowing smile, when they realised. That day it was damp and cold, but it wasn't raining, which meant I was walking faster than usual. When it rained I liked to dawdle; I liked how it felt when my school coat, my Burberry, became saturated with water; I liked the feel of the raindrops dripping off my hair and running down my face. Perhaps, if it had been raining that day, Malcolm Kennedy wouldn't have spotted me, and I would never have got to kill anyone.

He was several yards away when he called out. 'Hey,' he cried. 'I *know* you.' I realised he was talking to me almost immediately, but I tried the usual trick of looking the other way, pretending I hadn't registered. 'Hey, *you*,' he called again, louder than before, though he was, by then, almost alongside me. I looked at him. He was tall, bony-looking, a set of odd bulges inside a school uniform and, it seemed, inside his own pelt. It was as if his skeleton was too big for his skin, or maybe he had a few bones too many, an extra elbow here, a surplus shoulder-blade there, all of them vying for space. 'I know you,' he repeated. 'You're Michael Gardiner.'

This was astute of him. We had been going to the same school for six or seven years by then, and he had worked out who I was. I wanted to say as much, but I bit my tongue and nodded.

'You're in Miss Beansmeans class,' he added. Miss Beansmeans was a nickname some of the kids had given Mrs Heinz, a Scotswoman married to a German teacher from another school. I nodded again.

'What's up?' he said, grinning maliciously. 'Cat got your tongue?' *Cat got your tongue* was a favourite expression of Mr Connors, *his* class teacher. Nobody had a nickname for Mr

Connors, the man who gave the strap when somebody did wrong in a woman teacher's class. Women weren't allowed to give the strap, a rule that Miss Heinz, a former athletics champion, greatly regretted.

I didn't know what to say, so I nodded again. This was a mistake, and I realised my error immediately, but Malcolm didn't show the least sign of annoyance. In fact, his grin widened into something beyond a smile, something beyond any other facial expression I'd seen in a human being. His teeth were large and bony-looking; when he grinned, he reminded me of a chimpanzee. Finally, too late, I spoke. 'Yes,' I said.

He laughed. 'Yes?' he said.

I nodded.

'Yes, what?'

I wanted to go. He could see it in my eyes. I wanted to go running home and hide in the little room next to the landing, with my books and records and Airfix kits. When I went out for a walk with my parents, we would sometimes encounter a stray dog, a big, unkempt beast, part Alsatian, part something else, that seemed to run wild in the hinterland of dunes and fields above the point. My mother and I were afraid of this dog. When we saw it, she would take my arm, as if to protect me — and maybe that's what she thought she was doing. Naturally, my father's tactic was to ignore the thing. 'Don't be frightened,' he would say. 'Animals can smell fear. It won't do you any harm unless you provoke it.' I used to wonder how a person could just choose not to be frightened, but I never got round to asking him about it. Now, of course, I knew that I was supposed to *not be frightened* by Malcolm Kennedy — but I didn't know how. I did know, however, that there was enough animal in him to smell my fear. I looked around, hoping for the intervention of some neutral grown-up. There was nobody.

'I like you,' Malcolm said. 'You're smart.' He studied my eyes, still grinning. 'You're a real character,' he said. 'I think we're going to be *special* friends.'

Then he punched me. Not in the face, which was what I was expecting, but on the arm, a sidelong, jabbing punch that hit the bone between the elbow and the shoulder, where it hurts most. I didn't react. I could have hit him back, or run away, but life hadn't prepared me for either of the above, so I just stood there. I think I was waiting for somebody to come and save me.

Malcolm grinned. 'I'll see you later,' he said. He stood watching me for a moment, as if he expected me to reply; when I didn't say anything, his face dimmed and he hit me again: just a tap, a soft, friendly blow. 'All right,' he said. 'Catch you later, sport.' It was something from a book or a comic. Or maybe a film he'd seen on television. He was walking away, hands in his pockets, not looking back at me, and I was thinking: *you got that from a comic, you moron. You can't even think up your own lines.* It was almost funny. 'Catch you later, sport.' Who says something like that? For a moment, I almost felt sorry for him. Then I ran home quickly to the little room next to the landing, so I could make sure my Rupert books were still there, intact.

★   ★   ★

I didn't get the full version of the Birnie killings for a week or two. Mrs K went about her business, talking to people, listening, filling in odd gaps in the puzzle, piece by piece, but keeping her own counsel until she finally had it complete. When she was ready, she fixed me a cup of tea, set out a plate of Digestives and called me into the kitchen. I felt like a character from a Dorothy L. Sayers novel, but I couldn't help being pleased with the scene, as we sat at the table on what happened to be a suitably rainy afternoon, and I listened as the plump ghost of Ingrid

Bergman told me everything about my former girlfriend's life and death.

It seemed there really were three children, the boys, Malcolm and Jimmie, and an older daughter, whose name was Hazel. As the papers had reported, Hazel was fourteen. This meant she had been born out of wedlock, though people had always assumed Tom Birnie was the father, because Moira had been going with him at the time and she married him not long after. Moira had known Birnie in school, and they had stayed in touch, but the relationship had always been a wild one, and when they finally got married, much to everyone's surprise, the problems continued. 'How they stayed together, what with the drinking and the fights, was a miracle to everyone,' said Mrs K. 'And it wasn't all him. Moira could give as good as she got, when she was roused.' She sneaked a furtive little glance at me. 'But then, you'll know all about that, I imagine.'

'Sorry?'

She looked away coyly. 'Well, you used to go with her, at one time,' she said. 'Everybody knows that.'

I was surprised, though I'm not sure why. She would have done her homework, would Mrs K, and she was pretty dogged on the trail. It was one of the risks I had taken, hiring her in the first place. Though she would have found out for herself, anyhow: the story was too good to miss. 'That was a long time ago,' I said. 'Water under the bridge. Besides, when I knew Moira, she was just a kid.'

Mrs K nodded. Maybe she knew better, but that would be her secret, for now. 'She was a bonny wee thing back then,' she said. 'It always mystified me why she got tangled up with Tom Birnie and his crowd.' She looked at me wistfully. She could have been talking about herself. 'Still, we never know how things are going to turn out. The writing's there on the wall for all to see, and we go blindly on.' She took a sip of her tea. 'Anyhow, Moira wasn't quite herself for a long time before the incident.'

I wondered if it was for my sake that she steered clear of the word killings, the word they used in all the papers. It was touching to think she could imagine I still had feelings for Moira, after all that time. 'How so?' I asked.

Mrs K pursed her lips. 'She was drinking a lot,' she said, 'and she started going out and leaving the boys alone at home. Tom would come in at night and find Hazel cleaning up, making the boys' tea, instead of doing her homework. Not that he cared much about that. He loved his boys, I think, in his own way, but he treated Hazel just as bad as he did Moira. Still, he didn't want Moira skiving off all the time, sitting around drinking Southern Comfort when he needed his dinner.' She helped herself to a biscuit. 'Then, about two weeks before it all happened, Moira took it into her head that Tom was the devil. She told Maggie Croft that her husband was evil, and her sons were the devil's children. She didn't want to have anything to do with them. Maggie thought she was dead serious, and she even thought about calling the police. But she didn't.' Mrs K paused to break off a segment of biscuit, then dunked it in the tea. 'They say she tried to kill Tom, just before it happened,' she added suddenly.

'Who? Maggie Croft?'

She grinned happily. 'No, no, no,' she said, almost giggling. 'Moira. She went at him with a knife. Of course, they were both drunk at the time.' She shook her head ruefully. I knew her own husband was a drinker, but she never touched the stuff. God knows what miseries had been visited upon her by alcohol. 'That was just two days before. The rest you know, more or less. She got up that morning and for some reason Tom wasn't about. She told Hazel that she'd take her to school, then she drove her out to the edge of a field, just off the Balcormo road, and left her there. She gave the kid money and a bag of clothes, and told her to walk. Hazel tried to stay in the car, but Moira shoved her out and drove away.'

'The Balcormo road?' I said.

'That's right. Why?'

I shook my head. I knew the stretch of road she meant. That wasn't 'remote farmland', as the papers had called it, but a back road just a little way inland, five miles of nothing, a narrow, mostly straight lane that left the coast road and cut across to Balcormo before meandering away to who knows where. Nobody used it much, other than the odd farm worker hauling bales of straw or a trailer full of manure back and forth in the still of a summer's morning. It was an odd place to dump a child with nothing but a handful of banknotes and a change of clothing, but I thought I knew why Moira had chosen it. Just a hundred yards from that road, off a dirt track going nowhere, stood the limeroom, the abandoned farm building where her brother had died. 'I know that place,' I said. 'I used to play around there as a kid.'

Mrs K gave me an odd look and I wondered what she knew, or what she wondered, about Malcolm Kennedy's accident. Time, I decided, to move the conversation on. 'So she killed the others, but left Hazel by the road,' I said. 'Why do you think that was?'

Mrs K winced at the word *killed*, then gave me her Ingrid Bergman look. 'Well, I should say it was obvious,' she said grimly. 'The wee boys were Tom's children, but maybe Hazel's father was somebody else — which meant, to poor Moira, that Hazel wasn't evil like her brothers.' She shook her head sadly. 'Imagine,' she said. 'Two wee boys, just wee laddies not even in school yet. How could anybody think those wee boys were evil?'

I shook my head. 'The mind is a strange thing,' I said. What else was I going to say?

'That's true, right enough,' Mrs K said, then she stood. When the conversation strayed into *very* obvious cliché, it was time for her to wash up. It was a tacit rule we had for these gossip sessions, and I rather admired the way that she was the one to enforce it, whenever it needed enforcing. So it was something of a surprise when she came and found me later, in my little den on the landing to which I now refer, half seriously, as 'the library'. It appeared there was something she had forgotten.

'A funny thing,' she said, standing in the doorway with a tea-towel in her hand. It was approaching the time when Amanda usually got home, so she was looking slightly vexed. Amanda didn't approve of our little talks. I gave her a faint, but sufficiently encouraging smile. 'When Hazel found herself abandoned out there on the Balcormo road, she didn't do what you'd have expected her to do. Which was to walk back to Coldhaven, wouldn't you say?'

I nodded. 'That makes sense,' I said.

'Well, the strange thing is, she walked off in exactly the opposite direction,' she said. We could both hear a car coming down the drive. 'So why did she keep walking,' Mrs K added hastily, 'when she had a perfectly good home to go to?'

It was an interesting question. I had no opportunity to respond, however. By the time I opened my mouth, Mrs K had disappeared and was safely back in the kitchen before Amanda had finished parking.

★   ★   ★

In those days, I walked to town every day, no matter what the weather. I'm not sure why I always went in that direction, when all through my childhood our walks took us away from Coldhaven, out to the little inlets and skerries at the edge of the land, where the birds were. I didn't like the town that much. Down there, I always felt that I was returning to a realm of unending slumber: there was so much sleep there, huge storerooms of it, dark and heavy and dreamless. Even when the streets were busy, when people were going to and fro, out shopping, meeting one another on the streets, stopping for a chat in the post office or at the bus stop outside the old library, it always felt very still to me. Up on the point, it was perpetual movement, constant change, Heraclitean flux. Out here, the stars have always felt closer, the wind a participant in my daily life, giving me the dreams I dream, following me into the house on a blustery day like a familiar dog, snuffling around the hall for a moment or two before vanishing into the kitchen. Rain comes in suddenly and beats at the shutters; the morning light arrives like a telegram. In high summer, I will be out working in the garden and I will have to straighten up, or turn, to look for the presence I have just sensed behind me, a sense of someone coming home through the burnt August fields, someone who has been away a long time. Of course, it's nothing: a flock of starlings rising from the fringe of shelterbelt beyond the pea fields, a gull floating overhead, a gust of sea wind.

My walk never varied, by time of day or by route. I took the little path down the rise to Shore Road, then I followed Toll Wynd to Cockburn Street and down, through various little alleys, to the front. It hadn't changed much over the years and, for me, it was full of memories. I remember, I used to hang about outside the old Masonic lodge on John Street, watching the doves fly in and out through the one broken window that nobody had bothered to fix for years, whiter than it seemed possible for any living thing to be, like the white of starched linen or new-made sails from long ago. They would roost in there, up in the roof beams, and nobody bothered them much. In summer, the swallows would arrive and gather on the telephone lines all up and down the town. The trees opposite my old school were still covered in dark, blood-red fruits in autumn, up until three years ago, when the council cut them down to increase the parking area. Still, my principal memories were of my parents, and of the immense patience of Malcolm Kennedy.

Bullying takes time, and Malcolm took his time over me, I'll give him that. It must have taken so much energy just to keep track of where I was and when I would be alone, so he could spring his little traps without getting caught out. He was always very quiet-spoken, smiling, almost jovial. He would find me out and make me hand over the money I'd been given for a little snack at break-time, what they called the lief piece. He would walk up to me, hand outstretched, fingers beckoning and I would just pass the money over. This had to be done quickly, so he wouldn't get caught; all I had to do was hesitate for thirty seconds, for ten seconds, even, and he would have had to slide by, pretending he didn't even know me. But then, I didn't hesitate. As soon as I saw him I had the money ready, a tight clutch of warm, sweaty coins gathered up in my pocket. Now and then he hit me. He always hit in exactly the same place, between the shoulder and the elbow, on the bone. He was very good at this, as if he'd practised. He didn't do it every time, but he did it enough so I knew who was boss. Sometimes he would take my milk, drink the cream off the top, then hand me back the bottle; other times he would sneak up behind me while I was drinking and jostle me, so the bottle jarred against my teeth or I spilled the thick, yellowish cream down the front of my jumper. Naturally, I never said a word about any of this to anyone. Nor did I show that I was hurt or upset. I did nothing. I said nothing. Had it not been for an old woman who didn't much like me, to begin with at least, the bullying might have continued all the way through school.

I already knew who she was long before I met her. I'd known about her for years because she was one of the local characters. Her name was Mrs Collings, and why she took up with me is anybody's guess: she had no children of her own; she was lonely, up in her little cottage, half a mile up Clifford Road, between the town and the first strip of farmland; or maybe, as some of the kids in school suggested, she really was a little soft in the head. It didn't really matter, because I didn't choose her, she chose me, and it takes more skill than most children have, not to be chosen. Still, it has to be said that our first meeting was fairly inauspicious. It was deep summer and I was off by myself, as usual, wandering the hinterland behind the town. I had come armed with one of the usual instruments of childhood — an old pickle jar from my mother's larder — and I had found a big pool of rosebay willow herb in a dip between the road and the footpath that ran down to the shore. That day, I was being a scientist, a lone scholar of the natural world; when Mrs Collings found me, I was wading through the willow herb, waist deep in flowers and bees, the big pickle jar clasped in my hands, the lid just loose enough for me to lift it quickly when I found a bee at rest on a flower and snap it up. I already had twenty or more of them, a dark cloud of trapped, enraged creatures that rose and fell with every new snap of the lid, droning and throbbing against my right palm like a single crazed entity, but I wanted more — why, I had no idea — and I was still out there, fishing for bees in the heat of a July afternoon when this old woman came by. I immediately froze: I had heard stories at school, and I knew she had a reputation as a crazy person, mean-tempered and unpredictable. I didn't know, then, that she was only a few seasons away from death, or that she had just been told as much, on a visit to the surgery on Shore Street, but I couldn't imagine her wading out there into the undergrowth if she decided she didn't like the look of me, so I just kept on with what I was doing when she stopped on the path and stood stock still, glowering. Finally, she spoke. 'How would you like it,' she said, 'if somebody came along and snapped you up in a big jar?'

It wasn't a very original approach, but there was an intensity in her manner that captured my attention — enough, at least, to make me look up. She was pale, almost dead-white, yet fierce as a kestrel. I hadn't really seen her before: though I'd passed her on the shore-front a few times, I'd never really stopped to look at her. There was a vagueness about old people, an inbuilt distance, that kept them fairly remote from my child's world; I had no grandparents, and no kindly old neighbours to make a fuss of me, so I had always escaped the attentions of the elderly. That afternoon, however, even at a distance, Mrs Collings was unavoidable. What I saw was a silver-haired woman, brittle and thin as chalk, in a char-grey woollen hat and a Burberry, in spite of the heat; she was taller than I expected, and nowhere near as old, though she looked tired and weak, with that air people have when they are ill, of having to make an effort just to stay upright. It was her face, though, that held me: a face drained of colour and substance, but alight with righteous indignation, for these bees, and for all the helpless creatures of the earth. 'Well?' she said. 'Cat got your tongue?'

As it happened, the cat, or something, *had* got my tongue. I couldn't think of a word to say; or rather, I suddenly had a great deal to say but I didn't know how to say it. It had never occurred to me, before, to tell a grown-up about Malcolm Kennedy; now, faced with this fiery old woman, who sounded just like him, I wanted to let it all come tumbling out, the whole story, in all its ugly little details. But I couldn't; not then. I was afraid of her, a little; and I was fascinated, a little; but mostly I was just taken aback that she had even noticed me. 'I'm going to let them go,' I ventured, after a long pause for thought.

'Aha.' She shook her head sadly; then she gave me a tight little smile. 'And how are you going to do that?' she asked.

I stared at her. I had no idea; yet I had planned to let the bees go, because I wasn't the malicious little boy she thought I was, I was a scientist, a dispassionate observer of the natural world. What I was after was knowledge, not cruelty. But then, how *did* you release fifty or so bees from a jar? 'I don't know,' I said. I think I was hoping she would tell me.

'Well,' she replied, softening. 'Try not to get stung to death, won't you?' And without a second glance, she walked on.

       ★   ★   ★

That was the total extent of our first encounter and I imagine, from her point of view, there was nothing more to be said. For me, though, it was only a beginning. I tried, of course, to shrug the whole thing off: just some nosy old bag, who did she think she was anyway? That kind of thing. Then I proceeded to think about her all afternoon, trying to build a complete picture from the few scraps I'd heard in passing: she had once owned the florist's shop on Shore Street, but she had sold it and gone to live by herself in an old cottage up by Ceres after her husband died. Some people said she was rich and had piles of money hidden somewhere in her house; others said she was a witch. I knew this was nonsense, of course; but there was one other story that I'd overheard, and though I knew it was just as incredible, just as ridiculous, I still couldn't put it out of my head.

Everybody knew that there had been a woman in Coldhaven who had given birth to a baby with two heads. One of the heads was perfectly formed, quite beautiful, in fact; the other was a hideous mass of noses and ears, with tiny pinpricks for the eyes. The two-headed child died almost immediately, of course, but the woman never really got over it. She spent some time in hospital and by the time she was released she had turned into a kind of mental ghost, a physical presence, surely, but never altogether there, always somewhere else, away with the fairies. It's said that, a month after she was released from hospital, people saw her out and about, pushing an empty pram along the shore road, with a scarf covering her face, as if she were the one who was deformed. She was singing quietly to herself, they said, singing low and sweet in a language that sounded foreign. Several people saw her walking out like that, quite independently of one another; all agreed it was an eerie experience. Then, all of a sudden, she disappeared. Some people said that she had moved away; others said that she had drowned herself in the firth and that her body had never been found. The whole story was shrouded in mystery, a matter of hearsay and conjecture, and nobody could agree about anything other than the plain fact that this woman, dead or alive, mad or sane, had been in love with Frank Collings, and that he was the father of her baby. Whether or not this was true, the one other fact that could be stated for certain about the case, according to those who were alive at the time, is that Frank Collings, who owned the builder's yard just behind Cockburn Street, had died of a mysterious illness just three months after his lover disappeared. Not long after that, Mrs Collings, the youngish widow, had given up her florist's shop on Shore Street and sold off the yard. Now she lived in her little cottage, casting spells and counting her money, a mad old woman, with a heart of stone.

★   ★   ★

It wasn't until the Thursday afternoon that Mrs K continued to expound what was, for her, the final mystifying piece of her story. Apparently, she said, Hazel had been heading inland, on the road north of Balcormo, when a police patrol found her. This was hours after the conflagration, when Tom Birnie had come home and, finding the house empty, had called the police. The funny thing was, Mrs K said, it was as if the girl was sleepwalking and it took quite a time to get any sense out of her. They had found the burnt-out car by then, but Hazel had no idea what had happened.

'She was just walking along,' said Mrs K. 'Like someone in a dream.'

It was a striking detail, for more reasons than one. First because, as Mrs K had pointed out the previous evening, it made no sense for Hazel to be walking away from home, especially considering the circumstances in which she had just been abandoned. The second reason, however, was one that even Mrs K could not have worked out — but I could, because I had been a sleepwalker for a time, back in my early teens. Naturally, I had never done it under such bizarre circumstances and in the middle of the afternoon, but to me the fact that we were both sleepwalkers seemed highly significant, in those days when I was just beginning to go temporarily insane.

People who sleepwalk dream in the usual way, the only difference is that, while another dreamer lies in bed, the passive observer of his own inner newsreel, the sleepwalker gets up and follows it about, acting out events that he must imagine are real, following dark patterns of anxiety and longing that have already been imprinted on his mind by the business of the day. He goes out into the night and infallibly performs actions that no sleeping person should be able to perform; then he wakes up and remembers nothing. When I was twelve and thirteen, not that long settled in the Whitland house, I did some mild sleepwalking, but it was only a phase and, from what my parents told me, it seems not to have gone very far. It was exciting, for a while, to think that I might slip from my bed one night and go down to the water's edge, a sleeping boy gazing out, with his mind's eye, at the lights across the firth, seeing them just as they would have looked had his eyes been open. I've heard of people driving cars and operating machinery while sleepwalking, and I imagined myself being discovered, out in the middle of the channel, in a borrowed rowboat, under a sky full of stars, still asleep, but gazing up into infinity.

My father always made light of my sleepwalking, but that was because he thought I was afraid for myself, just as he was afraid for me. Yet I wasn't afraid. Not that I recall. I knew there was something in my mind, some corrective principle, some innate desire for a kind of dramatic tidiness, that would prevent my walking too far, or doing anything truly dangerous while I was asleep. I knew this; I was sure of it, and it was a relief, I suppose, to know that nothing terrible would happen in the night — but it was also a disappointment when my mother described how she had found me in the kitchen, filling a glass of milk almost to the brim and then drinking it, without spilling a drop, even though I was obviously unaware of what I was doing. It was a disappointment when I woke up in my own bed and there was nothing to show for my midnight rambles: no blood, nothing broken, no mysterious wisp of cotton or silk in my clenched fist. Most of all, it was a disappointment that my night wanderings weren't telling me anything I didn't already know. There was no hidden code, there was nothing to decipher or interpret. It was as if I had no secrets, and nothing to hide. Yet there must have been some connection between those episodes of somnambulism and the increasingly frequent, everyday cruelties that

Malcolm Kennedy was imposing upon me at exactly that same time, because the sleep-walking stopped for good on the night he died. I didn't even know he was dead, but I was released from something that day, when I left him out at the old limeroom and walked into town to buy myself a bag of doughnuts.

Now, listening to Mrs K describe the dream-walk that Hazel had taken that day, an idea began to form in my head. I wasn't aware of it forming, not then; only with hindsight can I say that it was at that moment, idly gossiping with my cleaner, that I began to go insane. A seed had been sown in my imagination and already it had begun to put forth tiny, probing roots. Moira's daughter was a kind of somnambulist, and I had also been a sleepwalker — which meant, did it not? that we had something in common. I hadn't begun to think in terms of blood, or I don't think I had, but everything begins before we see it beginning and, even if I wasn't conscious of the fact, I was making connections, fitting the pieces together, doing the maths. Mrs K was probably doing the same thing — and maybe I was taking my cue from her, as she talked on, watching me with her bright, sad eyes, sizing me up, contaminating me with her interest and her compassion, waiting for an appropriate reaction. Of course, I didn't react; not then. I only listened. I enjoyed Mrs K's gossip: it passed the time, it did no harm and, in an odd way, it preserved me, in my isolation, from the world she brought, one titbit at a time, to my lonely house. I had no idea that she was infecting me with a notion that, sooner or later, I would have to act upon. I should have known. I should have realised that every story is an infection, one way or another. I should have seen that, though she meant me no harm, Mrs K had her own ideas about how things should happen and, even if she didn't know it at the time, it was in her interests — or rather, it satisfied her expectations of how the world operates — that I should go insane.

★   ★   ★

Before I met Malcolm Kennedy, I thought I knew about fear. It was a phantom, out in the woods; or it lived in the old limeroom, a mummified creature wrapped in cold rags, soot-stained, raw, decaying slowly under broken strip lights. Or maybe it wasn't decaying, maybe it was returning, like Lazarus. Maybe it was changing: a man in the process of becoming a bird, or a bird that had started to become a man, hideously ugly, perhaps, but capable of inspiring pity, making its nest in the roof beams, cut off from others of its kind until the transformation was complete. I had read too many comic books, and I had seen too many films; that was why I could imagine fear in such a guise, and that was why I could flirt with it, wandering out along the old railway tracks on a summer's day, or sitting up in the limeroom, under the dark trees, watching for the phantom. That was why I was so numb, when Malcolm Kennedy chose me to be his special friend. I had wanted fear to be more beautiful, I had wanted it to be more thrilling. I could hardly bear it, that it was so ordinary.

And that it endured. Most days, it was the same routine, and I was as bored with it as I was scared and angry. Now and again, though, he came up with something new, some plan he had been nurturing for a while, just waiting for an opportunity to put it into action. Usually, it was just him, which was scary enough, but one afternoon — a Saturday, as I recall — there was another boy, someone I had seen before but didn't know by name. I had been up at the limeroom, idling away the afternoon under the trees, when the two boys appeared in my path, cutting me off from Whitland and safety. I didn't know what to do — because, of course, there was nothing I *could* do — so I kept on walking, just going about my business, hoping they would let me brazen it out. I knew the worst thing would be to run; odd as it seems, any attempt to escape would have been an admission of something — an admission of guilt, an admission that I deserved what was coming — as well as an insult to my special friend. The main thing was to show that he had the power, always, and that I accepted this as only right and proper. By continuing to walk homeward, head down, not looking at them, I imagined that things could be left open, and Malcolm Kennedy had the opportunity, if he chose, to be lenient.

'Hey! You!' It was the other boy who called me. There was no real need, he was only a few yards away, but he called out anyway, so I would have to look up at him. Or maybe it was just for the pleasure of hearing his voice ring out in the still summer air. 'Hey, kid! Where you going?'

I looked up. The other boy was a little too fat, but he was stocky with it, and he looked mean.

'You deaf?' the boy said. They were standing in front of me now, blocking my way.

'I'm going home,' I said, trying not to sound defiant, trying not to sound scared.

The boy laughed. 'Oh no you're not,' he said. 'You're not going home. Is he, Malkie?'

I looked at Malcolm Kennedy. He seemed serious, thinking about something that was his alone to think about. Finally, he spoke; but not to me. 'Shut up, Des,' he said. 'You're getting on my nerves.' He looked at me. 'Don't worry about Des,' he said. 'He's just rude. You know. Uncouth.' He smiled. 'What Des actually means is, we'd like you to come out to the loch with us. Don't you, Des?' Des didn't say anything. He was sulking. 'I said,' Malcolm Kennedy repeated, an edge of firmness in his voice, 'don't you, Des?'

Des nodded unhappily, and shot me an angry glance. 'We'd like you to come out to the loch with us,' he said, almost but not quite in a mocking singsong.

'So,' Malcolm Kennedy said, looking suddenly cheerful again. 'Are you coming? We can't stand here all day.'

'I've got to get home,' I said. 'My Dad — '

Malcolm smiled sweetly. 'You won't be late,' he said. 'We'll see you get home all right. Won't we, Des?'

Des nodded. 'Oh yes,' he said. 'We'll see you get home all right.'

⋆ ⋆ ⋆

It was fast coming on for that grey, slightly sooty time of the evening when the distance looks lighter and closer than the ground beneath your feet. We had gone down the dirt track that ran east, then north, where the Seahouses road gave out; then we had followed a sticky black footpath into the stretch of marshy land beyond, a place my father loved, for the birds he found there. At one point we had even passed within sight of our house, and I thought again about running, but I knew there was no point. Des walked on ahead, with a stick in his hand, slashing and flailing at the plants on either side of the path, while I walked silently alongside Malcolm Kennedy, my mind racing, wondering what fresh humiliation was in store. It was damp underfoot here, a little sticky, but the sky above us was clear. Finally, we had come to a sludgy area of reeds and water that some people called the loch, though it was really just wet marsh surrounded by squat birch trees and willow, a little pocket of it, within a mile or so of the seashore. 'This is the place,' Malcolm Kennedy had announced, and we'd stopped walking.

Now they were looking for nests in the wet patches at the edge of the loch, moorhens', or coots' nests that, out here, were fairly easy to find. I remembered, then, that Malcolm Kennedy had a collection of birds' eggs, a collection he was proud enough to have brought into school to show off at parents' day. I remembered seeing it: several short-bread tins full of brown and cream and blue eggs, all of them cold and empty, a little white ticket alongside each one, with the name of the bird written out in surprisingly fine calligraphy. The teachers hadn't much approved of that, but he'd said it was an old collection that his dad had given him, and that he didn't go out nesting himself, so they had let him bring it in. I imagine, looking back, that they were just trying to find some way to encourage a boy who otherwise showed no interest in anything. Of course, he did go nesting, but this wasn't the right time of year; now there wouldn't be any eggs, just empty nests and little broods of chicks, out on the water. I began to panic. I had been afraid before, but it had all turned out to be fairly ordinary, three boys taking a walk in the countryside on a Saturday afternoon, and I'd got my hopes up. Now, I realised that something bad was going to happen.

All of a sudden, Malcolm Kennedy stopped; then, looking down into the water, he raised his hand. 'Look!' he said.

I looked, but Des didn't seem interested. It

was a family of moorhens, the mother and about eight chicks, paddling around in a little pool of dark, sooty water. The mother looked alarmed, and swam between us and her brood making an odd, almost conversational piping sound that presumably signalled danger. The chicks stayed close.

Suddenly, Malcolm Kennedy exploded into movement, splashing into the water, scattering the mother and her brood and grabbing at something. At first I thought he'd seen a fish and was trying to catch it; then I realised what he was up to. Des came over and stood beside me at the edge of the water. He looked mildly interested now, recovered from his sulk. 'Come on, Malcolm,' he said. 'Come on.'

After several minutes of scrambling and splashing around, Malcolm Kennedy emerged from the water. He was holding something in his cupped hands. 'Got it,' he said. He looked at me. His face was wet, his hair was dripping water. 'You want to see it?' he asked.

Des sidled forward, trying to see the catch. Behind us, in the first grey of the twilight, the mother moorhen was calling again, bringing her chicks together, checking to see if they were all there. I assumed she would find one missing. Des moved closer.

'Not you, fucker,' Malcolm Kennedy said,

his voice ugly. '*Him.*' He held out the bony cage of fingers and knuckles, right in front of my face.

I shook my head. 'I don't want it,' I said.

'No?'

'No.'

'But I just caught it for you.'

'No.'

'Really?'

I nodded.

'Go on. It's for you.'

I shook my head. I didn't want to kill anything, and I knew that *that* was what it was coming to.

Malcolm Kennedy looked disappointed. Then, without taking his eyes off me, he opened his hands. The chick fell to the ground and started fluttering about madly, but before it could get away, he looked down, made out where it was in the summer gloaming and, silently, calmly, in no particular hurry, he crushed it underfoot.

'Bugger me,' he said. 'Now look what you made me do.'

That was enough. I knew it was over, that he'd done what he wanted to do. As he ground the chick into the mud and rushes, I turned tail and ran for it, splashing through water and mud, losing the path and finding it again, aware of nothing but the sound of my own breathing, till I reached the road and slowed to a halt, gasping for air.

There was no traffic, no noise. I crossed the road and started down the track to Whitland, noticing as I went how dirty and wet I was, all spattered with mud and marsh water. I was late, my parents would want an explanation; I didn't know what I would say. All I knew was, I couldn't tell the truth. I knew it would have hurt my father too much, though I didn't really know why.

* * *

For a week or so, I spent my idle moments running through the arithmetic. Hazel Birnie was fourteen years old, which meant that she was born some time in 1990. The year after my brief but potentially fruitful romance with Moira. Of course, there was nothing conclusive in that: for at least a part of that time, Moira had also been seeing Tom Birnie and, as Mrs K had hinted darkly, another, or possibly others. To complete my calculations, I needed to know Hazel Birnie's date of birth, and even then, I was working only in the realm of possibilities. But when I stopped and thought about it, I had to ask myself what the hell I thought I was doing. What difference did it make whether Tom Birnie, or I, or some other person was Hazel's real father? She had a father now, and that was that. I had no wish to interfere in Tom's business. I had no wish to acquire a child, either. The only thing I can say to explain those days of calculation and recalculation is that there was something compelling, something intriguing about the problem in its own right. Who *was* Hazel Birnie's father? The real answer had to be that nobody would ever know — and maybe that's why I was so preoccupied with the question. I wanted to know what I couldn't know. Nothing out of the ordinary about that. But what point could there be in knowing the knowable? I remember my father saying, once, apropos of nothing and, as far as I can remember, on the only occasion he ever spoke about things spiritual: If there were proof of God's existence, nobody would believe in him any more. I wish I could remember why he said that. I wish I knew.

I think my mother was a fully paid-up atheist. She liked things to be categorical. I imagine, when he talked that way, my father was just teasing her; usually these provocations took place during one of our rare dinner parties, when people would come from far away and stay with us for the weekend. My parents used to spend so much time alone up there, working and walking on the beach and reading, hardly talking even to each other, that when anyone came to visit they talked all the time, sitting round the table till the wee small hours, drinking and rambling on about nothing. Sometimes they let me stay up too, feeding me homeopathic quantities of wine, letting me try the cheeses or sweetmeats their guests had brought from the city, and I would sit listening, wondering what the point of it all was. When it was only family in the house, I never thought of them as lonely; as soon as guests arrived, however, it became all too apparent that they were. They had turned their back on a life they had known for years and, had I but known it, a life they had loved; then they had come to a quiet, almost empty place, not just because they wanted to work, but because they had a history of which I knew nothing. Or not till the very end, after my mother died. I wish I had known it then, known that they were lonely, that they couldn't go back, that these visits from old colleagues and friends provided the last connection to a world they had lost. Because I thought they had given it all up voluntarily. That was why, when they seemed unhappy, I judged them. They had chosen that life, after all.

Again and again, I redid the arithmetic and I could see, as she went about her business, that Mrs K was doing, or had already done the arithmetic, too. I don't know what she knew, or what she thought she knew, or to what conclusion she came. I suspect she left the case open in her mind, for lack of evidence. Sometimes I saw her watching me, a wistful look in her eyes, and I wondered whether it was because she felt sorry for me — because of the possibility that I still 'had feelings' for Moira, or that I had a daughter but could never know for sure and, even if I could, I would never have dared to spring such a terrible shock on the poor, bereaved girl, after all that had happened — or because she was judging me for my apparent coldness, or my inertia. If she had been in my position, I'm sure, she would have done something. But what was I supposed to do? What could I do with what I had to go on? Nothing. I couldn't do anything. I had no choice but to work through the sums again and see if I could come up with some conclusive proof that, whoever's daughter she might have been, Hazel Birnie was no daughter of mine: case closed.

★   ★   ★

It was Malcolm Kennedy who introduced me to Mrs Collings again, in a roundabout way.

It happened on a Wednesday, an hour after school; I know it was a Wednesday because I had been to my piano lesson. I was feeling good that afternoon, till Malcolm Kennedy caught me on the shore road, not fifty yards from home. Nobody else was around, but I could see the end of the track that ran up to Whitland, and it made me angry that he had deliberately waited till I was almost home before catching me up. Since the episode out on the marshes, he had kept his distance, just darting in every now and then, in the playground or when I was walking home, to mutter some dark warning, not hitting me, hardly stopping, but promising that something bad was coming to me, threatening to kill me, sometimes in words that were murmured so quickly and quietly that I couldn't make out what he was saying. What I could make out was the depth of his malice towards me. He was angry; he was determined to do me real harm. I knew it. He was waiting for his moment and, in the meantime, he was enjoying the simple pleasure of watching me suffer. He didn't need to hit me, he *had* me already — and he knew it.

'*You're dead, Gardiner.*'

'*I'm going to get you, Gardiner. That's not a threat. It's a promise.*'

'*What is it, Mikey? You scared?*' A big,

59

toothy smile, like the Crimson Pirate. '*You'd better be.*'

Now, he'd caught me where nobody could see us, just yards from home, and I knew the time had come for him to make good on his promises. 'Hey,' he said. '*Mikey.*' He had taken to calling me Mikey over the last few weeks.

I turned. There he was, in his school clothes, all bone and angle, a big smile on his face. I didn't say anything; there was no point.

'Well, aren't you going to say hello?' he asked.

I thought about making a run for it. There was something in his manner, an exaggerated lightness of mood that scared me. Today was going to be special. But then, if I ran, he would catch me. He was bigger, and he was always ready, always prepared. Really, he should have been a boy scout. He could see in my eyes what I was going to do before I did it; he could see, at that very moment, that I was thinking of running, and his tongue flickered between his lips in soft appraisal, as if he too were working out the odds that were going through my head. I crumpled. 'Hello,' I said.

'That's better.' He beamed. 'Now, come along with me, Mikey. There's a little experiment I want to try.'

He turned and led the way back down the rise, knowing I wouldn't try to escape. When we got to Toll Wynd, he cut in behind the first two houses and led me through a narrow, almost impassable alleyway that I didn't even know existed until that moment. It was dank and stony and smelt of pee. There were dead things in there, and tangles of old clothes amidst the broken crates and litter, all of it saturated with months of dirt and rain, but half dried out now, rank and matted underfoot; it was like walking on mouldy leaves, or mouldy flesh. Up ahead, Malcolm Kennedy gave an odd little snicker.

'Rats in here, I shouldn't wonder,' he said. 'Big fat ones.' He glanced back at me. 'Snakes, maybe,' he said. 'You like snakes, Mikey?'

I didn't answer. He turned away, snickering again, and I followed. Finally, we emerged into the smallest courtyard I had ever seen. At one time, it would have been overlooked by the first house on Toll Wynd, but the lower windows at the back of the building had been bricked up. To the rear of the house a low, sandstone outhouse stood disused, its door hanging open. Then I remembered: once, there had been a dairy here, but it had closed long ago and now only the front of the house, where the little shop had been, was still in use. The man who lived there, an ancient creature with the most astonishing goitre, restricted himself to the front room and the kitchen, both of which looked out on to the street. Here, it was just outbuildings and an old outside toilet, its green cistern crumbling on the wall, the rust stains dry now, but still dark, like freshly healed wounds. I looked at Malcolm. I just wanted it, whatever it was that he had in mind, to be over.

'Do you know where we are?' he said.

I nodded. 'It's the old dairy,' I said.

'So it is.' His face darkened. 'Take your jumper off,' he said.

'What?'

'You heard me.'

'No.'

He stepped forward and punched me in the face. I tried to back away and he grabbed me. 'Take your jumper off,' he said again, really angry now, but still quiet.

I pulled free and stood, watching him. He was calm again, confident, still in control. The tears were coming now. I was terrified. I thought he had a secret hoard of rats in there, rats or snakes, and he wanted to feed me to them. I thought he was going to do something unspeakable, something I couldn't even have imagined. I shook my head

62

desperately, and I felt my bottom lip go. It was the first time I had really cried in front of him. He'd made my eyes smart, he'd brought me to the point of tears, but I'd never actually blubbered in his presence.

'Take your jumper off,' he said again, quietly.

I kept shaking my head, trying to figure out what was happening, sobbing with fear. He could punch me all he liked, but he wasn't going to feed me to the rats. Snot was running out of my nose, the tears were streaming down my face.

He looked down, as if considering. 'All right,' he said after a moment. 'Suit yourself.'

He ran at me then and barged me to the ground. I fell hard, straight on my back, and I heard a damp, muffled sound: the thud of myself, falling. Shoulders, back, spine, lungs, ribs. He had winded me. I couldn't breathe, couldn't see, couldn't think. I just lay still, in an airless, bluish place, while Malcolm Kennedy got to his feet and leaned in over me, an invisible, breathing presence. He was immense.

I dream of him now, sometimes. Not often, and mostly as he was on that last day, treading water in the limeroom and calling out for help; sometimes, though, I see him as he looked that summer's afternoon, taller and broader and darker than he really was, an immensity, a demigod. I bestow upon this dream creature, this counterfeit, a gravity he never had in life, and then I wake to moonlight over the firth, or to the dawn birds, and I am glad to be alive; and I am glad that he is dead. That gladness is also immense, bigger than anything else I have ever experienced. It is as if the world had been waiting years to happen, waiting patiently through terror and grief and the weight of myself.

What happened next, I didn't really see or hear. I was still winded, still dizzy, coming back from the blue; only now I felt sick, and cold in my head, and I wanted to vomit.

'Hello?' It was another voice. A woman's voice. An old voice. 'Hello?' She was standing over me, looking down. Then she turned away. 'It's all right, he's just winded,' she said. 'We'll let him get his breath back.'

She came back a minute or two later, when, as she put it, the colour had returned to my cheeks. 'Are you feeling better now?'

I struggled to my feet. 'A bit,' I said. I looked at her and saw that it was Mrs Collings. For a moment, I was shocked: how had she come to be there? And who was she talking to? I couldn't see anyone else. She seemed to be alone, a thin, elderly woman in a blue coat, her face white, her mouth very red.

'Who was that boy?' she asked.

I didn't answer. I don't think she expected me to. I put my hand to my face. Something was happening, but I wasn't sure what: there was something sweet and wet in my nose, and I felt dizzy; it took me a moment to work out that I had a nosebleed. It wasn't the fall that had caused it, it was just the fear, and she knew it as well as I did. She reached into her coat pocket and pulled out a tiny, neatly folded handkerchief, embroidered at the edges with red and blue flowers.

'Here,' she said. 'Your nose is bleeding.'

I nodded. I didn't really want to take her hankie, it was so white, and so very small.

'Come on,' she said. 'I've got others.'

I took the handkerchief and pressed it to my nose.

'Put your head back,' she said.

I tipped my head back with the hankie still pressed to my nose. I could feel the blood running back into my throat and sinuses. I imagined it running into my ears.

'Stand like that a minute,' she said. 'Head back. Very still. You'll be fine in no time.'

I did as I was told. She didn't say any more then but turned around and started speaking to her unseen companion again. Still, I couldn't see anyone. I'd begun to wonder if she really was crazy after all, when I realised she was looking up, towards one of the upper floors of the building behind us. I looked up. There, leaning out, was an old woman, just a face and a pair of hands at the window, all wrinkles and wisps of flyaway grey hair. She was older than Mrs Collings, and she was tiny, like a doll, like one of those ventriloquist's dummies I'd seen on television.

'Say hello to my friend, Angela,' said Mrs Collings.

I took the handkerchief away from my face and said hello. The bleeding seemed to have slowed down, but it hadn't quite stopped.

'Well, boy,' Mrs Collings said. 'You've been introduced. Now you have to introduce yourself.'

'Michael,' I said, pressing the handkerchief back to my face.

'Beg pardon?' called Angela from above.

'He says his name is Michael,' Mrs Collings called, looking up.

'Oh.' Angela thought a moment. 'Are you from round here?' she asked, with genuine curiosity.

I shook my head. 'I live up there,' I said, pointing vaguely back towards home. 'On the point.'

'Ah,' said Angela, to Mrs Collings. 'He lives on the point.'

For some reason, Mrs Collings found this funny, and her laugh came as a surprise, much louder and deeper than I would have expected. 'So,' she said, 'you *are* from round here.'

I nodded. 'I suppose,' I said. It was all beginning to seem a little grotesque to me; all I wanted to do was to give back the handkerchief and get myself home. But then, I didn't know if Malcolm Kennedy was waiting for me, at whatever he thought was a safe distance. 'I live at Whitland,' I said, for no real reason.

Mrs Collings laughed again. 'We gathered,' she said.

'Do you live with your parents?' Angela asked.

'Of course he lives with his parents,' Mrs Collings said. 'Who else would he live with?'

'I don't know. He might live with relatives — '

'I'd better get home,' I said. 'They'll be waiting for me.'

Mrs Collings nodded. 'All right,' she said. 'But don't go out that way. Come on through the house.' She led the way to a door I hadn't noticed before; it opened on to a plain wooden staircase on one side and out, towards the front of the building, like the close in a tenement, on the other. 'Keep the handkerchief,' Mrs Collings said. 'You might need it.' She went to the foot of the staircase. 'He's going now, Angela,' she called.

There was a moment's silence; then Angela called, a little more loudly than she had when we were out of doors. 'Doesn't he want any tea?'

Mrs Collings grimaced at me. 'No,' she called. 'He's going home to his parents. Say goodbye.'

Another silence followed, then the same high, singsong voice called out. 'Goodbye Tom,' it said.

Mrs Collings shook her head despairingly. 'Never mind Angela,' she said to me. 'She's terrible with names.'

'That's all right.'

'Run along now,' she said. 'Watch out for that boy. He's a bad one, I reckon.'

I nodded; then I backed away into the front doorway and the sunshine, still holding the handkerchief. It was covered in blood.

★　★　★

The following Saturday, I climbed the rise up to Ceres cottage to return her hankie. I had told my mother about the nosebleed and about Mrs Collings, but not about Malcolm Kennedy. She had said she knew how to get the blood out, and she had washed and ironed it so that it looked as good as new, folding it as it had been when Mrs Collings gave it to me, a little square of linen, with the embroidered roses showing. Then she told me I had to return it to Mrs Collings and I had gone, my curiosity just strong enough to overcome my nervousness. It was another warm day, but the sky was overcast by the time I reached the cottage. I knocked. At first nobody answered, and I thought about giving up; then Mrs Collings appeared, her hands grimy, her hair a little untidy. She looked at me, then at the hankie.

'You brought it back,' she said. 'How considerate.'

'My mum washed it,' I said.

'So I see.' She took the hankie from my outstretched hand and studied it. 'And a very good job she did, too. Couldn't have done it better myself.' I had no answer for this, if it required an answer, so I said nothing. I wondered if it would be rude to go. Then I wondered if it would be rude not to. She put the handkerchief in her pocket; then she looked at me curiously. 'I suppose you'll want to come in for some cake,' she said. 'That's what old ladies do, isn't it? Make cakes all day, in case some hungry boy comes a-calling?'

I nodded, and she laughed. That was the beginning of our friendship, though I'm not sure that friendship is exactly the word. Which is to say, I'm not sure if she wanted to be friends with me, as such. She was always kind to me and she did, in fact, make cakes every time I came to visit. Still, I couldn't quite shake off the thought that what she was really interested in was my predicament with Malcolm Kennedy; she was old, and she was dying, and I think she wanted one last fight before she died. Not that I knew any of this at the time. At the time, I was flattered that she invited me to come again — very formally, with an odd little bow of the head — each time I went to visit. I was pleased to have someone to talk to about the things I didn't discuss with my parents and, though she didn't pursue the matter, I knew it was only a matter of time before she told me what I needed to do to escape the attentions of Malcolm Kennedy. I don't know how I knew this, but I was sure of it: she had an answer, and all that was needed was for me to show, in some way that I still couldn't guess, that I was ready to hear it.

Meanwhile, she talked about her life. She told me how she had bought the florist's shop

— it had been a bakery at one time, then a greengrocer's — more or less on a whim, because she had the money and the time to do it, and because she loved flowers. 'Even if you don't need any flowers,' she said, 'you should go into a florist's every now and then, on Valentine's Day for instance, just to see all that colour — all that crimson and damask and rose-pink.' She looked at me wistfully. 'Colour is good for the soul, boy,' she said. 'Remember that, when you're grown. Buy flowers now and again, it will do you good. Don't buy them for your girlfriend, buy them for yourself.' I winced at the idea of a girlfriend, but I managed a nod, and I remembered this, along with all the other pieces of advice she gave me. I kept them in my head and turned them over from time to time, wondering if they were true, or right. To some extent, I suppose I lived by them.

She also told me about her husband, Frank. I was a little shocked at that, because she didn't mince her words. 'Frank was an idiot,' she said, one day, when I asked her what he did. 'He inherited property, and he made money out of it, true enough. But he was an idiot, nevertheless.'

'Why was he an idiot?' I asked.

She laughed at that. 'Nature, I suppose,' she said. 'We all have our own natures. A man

71

can let himself go, or he can rein himself in, but that's as much as he can do. He can't change. The best he can do is to exercise some self-control.'

I had no idea what she was talking about, and my face betrayed as much. She laughed again, that big, almost manly laugh booming out in the front room of the little cottage. 'Never mind,' she said. 'You'll know what I mean soon enough.'

She told me about Frank and his girlfriend — that was the word she used, *girlfriend*, saying it with an odd little stress on the first syllable, so it came out sounding trivial and silly, something a grown man should have known well enough to avoid. 'Pretty girl,' she said. 'A sad waste, her getting involved with my fool of a husband. Tragic, really.'

'Was she the girl who drowned?' I asked.

She gave me a surprised look. 'Drowned?' she said. 'Where did you hear that?'

'I don't know,' I said. 'Somebody must have said it, once. Sorry.'

'Oh, don't be sorry, boy,' she said. She liked calling me boy. I liked it too. It made her sound like Miss Havisham. 'I know they all gossip about me and Frank down in the town.' She shook her head sadly. 'I have no idea why I married him. I must have thought it was a good idea at the time.' She looked at the plate where the four slices of cake she had cut earlier were now a distant memory. 'You like your cake, don't you, boy?' she said.

I nodded. 'I like *your* cake,' I answered.

She stood up. 'Flattery will get you everywhere,' she said. 'Let's see if I can find something else to fill the bottomless pit that you call a stomach.'

She never embarrassed me. It was all good-humoured, even when it came a little close to the bone. She treated me as an equal, and I always knew she didn't begrudge me the time I spent up at Ceres cottage, any more than she begrudged me the cake. It must have taken her hours, baking for me. She hardly ever touched the cakes herself, she just sat by the fire — there was always a fire, even in high summer — and drank huge quantities of tea.

'Anyway,' she said, reappearing with the freshly charged plate. 'I couldn't care less what they say, or what they used to say. Frank made a fool of himself, his girlfriend got her heart broken — for a while, anyway — and I watched him die with a certain feeling of relief.' She shot me a curious look. 'I know that probably shocks you, but that's how it was. Better the truth than a lie. He died as he had lived: an idiot. He never once saw what damage he had done, or how stupid he was.

As for me, I gave up the shop and moved up here. Been happy ever since. The only person I see now is Angela. She's totally mad, of course. Never leaves the house. I do a bit of shopping for her, go round for a cup of tea, listen to her insane fantasies. Still, she's alive and well. She's not drowned.' She scowled.

'You mean it was — ' I couldn't finish the question.

'It was.' Mrs Collings smiled grimly. 'Angela used to help me out at the shop. She loved flowers. I always preferred her to him.'

'But she — '

'What, boy? What did she do?'

I didn't know what to say, so I changed the subject. 'But why did you give up the shop?' I asked. 'When you love flowers so much.'

'I do,' she said. 'But I didn't want to have to go on talking to these people as if they were my friends and neighbours.' She poured herself another cup of tea. 'Besides, I didn't want to finish my days living over the shop, with the wireless and a tortoiseshell cat. I didn't want to sit there picking up on conversations that had finished twenty years ago. I didn't want to sit listening to the rain at the window — ' She stopped talking suddenly and sat gazing into the fire. When she spoke again, she was quiet, even quieter than usual. 'I didn't want to sit listening to the sea, hearing voices in the wind. All those lost men calling from deck to deck, as they go down in the fatal waters.' It sounded like a quote, and perhaps it was, something she had heard on the radio long ago, but it also meant something else to her. 'My father was a fisherman, and my brother. His name was Frank too. Maybe that was why I married the idiot, because he had the same name as my dead brother.'

'Your brother's dead?'

'Father and brother both,' she said. 'Lost at sea. We had some hard times, my mother, me, my sister. They're dead too, now. I'm the only one left. For now, at least.' She chuckled softly, as much to herself as anything. 'Last of the line,' she said. 'Just as well, really. There's nothing like leaving a space behind you when you go. A good, empty space for something else to fill. Wouldn't you say, boy?'

I didn't know. It struck me, then, that she was going to die. I just didn't know how soon. 'I don't know,' I said. I didn't want her to go. I didn't want her to leave a space.

She laughed. It never failed to startle me, that sudden, big laugh she had. There was no possible reason for a laugh like that to emerge from a body like hers. 'Have some more cake,' she said. 'I made it for you.'

I was pretty full by then, but I took another

slice of the rich, golden-brown fruit cake. It was delicious. Sweet, moist, just heavy enough. Rich. Fruit with just a suggestion of spices. The kind of cake that should only be eaten on a rainy day, beside a fire, in an old cottage with an old woman who isn't exactly clinging to life, but is in no mood, just yet at least, to let it go.

★　★　★

I don't know what I did to pass the test, but one day, with no particular fuss or fanfare, Mrs Collings began to talk to me about Malcolm Kennedy. By that time, she had found out who he was, who his parents were, what they did, who they were related to — all the things that matter in a small town. She didn't say much at first, she didn't really say that much at any one time, she mostly insinuated. She told me I wasn't really afraid of Malcolm Kennedy; I was afraid of myself. I was afraid of doing something final, afraid of acting. Most people are, she said. We turn our heads and look the other way, or we suffer for a while, so we don't have to do anything decisive. Because it's *doing something* — it's ourselves acting — that frightens us. And the thing to do with fear is to change it. You can't avoid it; you can't get rid of it; you can't throw it away. So you have to use it. You have to change it. If you need a weapon, it becomes a weapon. If you need a shelter, it can become a shelter — but, first, it has to be changed. That was all she taught me. Change your fear into something else. Righteous anger. Compassion. Fighting spirit. You can even make it into love, with enough work. That was Mrs Collings' lesson to me. I had to change my fear into what I needed most, and what I needed, at that particular moment, was cunning. A cunning person can become invisible, if he tries. He can become the hunter, not the hunted. If Malcolm Kennedy was tracking me all the time, I had to become invisible — and then I had to start tracking him. 'If you have an enemy,' she said, 'the first thing you have to do is get to know him. You have to know how he thinks and what he knows and, most of all, what he wants. Because what he wants is where he is weak.' Or she would say: 'It's not him you need to change, it's yourself. You have to stop caring, you have to learn to be patient. Bide your time, that's the secret. *Bide your time.*'

I'm not saying she always said as much as this, in so many words. Sometimes she told me stories, little parables of fear and cunning. She told me how the Samurai warriors would prepare for battle by deciding that they were dead already and so had nothing to lose. She told me about the Stoics, who freed themselves from mental and physical slavery by a sheer effort of logic. It wasn't so much a case of her telling me what to do, or teaching me about myself and the world around me, as an old woman telling stories to a twelve-year-old. Still, for a long time, I dismissed what she was saying. It was easy for her to talk about fear and cunning and being invisible, I thought, sitting there by the fire. But how was I supposed to become invisible? How was I supposed to become cunning? It was all just fancy talk, I told myself. It was like my father telling my mother and me not to be afraid when we met the dog on our Sunday walks. You were either afraid or you weren't, you couldn't control it. Besides, being afraid was a good idea, sometimes. Maybe most of the time. Being afraid was a pretty good preparation for the world, as far as I could see. Better, anyhow, than being stupid and just rushing into things.

And then, one day, all at once, I understood. I had been getting it wrong all that time because, to defeat Malcolm Kennedy, I had imagined I had to *be* like him, only more so. I had to be as big, then bigger, as cruel, then crueller, as strong, then stronger. Which was impossible, because I wasn't like him at all. Now, however, I saw that this was my big advantage. Now I could see that, to defeat him, I had to find the one way in which he was like me, the connection, the way in. I had to find the part of him that didn't want to be a forlorn child in a narrow seaside town, a boy among grim-faced adults whose only life was church and work, a boy who dreamed of getting away, of being elsewhere — in Tierra del Fuego, say, or crossing the Great Plains on horseback, alone in the world, under a wide sky. A boy who could be snared, from time to time, by a wisp of perfume when Miss Pryor leaned over his desk and, dizzy with a longing he didn't even begin to understand, forgets who he is supposed to be and exists only as desire. The boy he must have been, sometimes, when there was nobody to bully, a boy walking along a beach on a summer's afternoon. A boy capable of happiness; a boy capable of weakness. Of course, I couldn't have thought about it in these terms then, but I understood. I *understood*.

Mrs Collings noticed the change. 'Good,' she said. 'Now you're ready. Give yourself eleven days. Become invisible. Watch him. Find out who he is. See through him.'

I nodded. I was excited; I really did think it would work. The trouble was, I didn't stop to think about what Mrs Collings might want me to do. And maybe she didn't either. Which is a common enough problem, I suppose. It's all very well when the downtrodden and the victimised win back some kind of power, but the real trick is in knowing how to use it. Most of the time, I suspect, the easiest thing to do is just to turn it against oneself, and the only question that remains is how directly, or how indirectly, this is done. It's never really a decision, this seizing of power; it's more a sense of the inevitable, a sense of arrival. The moment arrives, and it seems possible, even necessary to act and, without really choosing to do it, we act. We do what we cannot avoid doing — as Moira did, when she escaped from the devil in Tom, taking the souls of her babies with her, and as Hazel would do, when she betrayed me, not because she wanted to, but because of a logic she couldn't see beyond, or a glamour that she couldn't quite deny, because there was nothing to put in its place, no logic, no glamour of her own.

★ ★ ★

It was about a fortnight after the Birnie killings, perhaps a little longer. Amanda and I were driving home after a party when we came upon a wreck. There were two vehicles;

80

they had come to a halt at the edge of Callie Woods, on the sharp bend just before the golf course. I had to brake hard to avoid the first car, which had spun round and blocked the whole road; it was dark blue, and it had finished up at an angle of forty-five degrees to the verge; all the doors were open and the ground on both sides was littered with junk — books and maps, picnic things, a straw hat, a scatter of cassettes. A brown crocodile-effect handbag had fallen out on to the road by the rear wheel, spilling lipstick and tampons and an identical crocodile-effect purse on to the tarmac. As far as I could see, there was nobody at the wheel. The other vehicle, a red minivan, had run off the road altogether and ended up in the ditch. Its lights were on full beam, and the engine was still running, but I couldn't see the driver. I pulled the handbrake on and turned to Amanda.

'Stay here,' I said. 'I'll go and look.'

She shook her head. For a moment, I thought she wanted to come too and I was about to speak again, to explain that there was no need for us both to go, when I realised she wanted me to stay, to pretend the wreck wasn't there and go about our business as if nothing had happened. 'It's better if we drive on,' she said, at last. 'We can go for help.'

'We can't do that,' I said. 'It's all right. I'll not be long.' I got out then, before she could say anything, and walked over to the first vehicle. Now I was out of the car, I could hear the music and was surprised I hadn't heard it before. It was quite loud. I recognised the track, it was one I particularly liked: Alanis Morissette's 'Mercy', the one with Salif Keita on it. It was an odd sensation, to think that whoever it was who had been driving the car was someone who liked the same music I did. Maybe they liked the same books, the same films. It made me hope they were all right, that they weren't badly hurt.

The car was empty and there were no keys in the ignition so I assumed that the driver was more or less unhurt and had gone for help. I began working my way around the open doors of the first car to check the van. Now that I was able to see through the lights, I could make out the driver, a youngish man, who was very obviously dead. As soon as I saw him I knew it, without a shadow of a doubt. Probably he had died on impact; it looked like his neck had broken. Already his face was grey and he resembled a tailor's mannequin, his body at odd angles with itself, his arms an afterthought. I stood looking at him for some time, curious, a little dismayed. It all looked very ordinary and, at the same time, not quite real. It wasn't vivid enough. It lacked drama — and I realised that I had never seen anything like this before, outside television or the cinema.

The girl appeared from nowhere, a sudden flare of white and red. At first I thought she was hurt, but as my eyes focused I saw that the patch of red at her throat was nothing but a polyester scarf, loosely knotted around her neck. She was dizzy, reeling; maybe she was in shock, maybe she had hit her head.

'Are you OK?' she said.

'Me?'

'Are you OK?' She stared at me. She had a wild look in her eyes, the look of blind panic you see in a hurt bird making ready for flight, even though it knows its wings are useless and in her fright I think she might have run off, or made to defend herself, if Amanda hadn't opened the car door at that precise moment and distracted her. The girl looked round then. 'Are you OK?' she asked Amanda.

'We're OK,' I said. 'We weren't involved . . . We just stopped to help you.'

The girl froze when she heard my voice, then she took a few reeling steps towards our car, her hand outstretched as if appealing to Amanda. Amanda recoiled — only a little, but it was visible, and the girl saw it. That confused her and she looked back to me.

'It's all right,' I said. I remembered something I had read, about the way accident victims become obsessed with the exercise of choice, with the idea that, by sheer will, they can make the impossible happen. An understandable reaction, of course, to the sudden fact of randomness in the world, a randomness that could touch them, and had touched them.

'Sophie,' she said. She pointed off into the woods.

'I'm sorry?'

'Sophie's gone,' she said.

I didn't understand. For a moment, I thought she meant someone called Sophie was dead, and I walked to the edge of the verge, to where I thought she had pointed, to see if there was something I had missed.

'She's gone for help?' Amanda tried to sound reassuring, even as she put the question.

'No,' the girl said. 'She's gone.' She tottered. It seemed she was about to fall; instead, she lowered her arms, let her knees give way, and sat down on the verge by the side of the road. I looked at Amanda. She was edging towards panic herself now, staring at the girl with an odd, offended look on her face.

'You should go for help,' I said. 'I'll wait here.'

She looked relieved. 'Yes,' she said. 'I'll go for help.'

She got back into the car, leaving me alone with the girl. I walked over and stood looking at her, feeling helpless.

'What's your name?' I asked her.

She looked up. Her face was ashen. 'Sophie,' she said. It occurred to me that she was the one who liked 'Mercy', and I wanted to ask her something, some question that would make a connection, make her see that we were alike, that she had nothing to fear. That we were looking after her. I wanted her to know that everything was all right, but then, that wasn't true. It's what we say for our own sakes, because we can hardly bear to witness the suffering of others.

★   ★   ★

I learned to be invisible in those eleven days when I was observing Malcolm Kennedy. Really. It was easier than I had expected, too; looking back, I can see that Malcolm Kennedy didn't know I was watching him. Why should I be following him around, watching his every move, risking another of his attacks? Why should I risk losing my supposed status of special friend and so become an outright enemy? He had no reason to suspect that the tables had been turned, because it was something that would never have occurred to him — and because he knew it was something that would never have occurred to me either. Still, I was surprised by my own patience and by my ability to stay hidden and watchful at the same time. I kept thinking of what Mrs Collings had told me. *Bide your time.* That was the secret. There was something very satisfying about that phrase. I was discovering this deep reserve of patience I never knew I had, and I was surprised at how rich it was. For eleven days, I observed him the way a field worker or a wildlife cameraman observes a dangerous animal: with all due caution, but also with a certain dispassion, without the fear or the awe, or even the pity, that had trapped me till then. For months I had wondered at the sheer single-mindedness, the sheer inventiveness of his malevolence. For months, he had been the hunter and I had been the prey. Now I became quiet, still, self-contained. I was learning him, just as Mrs Collings had told me to do. *Watch him*, she had said. *Get to know him. See how small he is. Find his weaknesses.* Finally, I was ready to act. I had my plan; I had gone over it carefully. It wasn't necessarily foolproof, but it had a surface innocence that appealed to what Mrs Collings had called my inner chess player.

It was a Friday afternoon, right after school. Most days, I now knew, Malcolm Kennedy hung around the gate after school, or he would wander home slowly, going the long way round, looking in shop windows, or standing outside the old library, killing time. It took me a few days to figure out why; then I remembered somebody saying that his mother worked late at the Spar, and I realised he couldn't go home, because he didn't have a key. He walked around in town, trying to stay warm, his hands in his pockets, his face reddening from the cold. He had his favourite stopping places: Mackie's, with its display of sheath knives and fishing gear, set right out alongside the lengths of copper tubing and dreening rods in the window; Henderson's, where they made those tiny, American-style doughnuts I liked, the ones that were all covered with sugar.

That day, though, I had a surprise for him. He hadn't seen me for so long, I think it took him aback when I suddenly appeared in his path, aware of him — *waiting* for him. Before he could speak, I walked up to him.

'You'll never guess what I saw,' I said, all breathless and propitiatory. 'It's amazing. You never get them round here, but my dad saw it, and he showed me where it was — '

'What are you talking about?' he said, annoyed. The spell wasn't working. He'd probably been about to hit me, just to shut me up and regain control of the situation, but there we were, right on Shore Street, with maybe teachers going by on their way home — and now, suddenly, I was offering him something. For the moment, at least, I had his attention.

'The icterine warbler,' I said. 'You read about it in the papers, didn't you? It's almost unknown — '

His left hand flared out, but he didn't make contact. 'Wait a minute,' he said. 'Slow down. Calm down.' He'd got that from television too. 'Where did you say you saw it?'

I grinned; naïve, trusting, hopeful. 'I'll show you,' I said.

He regarded me with natural suspicion. Why would I want to do that? But then — what harm could it do? I was no danger to him, not a little pipsqueak like me. What was I going to do, set a trap for him? It was ridiculous. I could see the wheels turning. 'All right,' he said. 'But you better be right. I got better things to do with my time than run off on any darned wild-goose chases.'

I smiled happily. I had to hand it to him, this guy watched a lot of TV. 'It's this way,' I said, with real and feigned excitement. Now that it was all set in motion, I was hardly scared at all. 'Follow me,' I said.

He was sceptical, still, but he couldn't resist the temptation. He had nothing to be frightened of. And if I was lying to him, he had a perfect excuse to really go to work on me. A risk I knew I was taking, of course. But I was excited. I was ready. I knew him, I had observed him, and I knew he was smaller in real life than I had ever imagined. So I led the way. I tricked him. I took him to the old limeroom.

The limeroom was an old stone building on the edge of a strip of farmland, just above the town. It had been abandoned for years; the roof was damaged and inside there were two long, deep pits full of black, viscous looking water. It smelt of diesel and old sacking and animals and rot, but most of all it smelt of lime. At the dark end, about thirty feet from the door, a row of galvanised iron troughs stood against the wall, full of cobwebs and dust and traces of leaf slime. I used to go there in the summer and sit around in the shade, doing nothing, just listening to the birds in the trees overhead, or the rain dripping off the boughs on to the roof. Nobody else attached any importance to the place; nobody ever went there. Even the name, the limeroom, was a private one that I had given it. I suppose other people saw it as some old farm building, but I thought it was the holy ground itself. On summer mornings, I would go out there early on my bike and watch the dawn from the half-open doorway. In that corner of the fields, the sun came up through the trees instead of over the water, and it looked completely different from the point, or the promenade. Sometimes it came up almost white and ghostly, and you had to look hard for it, through the leaves; other times, especially in early spring, it seemed to come bouncing off the horizon like a big red ball, suffusing the bare trees with wet, crimson fire.

We used to have a paper girl who rode her bike up the rise to Whitland in the morning at the end of her round. Ann Greer. She was two years older than me, and she was very pretty, with long silvery, almost platinum hair that she wore in a plait, most days — but sometimes she let it fall loose, a wild shock of it swirling around her face and her shoulders and down to the middle of her back. She was the belle of the school. Male teachers would freeze a little in her presence, trying to seem nonchalant, avoiding eye contact; the women thought she was wonderful too, because she was bright, courteous and smarter than the boys in her class. Her family wasn't well off, but she always looked good; even if her clothes were hand-me-downs, she had a certain natural elegance that could carry off anything. At the same time, she was modest, even a little quiet. Because she was two years ahead of me, I didn't really think about her that much, though I would always be glad to see her when she passed me in the corridor, or at the gate on the way home. Still, I didn't really fall in love with her till the night of the school play, when I was allowed to say a single, unmemorable line in exchange for a spell of hard labour backstage.

The play was *Macbeth*. Ann Greer was probably too pretty for Lady Macbeth, but she was the obvious choice, at least in the mind of the English teacher, Mr Connors, who also directed the school drama society. As far as Mr Connors was concerned, Ann Greer could have played Anna Karenina, Queen Christina and Hedda Gabler all on the same night. In his English class, she had been called upon to read a speech from

Romeo and Juliet and she had done it so well, acting, but keeping it all within the bounds of the classroom, that he had decided immediately that she was going to be a star. Me, he was less sure about, but I wanted to be in the play so badly that he let me walk on, towards the end, and say the immortal line: 'The Queen, my Lord, is dead' — thus launching Matthew Campbell, a nervous wreck, but a true thespian, into the *She should have died hereafter* speech. It wasn't much, but I got to tread the boards — not bad for a third-year.

As good as Matthew was, however, there was only one real performance on the night. I think grown men in the audience were close to tears when Ann Greer wandered across the stage, her hands wet with imaginary blood, her face pale as a sea mist, her eyes just a little too dark and her mouth just a little too red. After that scene, the play was over. It was like when you go to see a film and the actor you love most dies halfway through; you just sit there politely waiting till the end and thinking back over the handful of great moments you have just witnessed. Like *Marathon Man*, say, after Roy Scheider dies and it turns into a big hamfest, with Olivier and Hoffman going at it — *have you tried acting, dear boy* — energetic and competitive to the bitter end. Or *Henry V*, when you realise Falstaff isn't going to be there. By the time I got on stage to tell Matthew Campbell that Ann Greer was dead, my one line, which had till then seemed so lacklustre — not to mention syntactically unsettling — now took on a gravity, a charged, tragic quality, reminding us all, players and audience alike, that death was not only inevitable but terrifyingly *personal*. That was all Ann Greer's doing. Meanwhile, she had slipped outside for a breath of air, or maybe to talk to her brother, Nick, who was playing Banquo. She came back for the curtain call but, characteristically, she let Macbeth take all the glory — and Matthew Campbell was not about to refuse the exposure.

After that, I wanted to speak to her so badly. I didn't have any big hopes, I just wanted to speak to her, and then invite her to the limeroom so she could see what kind of place it was. Then we would be friends. I thought about it for a long time; then, one night, I lay in bed waiting till dawn, listening to the birds and for the sound of her bike coming up the rise. She used to finish her round about seven, I suppose so she could go home and get ready for school. I had thought about waiting for her outside, by the gate, or even on the path, but then I decided that would seem a bit too eager, so I got dressed and lay under the covers, waiting. Finally she arrived. She rode a man's bike, an old one, and she had a big canvas sack over her shoulders. Every day, she stopped at the gate and propped the bike against the hedge; then she walked up the path to the front door. I'd watched her a few times, and I could see the satisfaction in her face as she delivered this last paper and finished her round. That morning, as she came up the path, all fresh and cool in the early day, I opened the window as wide as it would go.

'Hello,' I said.

'Hello,' she said, looking up. She stopped a moment, a few feet from the door, and waited.

'Do you want to see something?' I asked. I sounded about five years old.

'What?'

'A place. It's not far.'

She studied me a moment, then she shook her head. 'I can't,' she said. She went to the door and slid the paper through the letter box. I heard it hit the hall floor with a soft flickering sound. Then she reappeared in exactly the same place as she had been before. She looked back. 'I can't,' she said. 'I'm sorry.'

'It's special,' I said.

She shook her head, then looked back to

where her bike stood, leaning snugly against the hedge, the handlebars beginning to settle in, the way they do. 'I can't,' she said again. 'Sorry.' It was heartbreaking, really. I couldn't think of anything else to say, so I nodded and ducked back inside. Every time I saw her after that, she gave me an odd little smile, but she never said anything.

Now, I was going to the limeroom for another reason. I had chosen that place because it was lonely, and because I thought it would bring me luck. Sometimes places bring you luck, if you know them well enough. I chose the far corner of the building, above the long, deep pit of black, rank water, for the icterine warbler's nesting place. I knew nothing about birds in those days, though I should have been an expert. My father just couldn't understand it, that I didn't want to go out birdwatching with him. He even bought me my own binoculars, to encourage me, but I still couldn't bring myself to. And I really did regret that, after he died. He loved birds so much, and he knew about them all, about their habits and their calls and where they liked to nest. Naturally, I had no idea where an icterine warbler usually sought shelter — probably not in a dank old building — but then, since they were birds that didn't normally nest in Britain, I didn't imagine Malcolm Kennedy would know any better. He wasn't a birdwatcher, anyway. He didn't even like birds. He just wanted to add one more egg to his collection. Still, one problem remained. I had got him to the limeroom: now I had to get him into that dark, dangerous corner, without seeming to be up to anything. I had to be cunning. I had to deceive him.

'God, it stinks in here,' he said, as we slipped through the half-open door. 'What is this place?'

I shrugged. 'I don't know,' I said. 'Just an old farm building, I think.'

He stood in the half-gloom of the interior, looking around. 'What's that big pit for?' he said.

'I don't know.' I advanced towards the back of the building. 'You stay here,' I said, starting towards the narrow ledge, a ledge about two inches wide, that ran along the back of the wall, overhanging the pit. I had crossed it once, safely, one afternoon — but then I had been on my own, with nothing to distract me. 'I'm going over to the other side. That's where the nest is.'

He grabbed my sleeve. 'What do you mean you're going over,' he said. '*I'm* going over.' He peered up into the darkness. 'Where is this nest, anyway?'

'It's all right,' I said, trying to free myself. 'I know exactly where it is. And I know how to get across. It's very narrow — '

He pulled me back again. '*I'm* going,' he said. 'Just tell me where the nest is.'

It appeared then that, with some reluctance, and feeling cheated yet again, I gave in. 'All right,' I said. 'But watch your step. It's very — '

'You said,' he almost snarled. 'Where's the fucking nest?'

I pointed up into the corner. 'See there,' I said. 'Where that dark stain is? There's a little gap, just above. You can't see it from here, but you can feel it. That's where the nest is.'

He looked up. He could only reach the gap — there really was a gap there, I had seen birds flying into it, once — by standing on tiptoe. That would be when he was most vulnerable. Standing on tiptoe, with his arm stretched as far as it would go, trying to feel where the nest was, trying to find the eggs — that was when he would fall. All he needed was a little help. At the time, I had no intention of doing him any permanent harm. I just wanted him to fall into that dark, greasy water and flail around for a while, wallowing in the muck. It would be him, this time, who would be humiliated; it would be him who looked like a fool. He would know I had tricked him, and if I could trick him once, if I could get the upper hand once, I could do it again. I wasn't afraid — or I wasn't as afraid as I'd thought I would be. I was perfectly focused on the image of him in the pit, treading water, calling out for help. Help that only I could offer. And I would refuse. I would laugh at him and walk out into the fresh spring air and leave him there, floundering.

He took a moment to get his bearings, to fix in his mind the place where the supposed nest was; then he set off. He was pretty agile, edging along, his back to the wall, using it to balance as he went, carefully, not hurrying, but not overcautious either. He took his time, but then I think he was also showing off a little. He wanted me to see that he could do it, better than I ever could, probably; he wanted me to take back what I had said about how narrow it was, and how difficult it would be. Slowly, his face set in concentration, he edged his way across. Soon he was close. 'You're almost there,' I said, a little too loudly. I wanted him to think I was encouraging him. I was exactly where he wanted me, servile, obsequious, the dumbstruck witness of his superior boyhood. The trouble was, I startled him a little, and he wobbled, just perceptibly.

'All right,' he said. 'No need to shout. You'll disturb the birds.'

I nodded stupidly. 'Sorry,' I called, not quite as loudly.

He looked back at me and grimaced. 'All right,' he said. 'Am I there now?'

'Yes,' I shouted. 'You're right below it. If you turn around and put your left hand up, you'll find the gap.'

'Will you *stop* fucking shouting,' he shouted. 'I'm trying to concentrate here.' He turned carefully, shuffling his feet in tiny steps like a dancer, till he had his back to me. He was right in the far corner, pressed against the wall. He lifted his left arm and started feeling about above him. 'I can't find it,' he said. 'Are you sure — '

'A little to the left,' I called, as I fetched the pole. It was something I had found on the waste ground next to the lime-room, a long wooden pole, a little like a clothes prop, but without the V-shaped nick at the end. I had no idea what it had been used for before it was abandoned there, but I had a use for it now. Because he wasn't looking back, and he was stretching as far as he could, and he was preoccupied with something, an avid child with his mind set on what he was going to get out of this day's business, he was an easy target. I had rehearsed it any number of times in my mind, and in that dark corner of the real world, and I knew it was possible, with some luck, and more judgement and, most of all, resolve. I had to steel myself. I had to stop being afraid. Now I knew what my father meant, when we met that stray dog on our walks. 'Don't be afraid,' he had said. Now I knew, and I wasn't afraid. It was simply a question of will.

'That's it,' I called. 'You're right there.'

'Yes, but — '

'Reach right in. I'm telling you — ' I raised the pole and trained it out over the water, like some huge fishing rod. It trembled and wavered and for a moment I was afraid that it wouldn't be up to the job.

'There's no nest here — ' he said. He was just beginning to sound genuinely annoyed. The pole was behind him. All I had to do was swing it and push. I had practised this — but I hadn't taken into account the possibility that he might turn and see what I was doing, and I hadn't taken into account how much heavier he was than any of the objects — a sack, a tree branch — that I had practised with.

'You'd better not be mucking me about — ' Malcolm Kennedy turned and saw what was happening, but it was too late. Maybe it even helped me, that he was turning, and so off

100

balance and distracted, when the pole swung in and hit him hard and square, almost slipping from my hands as I pulled it back and prepared to swing again, excited now, suddenly certain of victory. I saw his face — he was confused, of course, but the confusion only lasted for a moment, as he saw what I had done, and that he couldn't hold on. Then he was falling, hanging in the air for a moment before he went, like a cartoon character who has just run off the edge of a cliff — and now he seemed genuinely upset, as if he had been betrayed for no reason by a true friend, and not some miserable boy he had victimised for months.

He hit the water hard. I was impressed. It was a flat, slapping noise, not a splash so much as the sound the wind makes filling a sail, or the sound I had made hitting the ground, the day he had winded me. I'd got him on my first try and he had no idea what had hit him. He went right under, then he came up, choking, splashing about desperately, the water in his nose and mouth, his face scared. With only a fleeting sight of him to go on, I could see he really was afraid. He was frightened. He didn't know what had happened, and now he was in the pit and there was no way out. From the level he was at, there was no way he could reach up and pull himself out, all he could do was swim about, or tread water, waiting for someone else to help him. I stood for a moment, watching him surface, wanting to be sure that I had accounted for everything, that there was no way he could climb back out and come after me. Then I turned and walked far enough into the shadows that he couldn't see me. I couldn't see him either, but I had already seen enough. He was afraid. He didn't know what had hit him. That was all that mattered.

Finally he spoke. 'What the fuck!' he said. 'Hey!' I could hear him splashing around in there, trying to get to the side. Not that there was much point. He wasn't going anywhere. I stood listening, savouring the moment. Then he shouted again. 'You better get me out of here,' he said. 'Or your life won't be worth living.'

I didn't say a word. It was time to go. Leave him to stew. Let him know how it felt to be afraid. Let him know how it felt to be humiliated. I was tempted to take one last look, just to see him splashing about in all that filthy water, but I exercised self-control. I reined myself in. After all, I was there to make a point, not to gloat. Mrs Collings would have been proud of me.

* ★ ★

All the way back to town, I was sure he would come to no real harm. He would be found, after a suitable delay; someone would hear his cries and haul him out and I would see him at school — chastened, or in vengeful mood — the following Monday. He would have had the whole weekend to think about what had happened, and maybe to plan new attacks against me, but I didn't care. For that day, at least, I felt I had done something, I felt *strong*. If it all began again, I would begin my own campaign again, and I would catch him out, too, sooner or later. I knew my own strength now. And who knows? Maybe he'd decide to get himself a different special friend.

At the same time, I have to confess that the thought crossed my mind, not once but several times, that he might drown out there and, though I didn't linger over this notion, it didn't bother me. I didn't care about him, and I knew there was nothing that could connect me with his apparent accident. For that next hour or two, I felt elated at having done what I wanted to do and, if I gave thought to it at all, the only thing I was certain of was that, if Malcolm Kennedy drowned, I would be free of him. Not that I ever considered this a serious possibility. He wouldn't drown, because nobody drowned in a twelve-foot-deep pit of water, a few miles from the town. People drowned at sea. Like Mrs Collings' father and brother.

When I got to town, I went into the baker's and bought myself a little bag of doughnuts, the ones I liked. It was starting to get cooler, and the doughnuts felt warm in my hand; I ate two, then I closed the bag, so I'd have some for later. They tasted delicious, those two doughnuts. Sugared, warm, doughy, a little chewy. I felt good, too good to just go home. I decided I would walk over to Sandhaven, then come back the roundabout way, along the old railway line. The sun was starting to dip over the water, but it wasn't cold, just pleasantly cool. To be honest, I didn't think about Malcolm Kennedy. I think I kept him out of my thoughts on purpose, not to spoil the moment. Because some moments you want to last for ever. Moments of freedom, moments when you know exactly who you are and that what you are doing is exactly what you were meant to be doing. I walked to Sandhaven and stood looking at the sea for a while; then I turned for home. As I crossed the old railway line, on the way back to Coldhaven, I noticed a row of houses, quite large and old, with their upper windows on a level with the embankment, so I could see in. It was already evening: the curtains were drawn in some of the houses, and some of the rooms were dark and cold-looking, but there was one window that was lit, with no curtains that I could see, or even very much furniture, just a standard lamp and a wardrobe with a long oval-shaped mirror at the back of the room, against a wall. Someone had hung a blue dress over the door. I stopped. The colour of the dress attracted my attention; I thought I had seen it before and I was trying to think where. I could have sworn that the window was empty when I first stopped, but after a moment I realised someone was in there, watching me. I didn't recognise her at first, she was just a young girl with blond, shoulder-length hair, in what looked like a very old, rather dirty nightdress. A young girl, a child really, standing at the window, with her back to the light. She was looking directly at me. I didn't know who she was, she was just a girl from the houses on the old railway that meandered along the coast, or at least, I thought she was. Then I recognised her. It had been earlier that spring, and I had been up on the point. I was alone, as usual, wandering about, doing nothing in particular, enjoying the first warm sunshine. I'd thought myself alone then, too, and I would probably not have noticed her, had it not been for the blue dress and the fact that she was bare-legged, a fact that had excited me at the time. And, though it sounds ridiculous now, this scared me, all of a sudden. The girl looking at me, and the memory of her bare legs, excited and scared me, and I immediately looked away; then I walked on quickly, annoyed that I had allowed myself to be seen. For the ridiculous, utterly irrational thought had entered my mind, at the very moment I recognised this girl, that she knew everything. She had read in my face what I had done, just as she had read, on that first day, the secret desire I had felt when I saw her, barelegged and slightly wet, standing on the rocks beyond the point. Then, absurdly, as a gesture, to show my indifference, I stopped and looked back. The girl was still there, framed in the window, and it occurred to me again that she was beautiful, but not in the most obvious way. She was like one of those children in old films who seem happy and blessed, insulated by the brilliancy and malevolence of their own innocence. I stood watching her, taking her in, expecting at any moment that someone would come to the window and fetch her away. Then an odd thing happened. When she saw I was still looking, she raised her arm

106

very slowly and waved — and before I could stop myself, I had lifted my arm and was waving back, out of fear or love or defiance, I couldn't say, but at that moment it was more than I could do to prevent myself responding. A moment later, somebody did come into the room and she was gone. I looked at the half-eaten doughnut in my hand, cold and small and white in the near-dark, and I threw it away down the siding, for the rats.

Le Reniement De Saint Pierre

It was my mother who taught me about looking. Some days, she would go about the house trying not to see things as themselves — the furniture, the shrubs in the garden, the coats hanging in the hallway — so she could see their shadows better. It was a game she played, but it was serious, too, because shadow was what she worked with: shadow and light, complements rather than opposites. She would find paintings in her library of art books and she would give me them to look at, sometimes, pointing out the light source and showing me what to look for in the shadows, how some were deep and dark, others faint, or indistinct, and all of them — a commonplace, of course, but also a source of pleasure — all of them with their own distinct, sometimes surprising, colour. She didn't give me formal art lessons, she would just point out something, in the world that I was taking for granted, or in a book she was studying, and some shadow would become visible, another aspect of an object or a person that I had missed until then. One of her favourite paintings was the one by

Georges de la Tour where the angel appears to Joseph: Joseph has fallen asleep beside a lighted candle, his head resting on his right hand, a book just beginning to slip from his left. The angel, who looks like a young woman, is standing over him, one arm raised so that it hides the candle from the viewer; this is the only source of light, so that, although her face and hair, and the silver and black sash she wears around her waist, are bathed in light, we see only the very tip of the candle, and Joseph has become a play of warm shadows, running from gold and tan to nearly black. On the facing page, in *The Denial of Saint Peter* of 1650, we see a timid-looking, rather elderly man, at the point where his world has just vanished into thin air — and here, the dramatic effect is achieved by concealing a candle or a lantern behind one of the group of soldiers casting lots around a table, their manner at once casual and threatening, their faces coarse and avaricious, men with whom the old fisherman is very obviously out of his depth. Here, the effect is doubled by the addition of another obscured light source, the candle held by the serving woman, which is, like the candle in Joseph's vision, barely visible. Yet where the hidden light source picked out the inspired face of the angel in the first of these two pictures, light only serves, in *The Denial*, to accentuate the ugliness, the threat of discovery and, most of all, the sheer coarseness of the soldier in the red cap.

Malcolm Kennedy died in the pit. I picture him now, going under, his lungs filling with that black, greasy water, and I ask myself if I knew, all along, that it would happen. I have no answer. I must have known, and I must have wanted him dead, but at the time I wasn't aware of having that intention. I just wanted to punish him for what he had done to me and, when I heard the news, the following Monday, at school, I was genuinely surprised. I didn't feel guilty, though. I didn't feel bad for him. He was nothing to me, after all. I wasn't even afraid that I would be found out — or not by the authorities, at least. When the news of his drowning broke, an odd wave of excitement swept through the school: somebody we knew was dead, and he had died in mysterious, or tragic, or just novel circumstances. Everyone was speculating as to how he had come to be in the pit, but nobody ever thought of it as suspicious. Later, people would say he had died by misadventure, and I went to the dictionary and looked up the word, because I thought I knew what it meant, but I wasn't certain.

MISADVENTURE NOUN 1 A PIECE OF BAD LUCK. 2. *LAW* AN ACCIDENT WITHOUT CRIME OR NEGLIGENCE; *DEATH BY MISADVENTURE.*

Misadventure. It was an event that happened in the shadows, back in the far corner of an old farm building, and it was an event for which nobody could be held responsible because, in that shadow place, the usual laws did not apply. I told myself this, in different ways over the next several months and, mostly, I believed it, just as I believed that it was an accident without crime when I met Moira Kennedy and — at first not even knowing who she was, but then realising, with an odd rush of excitement and revulsion — entered into something that I knew from the first was grotesque and unseemly, perhaps from perversity, and perhaps because it had already begun, because the ball had started rolling and it was something that could not be prevented. Like the visit from the angel, or that moment of terror before cock-crow, a flicker of light revealed how, mostly, we are creatures of chance — how, when the devil has work to do, he makes it look like an accident, at least to begin with, in order to lure us further into his trap, protesting mildly, if at all, but willing accomplices at the last.

111

Before we came to Whitland, we lived in the town, in a high, old-style fisherman's cottage on Cockburn Street that my father bought when he first came to Coldhaven. At that time, he was an unsuspecting incomer with a strange accent and an American wifc who was somewhat younger than himself; he was also a person of independent means, a successful photographer who, having decided that he wanted to work on something new, had chosen the land and seascapes around Coldhaven. None of this was designed to endear him to the locals, though I don't imagine that mattered to my father. It was the light that drew him to this place: the weather, the sea, the sky, the light reflecting off the water. There are stories, in these parts, of how the herring fishermen could follow the harvest by looking for a reflection in the clouds — and I am sure it was true, for the vast shoals of fish would be visible for miles, on the top plane of this double mirror, alive, bright, always moving. There were other lights here too: the silver and paled gold of the night boats going out to the fishing grounds; the reds and greens of the warning lights at Coldhaven harbour; the ghosting flash of the lighthouse out by the point. My father cared about such things much more than he cared about people; his well-being depended, for the most part, on the atmosphere, rather than the goodwill of his human neighbours. I imagine he would have preferred to get along with the townsfolk, but he wasn't going to put any effort into it. He and my mother chose the cottage on Cockburn Street because it was sufficient to their needs: it wasn't ostentatious or out of the ordinary, and it seemed to offer the quiet seclusion they wanted. They were, when all is said and done, a pair of silent, abstracted, slightly defeated souls, who wanted nothing other than to get on with their work. Knowing what I know of them, I have to assume that their strategy was to live and let live, to keep their own counsel and follow the way they had chosen, resigned to a single-minded, almost ascetic life, dedicated to their respective arts, and to the subtle craft of forgetting whatever it was they had come here to forget. For a long time, I knew nothing about their past history, but I did know that the world had injured them both, long before they came to Coldhaven, in ways that I didn't begin to understand. What they wanted was to render unto Caesar and be left alone; but they were out of luck. Neither of them ever worked out what they had done to offend the town of Coldhaven,

113

but it seems it was only a matter of time before a handful of the locals decided it was their business to make my family's life uncomfortable. Some did it openly, some in secret; but they knew what they were doing. I don't want to say there was some kind of concerted action, some plot. No: they were united by a common sensibility, by a shared recognition of the possible victim. They were only a handful, just a few of the more vicious members of the uglier clans — the Kings, the Gillespies, the Hutchisons — and their unwitting instruments, like Peter Tone, the town drunk, the one who killed my mother. I'm not going to say those people were working together, because they hated one another just as much as they hated people like my parents, but the sum total of their malice combined to make for something greater than all the petty, individual insults.

My parents' offence, of course, was to be who they were. I think my father saw it quite soon, and it didn't matter to him anyhow. He liked to be alone, at work in his studio or out walking on the east shore with the birds. Still, it affected my mother badly. They both wanted to belong to the place, but to my father belonging had nothing to do with blood or birth, nothing to do with community or kinship, it was all about the land and the sea, it was all about imagination, about choice. He belonged here because this was his sky, this was his light, his stretch of sea. It wasn't that he was entirely indifferent to how the locals behaved, he could talk about it, and he obviously saw the situation clearly. One night, not long after we moved up to Whitland, an old friend of his was visiting from London, on one of those rare occasions when my parents had any contact at all with the outside world. This friend, John, was a writer, with an interest in the local landscape; he and my father had worked together on a couple of books.

'So,' John said, 'what's it like, living in the back of beyond?' He was mostly joking, but my mother gave a big sigh and looked forlorn. I thought she was going to say something, maybe something too serious, but she just sighed again and looked at my father.

He smiled. 'Well,' he said. 'It's beautiful, as you can see. And up here, it's quiet. Loads of birds, amazing skies — '

'And the locals?'

My father smiled ruefully. He knew he was being provoked. 'They're all right,' he said.

John shook his head. 'That's not what I heard,' he said. He shot a glance at my mother, who bowed, clasping her hands over her head, like someone trying to hide.

'Oh, they're all right,' my father said. He wasn't annoyed. 'They're very different from us, I'll give you that. They have different — ideas.'

John wasn't giving up. 'How so?' he said.

My father took a moment to think about it, then launched into one of his wordy, mock-serious analyses. 'Well,' he said. 'Imagine you have been set down in a strange place, amongst strange people, people who resemble you, superficially, physically — '

'Speak for yourself,' my mother put in.

'Superficially,' my father went on, ignoring her. 'They speak the language you speak — '

'I hadn't noticed — '

' — but in an odd, inconclusive way, as if there was nothing really to be said, other than nonsense or mild pleasantries. And, of course, you are new in their territory, you are a stranger. Worse still, you are a stranger with new maps, maps they have never seen before, and they think you have come to tell them that their maps are *wrong*. Which they are not about to accept — '

My mother tossed her napkin on to the table. 'Oh come on,' she said. 'Nobody's trying to tell anybody they're wrong — '

'Not in so many words,' my father said. He looked at John. 'It's just how we are. Who we are. For them, we're a threat. Which is understandable.'

My mother shook her head. Unlike me, she knew better, but she bit her tongue. I don't suppose she wanted to tell John what had really been going on, or not, at least, in front of me. Because I didn't know, and they never let me see. I thought it was all trivial, just the usual problems amongst neighbours. I didn't know what they'd had to endure. I look back now and I wish I had known, or had even just met, the blithe couple who came to Coldhaven that morning in early summer when they first moved to Cockburn Street. They had come from cities — my father from Edinburgh, then Paris and London, my mother from Boston, then Paris — and from disappointments, betrayals, disillusionments they no longer wished to think about. Moving out, moving away from the centre of things, they had only dreamed of a better life. Nothing specific, I imagine, just a shared dream of space and sky. Maybe they thought of a white cottage lost in an acre of goldenrod somewhere to the north, or one of those lonely coastal towns high up on the map; the two of them turned to the sea, their bodies tuned to the sway of the tides and the migrations of shore birds. Maybe they considered the dark, sweet air above the reed

117

beds up and down the coast, or some dark villa at the edge of woodland. There were other places they could have chosen, besides Coldhaven, but then, at that time, how could they have known what the future held? They could have gone to some pleasant corner of France — the *côte sauvage*, say, or La Brière — but I think they liked the idea of a place where the people spoke English, and when they found Coldhaven, they quite literally — as they always said — fell in love with it. It had what they needed and I imagine that, even from the first, it was a dream they shared without really needing to talk about it, each of them taking for granted that the other knew exactly what they meant by the word *home*. They never talked about it to me, either, but they didn't have to; when we moved to the house on Whitland Point I knew exactly what they meant, and I agreed, I utterly agreed with them, in my blood and my bones and my soul.

I'm sure the house on Cockburn Street seemed to them a realistic compromise, at first. I don't think, really, that they meant to withdraw from the world entirely, not to begin with. When they came to Coldhaven, they recognised something about the place: they had found everything they wanted in the light and the water and the crowstepped gables of the old houses on Shore Street, and it probably took a while before they noticed the people. Or rather, before the people noticed them. As I was growing up, I didn't really understand what was going on; all I had to go on were clues, remarks overheard in passing, my father's attempts to calm my mother when she was angered by some injury or slight. He took it better than she did, which wasn't necessarily a good thing; I think, at the time, I was glad that at least one of them had enough self-control to keep going, to stay on course. Had I known how bad things were, however — if I had known where it was all leading — I think I would have been in my mother's camp. But, of course, nobody knew where it was all leading. Nobody planned the events that unfolded during my nineteenth year; they just happened. And yet ... Everything that happened could have been foreseen, from everything that had gone before. Surely that is what we mean by destiny, that long, slow sand-pile effect where, grain by grain, word by word, something becomes inevitable, though nobody could have said when one thing turned into another.

Besides, everything seemed so petty at the time. I remember, once, as we were leaving

the house on Cockburn Street, we encoun-
tered the family that lived across the way, an
odd, strangely homogenous clan of plump,
rather downy creatures called the Kings.
Their youngest was Alec King, until recently
Mrs K's lord and master; at the time, though,
he was a soft, hairy boy, just a little older than
me. He would have been there that day,
bringing up the rear, as the entire clan
— mother, father, father's brother Rex and
his wife, Grace, sisters, brothers, cousins
— promenaded out from Sunday lunch for an
afternoon drive. We were going for our usual
walk, along Cockburn Street and up the hill,
away from the shorefront, towards the woods
and the fields inland. Usually, we missed the
Kings, but that day our paths crossed. Not
that there was any commerce between us,
ever. The Kings were, at the time, mere
onlookers in the war that was being waged
against us and, though that would change
later, we had no real reason to do anything
but ignore them. Still, as far as my mother
was concerned they were complicit in
everything — and, to a disturbing, for me
almost frightening, degree she disliked the
passive onlookers more than people like the
Tones, who sent their kids round to put
dogshit through the door, or let them climb
over the back wall to trample her flowers. My

mother despised the Tones and their ilk, but she *hated* the Kings. Now, as the entire clan trooped to their cars, the father — a slick, round boar of a man — leading the way, the rest following along behind, muttering and sneering, she could hardly conceal her loathing. I sensed it, and my father sensed it too; putting his hand on her arm, he started to lead her away. For a moment she resisted, then she surrendered, smiling grimly to herself as she turned to him.

'Look at them,' she said.

My father kept walking, still holding her arm, but he didn't respond. I looked back at the King clan, trotting along the pavement. I wasn't even sure their remarks — unintelligible, muttered into their collars — were aimed at us. There was always that smug look, that half-smile intended to conceal a raging inferiority complex, but that was all. All I could see, at least.

'They remind me of something,' my mother said. 'I just can't remember what.' She glanced back at the tail end of the procession, a gaggle of snub-nosed children, Alec among them, the whole brood glad to be out of the house, snuffling at the air and at one another as they scrambled into the back seats. Then, illuminated, she laughed out loud. 'Oh, I know what,' she said.

My father smiled carefully but he still didn't say anything. He had already guessed at some further unpleasantness, but he let her go on, for the pleasure, or the relief, of getting it out of her system. For my part, I was perplexed at how vehement she seemed.

'They're cartoon pigs,' she said. 'Big pink piggies from a Disney film, all that fat washed flesh and wisps of hair combed back off their faces.' She laughed again. 'Cartoon piggies in suits and summer dresses,' she said. She looked at my father, then at me. 'Do you see?'

I was embarrassed now. She was right, of course but, to my child's mind, it behoved her not to talk that way.

'Little piggies, little piggies,' she went on, somewhat breathlessly now. 'Come out, little piggies, or I'll huff and I'll puff and I'll — '

'All right, Catherine.' My father looked grim now. He usually called her Kate, or Cat, so I could tell something was wrong. And as soon as he spoke, she gave it up. I could tell it was what she had been waiting for, an admission that she was right, an admission that he was avoiding the problem — though at the time, I had no idea what the real problem was — and, at the same time, a reminder of the authority he presumed upon, an authority that she no longer believed in, because *he was wrong*.

That shocked me. I had never imagined my father being wrong about anything, and I had never imagined that my mother would imagine such a thing either. It felt like a betrayal, a kind of complicity that had reached out, from the Hutchisons and the Kings and the Tones, and had finally touched her. My father must have felt it too, because he broke stride a moment and said, quietly, though not as quietly as he had probably intended, 'Why are you doing this, Catherine? Why do you let it get to you?' He stood waiting for an answer, and I guessed, for the first time, that things were worse than I thought. Of course, my mother didn't answer. Her point was made, as much by my father's reaction as by her own behaviour. Finally, he shook his head and turned away. 'They're nothing to us,' he said. 'Nothing. Why can't you see that?'

At the time, I thought it was to my father's credit that he didn't let those people get to him. Not till the end. But then, his approach didn't really work, either: my mother got angry and, though it didn't do her any good, she got it out of her system. My father, on the other hand, seemed unperturbed, but this outward calm was a pretence. A mask. He was just as upset and disappointed, because he couldn't see the point to any of it and it always seemed so petty to him. I think he clung to the house on Cockburn Street for a long time, determined not to have his new start ruined by the small-minded resentment of his neighbours. It was pride on his part that made him want to stay, but it was also the hope that my mother would learn to ignore the problem. I think he believed, far too easily, that if such things were ignored they would just go away. He didn't want to be driven out, not over such trivial nonsense. Eventually, however, he gave in and, two days after my ninth birthday, we moved to Whitland.

On that last day, I sat at the upstairs window while the men were loading the van, and my parents came and went, my mother excited by the idea of the new house, my father, I think, saddened by it all. It was a weekday, but that didn't stop the neighbours coming out, under the pretext of going to the shops or just to stand at their gates in little gaggles, talking about nothing in particular, pretending indifference to this flitting. At various times, the Kings were there, the Hutchisons, the Gillespies, even little Peter Tone, who normally would have got the cold shoulder from people who were so obviously his betters. They gossiped, they passed the time of day, they came and went about their real or imaginary business — and all the time they watched, as the removal men carried the visible evidence of my parents' life from the house — the books, the music, the Chinese ceramics, the pictures, the furniture — and they could barely conceal their annoyance. It should have been a victory for them, it should have been a matter of satisfaction that we were going, but it galled them to think that it was the Whitland house we were going to. It galled them to see my mother happy again, fussing over her things, making sure everything was properly managed.

By that time, my parents had been waiting for the right house for years. The house on the point was ideal, but they weren't very confident of success when it came on the market. It had been in the same family for years, handed down from father to eldest son over generations, but the last occupant, a devout old queen to whom the locals referred, rather quaintly, as a confirmed bachelor, had died without issue and his cousin George, whom he had disliked, put the house on the market. My parents went for it right away. It had everything they needed: a good-sized piece of land, high windows facing the sea, a walled garden and — most importantly — it stood on the point, by itself, away from Coldhaven. Not surprisingly, they made a generous offer. Still, they were lucky the vendor was an outsider — the cousin had moved to Yorkshire as a young man, and had lost all but the most formal contacts with the town — and they were lucky that this particular outsider disliked, not only his cousin, but the townspeople in general. In Coldhaven, what mattered first was what a man owned; but how he came by it was almost as important. People in Coldhaven enjoyed talking and thinking about deals and intrigue. How much property a man possessed wasn't always clear, you had to be in the know and, when you were, you had to take the trouble to find out the details of ownership and the scandals around the exchange. My mother used to say that all those people cared about was who owned what, and who they had betrayed to get it. If so, Cousin George betrayed the whole town when he accepted my parents' offer, and there were those who said as much aloud. I can picture them now, huddled in little groups at the post office, or outside the fishermen's co-op. 'He'll no be wanting to show his face around here in a hurry,' a King would say, 'not after selling a place like that to outsiders.'

'Ach, leave wee George alone,' one of the Hutchisons would put in. Not that they had any choice in the matter. Wee George had rushed back to Halifax as soon as the deal was done. 'The man took the best offer that was on the table. Ye canna blame him, if it came frae the Gardiners.'

'Aye, well at least it gets them awa frae Cockburn Street,' muttered old Joe Belcher, who lived just along from us and looked after the Social Club. Joe Belcher was a small, bald-headed man with a grim stare; retired now, he spent his days painting the gates of the Social Club in black and gold, or raking leaves in the courtyard, where he could keep an eye on things. My mother had complained to him once, when some drunk on his way from the regular Saturday night ceilidh had trampled through our front garden, and Belcher had never forgotten it. 'They dinnae belong in the toon.'

It was true, of course: my parents didn't belong to Coldhaven. They belonged to the land and the sky and the light and, maybe, they belonged to an idea that had become untenable even before I was born. I think, when they first came to Coldhaven, they hadn't entirely given up on that idea; they were just biding their time, waiting for it to reappear in some new form. They were conserving their energy, building on what they had. *Reculer pour mieux sauter*. But

127

nothing had happened and, gradually, they had come to see that *this* was their destiny, *this* was their life. My father was contented enough, making a different kind of photograph, drawing on the way the light worked on the point, and I suppose he realised that he'd been obliged to come to this one place, to this particular weather, to find his best work. My mother never really settled, though, even after we moved out to Whitland. She wanted to go back to something. I never quite knew what it was, and I'm not certain it even existed.

That first night at Whitland, I woke in what, at first sight, seemed to be the silvery gloaming of festival. I thought someone had turned on a huge lantern just outside my window, an immense, intimate body of light that was part of some piece of theatre, some celebration. I sat up. I was in my little room next to the landing, the one I had chosen earlier that day, when we had gone about the house deciding what would go where, while the removal men stood patiently by, letting my mother talk her way through her decisions, as if someone were listening to her. I had chosen that room, even though I could have had a bigger one on the third floor, because it had this single, wide bay window that looked out over the sea, and because it seemed haunted by the history of that place, a history of summer warmth seeping up through the pipes and the sweet vapour of milk rising from the kitchen, a good haunting, a warm presence, like the heat that still remains in the embers of a fire long after it burns out. There were no curtains in the window, and the room was full of light — and there, directly opposite the bed, the moon hung, almost perfectly round, in a vast dark blue sky. I was happy, then. I felt that we had come home. I didn't know the real extent of the troubles we had just left behind, the little gifts of dogshit, the anonymous letters, the threatening encounters on the street, the nasty phone calls. I had never experienced the hostility my parents had endured for so long. I thought my mother just didn't like the locals, that she was making a big fuss about nothing, and I wanted to operate as my father did, turning the other cheek, and so getting to look like a reasonable man. People think tolerance is a virtue, but there are things that shouldn't be tolerated. I learned that from Mrs Collings, I suppose, but I didn't really understand what it meant until I met Moira Kennedy.

★   ★   ★

From time to time, I would find my mother at work about the house, cooking, or mending something, or sitting on the landing by the big window that looked out over the point, working at her easel, and I would observe her, an unseen witness to a life that was, for me, a complete mystery. I thought I understood something about my father, but my mother was an unknown: unpredictable, faraway, volatile. At other times, she would drift away in an armchair, and I would be fascinated by how different she looked, asleep. I was at that stage of early adolescence when everything seems like a huge philosophical discovery: the fact that we are essentially alone, the idea that we never see ourselves as we seem to others, the realisation that we lie, to ourselves mostly, in a vain attempt to cheat time, to cheat death. It's all linked; it all fits together, in this childish philosophy: we go through our lives in a dream, living one life and imagining another, hearing our own voices as nobody else hears them, seeing ourselves from inside as we never appear to others. Occasionally, we catch ourselves in passing, in a mirror or a shop window, but that glimpse is fleeting, almost instantaneous. A moment later, the assumed face appears, an appropriate mien of indifference or seriousness, or good-humoured self-mockery, as we adopt for ourselves the mask we assume for others. But when we sleep, we are occupied with our own looking; we do not feel the gaze of others. Watching my mother sleep was the only time I ever felt that I could really see her; the rest of the time, her presence was an illusion that she created, even when she was angry, or upset about something. She was never herself, not for me. It was like living with an actor who was forever working on a new role, preparing who to be, performing a walk across a room, the lifting of a glass, the saying of a phrase.

Sometimes she would fly into a rage, or she would become despondent, and the reason — the official reason, at least — was always the behaviour of the locals. She was always ready to find fault with them, always ready to see a slight or an insult in the most fleeting exchange. I couldn't understand that and, after we moved to the point and everything seemed more settled, I suspected something else was at the root of her problems. Her dislike of the locals had always seemed trivial: a storm in a teacup; much ado about nothing. But then, I really didn't have any idea of what was still going on in the background — the telephone calls that came late at night, while I was asleep; another wave of poison pen letters; the extravagant silences that would descend whenever my mother entered the post office or the pharmacy — because my parents had agreed that, for my own good, I should *never* know. They chose, in other words, to keep these events a secret from me, just as I chose — for my father's sake, I think — to say nothing about what I was enduring at the hands of Malcolm Kennedy. Oddly enough, I think my mother would have coped with knowing what was going on. She would have done something decisive, perhaps she would even have taken me out of school and taught me herself, at home. But then that was the last thing I wanted. My father would have responded altogether differently, however, and I am sure that, had he known about the bullying, he would only have made matters worse. He probably would have gone to the school and talked to the Headmaster, a kindly but utterly ineffectual little man called Mr Allman. There would have been face-to-face meetings and resolutions to do better on both sides, and then it would all begin again, only this time it would be much worse. And by then, of course, I would have learned, once and for all, that nothing could be done.

So it was that, at various times, I had my secrets and my parents had theirs. Some of those secrets, on both sides, were pleasurable to keep, all the hidden joys and fragments of knowledge that demand concealment, because

132

we know they will evaporate if we talk about them, and the secrets that are impossible to betray anyway, because there are no words sufficient to convey them. The secret pleasure of leaving the house early, when everyone else is asleep, and going out along the shore beyond the point, the birds rising in tens and twenties at a time and flickering away; the pleasure of waking with a dream, or the wisps of a dream, in your head, and lying very quiet, trying to put it all back together again, working out what the hidden message was, in a story that would seem absurd in the retelling, though it made perfect sense as it unfolded. There is always a tension between the desire to keep a secret and the perverse desire to give it up; or there is, at least, when the secret is a good one, a matter of pleasure or understanding. But those other secrets were burdens, to my parents as much as to me, I am certain, and I wish they had told me everything rather than bear that load, even though it would have made not the blindest bit of difference, and would only have caused me unhappiness. And I wish I had told them about Malcolm Kennedy, first about the months of bullying, then about the way he died, which both was and was not my fault. I didn't want them to share in my misfortune, however, just as they didn't want me to share in theirs. So, out of kindness, out of a perverse consideration, we had nothing to say to each other.

After Malcolm Kennedy died, I had nothing to say to Mrs Collings either. She suspected something untoward had happened, that I had been involved in some way, but she grimly refused to ask me about it. It wouldn't have taken much for me to tell her, to explain that I hadn't really meant him to drown, that it really had been an accident. She would have known, too, that I was lying; she would have seen right through me — and that was why she didn't ask the question that was forming in her mind, all through that last summer. If she were to ask me, and I were to answer, she would have to look into my eyes and see that, at some level, I had planned it, and that meant, did it not?, that she was implicated. She was the one who had told me to find the cunning in myself, she was the one who had been my guide. I'm not blaming her — I would never blame her, any more than I would blame myself — but she would have held herself responsible. Had she asked the question she could have asked, at any time, she would have been obliged to take the blame for making me into a killer, and by that time she was too ill, and too weak, to do that.

It must have surprised her that I thought we could just go on as we had done, being friends. I was too young, I suppose, to recognise that the only way we could keep our secrets, the fact and the recognition, the expected question and the dreaded answer, was to retreat. Besides, I had already guessed that, when the time came, she would want to die alone. She had said as much, often enough, when she talked about her move to Ceres cottage: she would die alone, like a good animal, listening to the quiet, letting the silence take her away. She didn't want to live in the town, like some stain fading slowly on the air, she would be a quiet note fading away, disappearing into the hinterland. It's what people mean, when they talk about a dignified death: a silence, a special fastidiousness. After my father died, I thought that idea was a lie, something we tell ourselves to put off the recognition of the inevitable mess, but it's a lie I understand, and I understood it in Mrs Collings' situation, even if I didn't quite believe it. It was all she had, perhaps — but to keep it, she had to send me away sooner than she had expected. Oh, subtly, kindly, with a certain visible regret that heartened us both; but it was another accident that should have been avoided, and when I left, on that last day, I felt like Peter when the cock crowed, denying something, or someone, though not quite sure who it was I was betraying.

* ★ ★

I was away at college when word came that my mother had been killed in a car accident. It was all handled very carefully, with tact and compassion and yet, at the same time, it was also rather businesslike. I was taken aside after a lecture and told that my tutor wanted to speak to me. This struck me as odd, and I immediately assumed bad news, but it didn't cross my mind that anyone had actually died — or not, that is, till I saw my tutor's face. Dr Wright was a cool, detached, scholarly man who had recently been divorced by a much younger wife and I have to confess that, though he had my respect, I didn't really know what to make of him. He planned everything so carefully, down to the very second he would conclude a lecture or a tutorial; he seemed to know exactly the limitations and the possibilities of every one of his students and yet, considering how much work went into all this, he had the look of someone going through the motions, with his mind on something else, much of the time. I'm not talking about his divorce. That seemed not to matter at all. No: I think he was a man with a secret passion, real or imagined, a man who had a carefully concealed lover somewhere, or a secret fund he was building up slowly, in order to buy a boat and sail away. Until that day arrived, he just wanted everything to go smoothly. My mother's death was a glitch in all this careful organisation. Now he would have to reach into himself and pull out an inordinate amount of — something — and it was immediately obvious that he had no idea what that something was. That was when I knew someone had died, when I saw his face: that terrified look, that tenderness for his own predicament.

'Come in,' he said. 'Come in, and sit down — ' He had come around his desk to welcome me and stood, with his left arm half extended, a little like the anatomical figures in Vesalius' *De humani corporis fabrica*, as if he was on show, or performing some ancient social ritual — and the ridiculous thing was that I didn't need any of this, I just needed the facts, so I could get on with things, so this part could be over. I sat down quickly, because for a moment I was afraid, if I remained standing, that he might touch me. A gentle touch, a cool palm of the hand on my forearm, something of that sort, but unbearable nevertheless.

'Is it my father?' I said, quickly.

He looked even more worried now. I was rushing him. He didn't like to be rushed. For a moment he couldn't quite bring himself to continue; then he shook his head.

And so I knew. 'What happened?' I said.

A glimmer of relief passed across his face. We were back on the script he had prepared. 'I'm afraid there's been an accident,' he said, straight out of those old films they used to show for the Sunday matinée.

I didn't listen to the rest, or not all of it. I just sifted out the few factual details he had to offer: my mother had been walking, alone, on the coast road, and a car had gone out of control. Those were his words: *a car had gone out of control*. It sounded abstract, theoretical — but I knew, immediately, and I almost said it aloud, came close to jumping up and shouting at him the one thing I knew for sure, the one thing I had known even before it happened. *They did it*, I thought. *They killed her*. And before he could say any more, I got to my feet — slowly, a little unsteadily — thanked him, and walked out of his office, out, along the corridor, through the foyer where the student pigeonholes were, and away, into the cool February air.

Everybody knew Little Peter Tone. Everybody always knows the town drunk. Little Peter had been just plain Peter once, but over the years he had grown smaller and sillier with each new disgrace. Like the day he was found fast asleep on the War Memorial clutching a bottle of Buckfast, his trousers down around his ankles, soaked in urine. Or the time he stole his brother-in-law's car and tried to sell it in the local pub. He was the town joke, the fool. Some people said he'd been all right before he started drinking, that he'd once been quite a talented footballer; mostly, though, they knew him as an embarrassment, a man whose own children wouldn't talk to him. He had been written off as mortally ill more than once and went about the town looking like he was at death's door, but he was always cheerful, with a ready grin for everyone he met — and an outstretched hand in hopes of a hand-out.

Little Peter was the one who killed my mother. Nobody knows now if he did it on purpose: he had borrowed his brother-in-law's car again; and was driving it up and down the coast road for no good reason, going nowhere, but sober for once. *Just out for a drive*, he would say later. He couldn't actually drive, he didn't even have a licence, but that didn't bother him. What did bother him was the accusation that he'd lost control of the car because he didn't know what he was doing, and at least two people heard him boasting that he'd hit that Yank bitch on purpose. That was probably just talk, of course. He'd been driving a car he didn't know how to drive, and my mother had been in the wrong place at the wrong time. The police investigated as well as they could, but it was determined that Little Peter was sober at the time of the accident and, in the end, he got off fairly lightly. There had been no witnesses to the incident itself, and there was no evidence to show that he had been speeding. He hadn't left the scene of the accident; he had stopped — probably because there were witnesses — and he had stayed put till the police and ambulance came. That was a surprise for most people, and it probably counted in his favour. Nobody could work out why he didn't just run away.

When I got home, my father was in a daze. The doctor had been up to the house and had given him some friendly, mind-numbing drug, but the shock was more than he could stand. He was already ill, it turned out, and not long after the funeral — a private event, attended only by family and a few friends from London — he took to his bed on doctor's orders. I seriously considered giving up my studies and coming home to look after him, but he wouldn't hear of it. He hired a woman from Sandhaven, an early incarnation of Mrs K, to keep house and cook, and he spent his days in bed reading or staring out of the window at the birds circling over the point. I hung around for a fortnight — and it was during that time, if I recall, that I had my last little fling with Moira, a fling that might well have resulted in yet another misadventure, if the arithmetic was to be trusted — then I took the train back to college and arid tutorials on *The Parlement of Foules* with the well-prepared Dr Wright. By the summer, I felt desperately guilty and I couldn't wait to get back. I wanted to be there if my father died too, and I wanted to talk to him properly, at least once, about something other than birds and pictures.

★ ★ ★

By the end of the summer, Amanda and I were barely talking to one another. Mrs K had become a little remote, too, and I spent the days alone, thinking, dwelling on the past, mulling things over. I was becoming obsessed by the story of Hazel Birnie. I wanted to meet her, or at least see her, maybe talk to her in passing, incognito. I had seen a picture in the paper, but it wasn't much to go on. She was in her school clothes, standing perched on a bike, squinting at the camera. She looked about ten. I saw nothing in her face that suggested she and I might be blood kin, but then I didn't see anything to suggest that she was Tom Birnie's child either — nor, for that matter, did she look anything like her mother. She seemed to have emerged from nowhere, manufactured according to some abstract plan, some blueprint of a child. But then, all I had to work with was a grainy photograph in the newspaper. If I could only see her, I might find an answer to the question that had come to dominate my thoughts. Was Hazel actually my own flesh and blood? How could I know? How could I be sure, one way or another? To be honest, I have no idea, looking back, why I cared. I had no desire for children, much less for this particular child. I had never even discussed having kids with Amanda and, as far as I know, she had no inclinations in that direction either. Of course, I had probably done more than I admitted to avoid the subject: early on, perhaps, before we began to sleepwalk through the marriage, there might have been some notion in her head that it was only a matter of time, that children were to be part of the normal course of events. After a while, though, she had probably given up on the idea — or maybe she had just given up on me — and she confined herself to having fun with friends and keeping up with the arts and current affairs. Or so I thought, at the time.

One night, she was having one of her dinner parties. This meant two things: first, I was to help her prepare the table (she made the food herself, on principle) and second, I had to behave. This wasn't quite as difficult as it sounds: I was in my own house, I could create diversions, escaping from the company every now and then, to put music on, or to fetch something Amanda wanted to show off. For a while I even took up smoking, so I could retreat to the garden for a cigar. Amanda fumed about that for a while, but I kept it up and eventually it became an accepted part of the soirée: she stopped fuming and I was allowed to go out for a smoke. Luckily, none of her friends smoked. Most of the time, neither did I.

It was a warm evening. By that time, I had started to think about taking things further, maybe taking some kind of drastic action, in order to get some answers — but I hadn't yet figured out what I meant by that. Still, the evening promised plenty of time for reflection: Amanda's dinner parties were nothing if not predictable affairs, and the people she invited were easy to humour, women she had grown up with ('the girls'), and their husbands or boyfriends, people from work and their spouses, sometimes her sister, Mary, and her sister's girlfriend, Maria. I

143

liked Mary and Maria best; they lived in Edinburgh, though, and didn't get through that often. That night, the guests included Michelle (*Shell*: apt nickname) and her boyfriend Mark. Shell was one of 'the girls' — and Mark was definitely one of the boys. Dull, but perfect auto-pilot material. The other couple, a new colleague of Amanda's and his thin, pinched-looking wife, were people I hadn't met before.

At one time, I had regarded Amanda's friends with awe and wonder. They were all the same, and they loved it. They came from Coldhaven, or from places nearby; most of them had gone to college or had spent some time away, but now that they were back, their local accents were more pronounced than they had ever been, and you could tell they had been unhappy during their absence. You just knew they couldn't wait to get back to the old rivalries and secret attractions and rituals. At school, they were the clean children, the ones who worked hard and did well at games, the ones who participated. They would have been quick to point out that they were no better than anybody else, but they were always well turned out. Like their mothers before them, they made an effort. As children, they collected something — stamps, coins, cigarette cards, train timetables — and the need to gather and store away goods stayed with them for the rest of their lives. One of the husbands, a guy called Murdo, turned up for his first dinner in a mauve shirt and a pink and yellow tie; he was a collector of words. You could see it in his face: though he was a born and bred local, he still delighted in the place names of Fife: Freuchie, Limekilns, Star, Burntturk. He genuinely loved those sounds — but it was also his way of explaining, in a neat and socially acceptable code, why he had never moved on to bigger and brighter things. He just loved it here; he just enjoyed being part of all this quaint nonsense. As dinner guests went, I rather liked him. What I liked best about Amanda's dinners, however, was doing the washing up afterwards. For one thing, it meant I could escape the company, while they went through to the sitting room for coffee — and I did like to escape from her friends, just as they liked to have me off their hands for a while. Sometimes, somebody would offer to dry up, and I had to insist a little; most of the time, they let me get on with it, especially if they were regulars.

The other good thing about this little chore was the look of the dining table when I was clearing up. It was much more interesting, afterwards, than it had been before the guests

145

arrived, when everything was neat and nicely set out and clean. There was something forensic about it, all the coffee dregs and crumbs of oatmeal, smudges of fish oil on the rim of a plate, little pools of cream on a spoon, or the tatters of a label someone had peeled from a wine bottle, more or less unconsciously, all the way through the evening. I liked the after-scent of tallow when I snuffed out the candles, and finding the right way to stack the plates so pieces of food didn't get trapped in between, to end up in the sink, floating amid the soapsuds. One of Amanda's friends, a fat woman who worked in her office, had a habit of spilling little piles of salt in various places all over the table, and I would go around afterwards, finding them, trying to work out what it meant, if it meant anything at all. Amanda herself had toothpick syndrome: she insisted on having toothpicks on the table in small plastic boxes and, as soon as the dessert course started, she started removing the toothpicks in the box nearest hers, and spreading them out on the tablecloth, picking them up from time to time, fingering them, so the wood got stained with faint traces of cheese or clementine. Nobody else seemed to notice this.

When I had finished clearing up, I went outside and stood in the garden. It was cool, after the close, packed human warmth of the dining room, and I stepped away from the house, into the colder space beyond the patio. Now I could feel the full contact of the night air on my skin, the simple, clear pleasure of it. The delicious *frisson* of cold. When the winter days began, I came into my own element, but even in autumn, or late in the summer on nights like this, I could go out into the night after a few days of warmth, and I would feel restored to some initial state, some origin. *Home*. It was like those occasions when you catch a regional airline, one of those little planes that you have to cross the tarmac to board: I would always wear a thin shirt, with the neck open, and I would wait till the other passengers boarded, to stay out in the cool air for as long as possible. Finally, when I couldn't put it off any longer, I would climb the steps to embark, lingering on the top stair, in the eye of the wind. I feel at home in the wind. It feels like a companion, whenever it finds me — a companion, not necessarily a friend, but something I know intimately. Amanda thinks it odd that I like the cold so much. She says it reveals something about me, something Freudian. I suppose, if that were true, it would reveal something about her too. But then, I don't really see her point. I like to be a little cold; I like the wind on my face and hands. What harm could there be in this obscure pleasure?

Usually, the guests at Amanda's dinner parties were, at best, a mere distraction. That evening, however, a surprising thing happened. I had just stepped back into the kitchen when the thin wife appeared, a curious look on her face. I felt a little annoyed, like a *chef de cuisine* who finds some diner wandering around his domain, poking among the dishes and saucepans. I tried to conceal this; it wasn't worth the trouble I'd have with Amanda later, if I were to upset one of her guests. I tried to remember the woman's name, and failed.

'Hello,' I said. 'Can I get you something?'

Everyone but me had been drinking white wine, and the woman appeared a little tipsy. 'This was your father's house,' she said, looking around. 'It's not as I imagined it would be.' She went and stood at the French windows, looking out at the garden.

'Well,' I said. 'It's changed some, over the years.' I tried not to sound too eager, or too curious. 'Did you know my father?'

The woman looked at me and made an odd little sound, a kind of apprentice shriek. 'Oh no,' she said. 'Not personally.'

'Ah,' I said. She had meant that she knew

his work. Sometimes people did, though not usually those in Amanda's immediate circle. But then, she was the wife of a colleague. She had a life of her own and, I suddenly saw, she was as bored by evenings like these as I was.

'I love photography,' she said. 'Especially landscapes. I admired your father's work very much.'

I nodded. There was something else she wanted to say, but didn't know how. I hoped it had nothing to do with the accident, or with my father's death.

'Do you know,' she said, 'I wrote him a letter once. A fan letter, I suppose.' I was surprised by this. I didn't know of my father receiving fan mail. All at once I remembered the woman's name: Emma something. She was older than her husband, and a little too delicate, perhaps, for him. She was one of those people who lives slightly apart, with the solipsist's habit of speaking, all of a sudden, halfway through a train of thought that had, until that moment been running silently in her own mind. 'It was because of a photograph of his that I saw, one of the Brière series.' She smiled. She should have smiled more often, for it lit her face so that she no longer looked so pinched, so very drawn. 'I used to go there, *en vacances*,' she said.

'Into the black marshes. It was a very happy time for me.'

'I'm sure he was glad to know that,' I said. 'To know he had communicated his love for the marshes — '

She laughed softly. 'Perhaps he was,' she said. 'But he didn't reply. I can't imagine he even read it. It was a foolish letter and he must have been very busy. It was long ago, before he came here to live.'

'Ah.' I was ashamed, a little, of how glib I'd sounded. 'Well, I'm sure he was busy. He was never very good at remembering things.' Something of a solipsist himself, I thought. It hadn't occurred to me, in so many words, but I don't think he was altogether persuaded of the existence of others. The birds, yes. The sea. The wildflowers out on the point, but not other people.

She smiled. 'No,' she said. 'Well, he was an artist.' She studied my face. 'Terrible thing about his friend, though. That must have been hard to bear.'

'His friend?'

'Oh — ' She looked horrified, as she realised that I didn't know what she was talking about. 'I would have thought . . . I assumed you knew.'

'Knew what?'

'Well.' She looked uncertain whether she

should proceed. I tried not to look worried or upset. I wanted her to say what she had to say quickly. 'They were both working for the same paper. When he was still a news photographer. In Guatemala, if I remember. They kept them prisoner for several days, and they tortured the friend. Not your father, though. He escaped.' She looked aggrieved. 'I'm sorry. I thought you knew — '

'What happened to him?'

She looked confused. 'He escaped,' she said.

'The friend?'

'No. Your father.' She shook her head. 'His friend died.'

'What was his name?'

'I'm sorry?'

'The friend. Do you remember his name?'

'Oh, yes.' She looked more frightened now, as a new fact registered, something she didn't want to have to say. And yet she had come in here, into my golden kitchen with its various lights and coloured shadows, to have this very conversation. She couldn't help herself.

'It was Mallon,' she said. 'Thomas Mallon.'

I nodded, and she looked away. My mother had been a Mallon, I knew that from idle conversations they'd had about the Gardiners and the Mallons, how the Mallons were so volatile, the Gardiners so patient and

151

painstaking. Hotheads versus cardigans. Irish Catholics versus Scots Presbyterians with a soupçon of Huguenot for good measure. It was a game they played sometimes. My mother's name had been Kate Mallon, Catherine, Cat, and she'd had a brother called Tom. He'd died young, they'd said. That was what they told me. He'd died young, that was all.

★ ★ ★

I used to think the dead travelled away, out to some great distance, as they decayed, over weeks, or months, or years. I didn't believe in the stories they told at school, stories of heaven, little fables of the afterlife; I thought the dead went back to nothing, breaking down slowly, like fallen leaves, or the scatter of bones you find out in the marshland, the bones of a dog or a bird, whitening and breaking down in the sun, everything going to powder, then scattering on the wind. After my mother died, I still thought that was how it happened: she seemed far away, buried in the earth, unseen, her spirit, or soul, her *essence*, decaying somewhere on the air or among the stars. They didn't let me see her, of course, after the accident. She was badly injured and they thought it better that I didn't see that, but I'm not sure they were right. They put a distance between us, the kind of distance we learn about, one way or another in school, in religious studies: the distance of heaven, the distance of some other world. When I wanted to think about my mother, I would close my eyes and I would see objects: a necklace with red and green beads on a silver chain; the sweater she used to wear when she was painting, a deep terracotta colour, smudged at the elbows and cuffs with blue or yellow paint; the antique silver hairbrush my father had given her. When I came back for the funeral, I began to notice things about the house at Whitland, things only a stranger would notice: the smell of her paints; the bakery smell in the kitchen from years of her special cherry cakes and fruit crumbles; the sound the wind made in the chimney of her studio; the splashes of paint on the floor. Walking to the grave, with that sealed box, I remembered her shoes standing in rows on the little stand in the hall — small, narrow, lace-up shoes, with flat heels and round toes, newly polished but already flecked with dust — and I realised that, earlier that morning, I had been in the hall and they weren't there any more. Someone had taken them away. I hadn't really registered at the time but, as I stood by the grave, that was how I knew she was gone. The shoes. I could close my eyes right now and picture them, but I cannot see *her*. Afterwards, when I went home for the summer, I used to go out to the cemetery to visit the grave. My father wouldn't come; he said he wasn't up to it but he could feel her all around him anyway, in the house, in the air, in the light, in the calls of the birds beyond the point. He could feel her there; I couldn't. Then, that summer, when he was dying, I would hear him, sometimes, mumbling to himself in the bedroom, and I knew he was talking to her. For him, she was an indelible presence; for me, she was, quite simply, gone. And he wasn't really there, either, he was already absent. Maybe he always had been.

Out at the cemetery, I would take the vase from her grave, remove the old flowers and rinse it clean under the free-standing tap not far from the headstone, wiping away the film of green algae, my fingers thrust into the neck of the thing as far as they would go. The rushing water was cold, and I would let it run a while, till my hands were chilled to the bone. When I looked up, over the ranks of white crosses and angels, I could see the church tower rising above the slate roofs and red chimneys, and a flock of cream and grey pigeons wheeling around it in formation, catching the sun on their wings then turning, darkening, becoming different birds, like an Escher print, or a conjuring trick. The clock had been stopped at five minutes to twelve for as long as I could remember, and I recalled a story my mother would tell about the old town clock where she grew up, how she had climbed once into the works of it to see the town, spread beneath her like a coloured quilt, through the cracks in the face. There had been nests in the beams, and she remembered seeing the eggs among all that machinery of cogs and wheels. It always surprised me that I knew things about my mother, because I didn't remember her telling me about her life; it always seemed to be about art and books and places she had visited, not about her. Yet I knew more than I would have expected. That I didn't know about her brother hardly came as a surprise: all my life, I had suspected my parents of being on the run from something, and she had carried with her this spark of anger, of grief — of who knew what else? Did she blame my father, that he survived? What had he done to save himself? Had he ever told her? And, if he

155

had, was what he'd said the whole truth and nothing but?

★ ★ ★

After my father died, I was alone out on Whitland — and I was happy that way. At that time, I would have said that my only desire was to remain out there, alone, with nobody to accommodate. No ghosts, no memories. No others. Just me, myself, in a house full of instruments and measuring devices, needles stealing across sheets of graph paper, sensitive monitors gauging the risks of intrusion. That was all I wanted: a house that was, in itself, a sensitive membrane, a register, where every shift in the atmosphere — weather and gossip and the most subtle demographics — was brought to my awareness in real time, as it happened. I wanted to be alone, and true to something. I wanted to be certain that nothing could intrude upon that solitude. I had no reason to leave the house: I had all I needed, and the walks I took were nothing but a whim or, rather, an appeasement, an offer to meet the world halfway, and so dispel curiosity. And so keep it at bay. I wanted to be unavailable. Then I met Amanda, entirely by chance, and before I really knew what was happening, I had married her.

To begin with, I would have said we were happy enough. Or if not happy, then contented. It was an absorbing exercise, moving her into the house, as we got to know each other, learning how to occupy the same space. It was absorbing, and it made the house different, oddly larger, and lighter, like going from room to room and throwing open all the shutters. Amanda wanted to buy all new things — furniture, rugs, things my father would have hated — and I enjoyed going along with her to pick them out. It was important, she said, that we choose these things together; in the end, though, she was usually the one who decided. I didn't mind. I liked the old stuff well enough, but when she suggested selling off a few of the more careworn pieces, to make way for the new, I went along with her. There were things I didn't want to part with, and they stayed. My father's books, his instruments, his materials, his darkroom. My mother's studio. My own little room next to the landing. All these remained intact. Only the main bedroom and the living room were seriously affected by the alterations. Amanda wanted a brand new fitted kitchen, but I couldn't bring myself to have one. We managed a compromise on that.

So it went on — and I suppose I thought it would go on for ever. Or maybe I didn't think anything. Maybe I just took it all for granted. I can't say, now, when things first started to change but, looking back, I see that there was a first, silent shift, an almost overnight slide from being newlyweds one day to a typical married couple the next. All of a sudden, it seemed we were going to be awkward with one another. I started to dislike the changes she was making; then I began to resist them. She started to make little digs about the fact that, with my private income, I had it too easy, that I was shirking a duty to get out and *do things*.

'You ought to get a job,' she said, one day, out of the blue.

'What?'

She looked at me curiously, as if she had only just noticed that I was a man who spent his days at home, rearranging his books and listening to music. 'You should get a job,' she said. 'You spend too much time up here by yourself. It's not healthy.'

'I don't need a job,' I said. 'I already have enough money.'

She laughed. 'I'm not talking about money,' she said. 'I'm talking about *doing something* with your life. You could work for a

158

charity, if it's the money thing that bothers you.'

'I don't want a job,' I said. It was nothing more than that, a conversation in passing, a conversation within a conversation, really, but all at once I saw that she didn't like me as much as she had done. It had nothing to do with love, it was all to do with liking — and I suppose, now that I'd noticed, now that she'd brought it to my attention, I began to wonder, for the first time, whether I actually liked her. I didn't come to any conclusions, it was just that the question passed through my mind. It wasn't some big drama, some turning point. At least, I didn't think so at the time. Yet what happened a few months later, the real turning point, depended entirely on that moment, and the mood of vague unease, the guardedness that evening created, a guardedness that would eventually settle into a calculated neutrality, a process that was at once formal and entirely collaborative, like the enactment of a ritual.

We were driving back through the country-side in late summer, on one of those astonishing Fife nights when you think the whole world will turn the darkest possible blue and stay that way, a merest glimmer of light over the firth, a thick darkness close to, rabbits appearing suddenly in the headlights from time to time, picked out in the light then disappearing into a nothingness that was only inches away. Illumined by our passing, the trees on that road, combed sidewise — *thrawn* — by the wind over decades of desperate, drunken growth, seemed as fleeting and translucent as the porch lights of the cottages and farms I glimpsed in passing. The road was empty. For once, the car radio was switched off, and I thought what a pleasure it would have been had I been alone on that road, without Amanda. I loved driving at night, especially on my own. The thought passed through my mind that I could have stopped the car and got out, to look up at the sky. To look up, to taste and smell it.

'Are you all right?' Amanda was staring at me as if in the presence of a madman.

'Yes,' I said. 'Why wouldn't I be?' I turned back to the road.

'You were talking to yourself.'

'No I wasn't.'

'Yes you were,' she said. She seemed genuinely concerned. 'I heard you quite clearly. You were talking to yourself.'

I laughed. 'Oh, really,' I said. 'So what did I say?'

She didn't speak for a moment. I looked at her. 'This isn't a joke, you know,' she said. 'I'm worried about you — '

'What did I say?'

'You've been acting strange recently,' she said. 'It's not healthy, the way you sit up there all day in the house, not seeing anybody, not doing anything — '

'*What the hell did I say?*'

I said it too loudly, I know that. I almost shouted, in fact — but then, I was exasperated. I wanted to know what I had said. All she had to do was tell me. But then, I hadn't said anything. I felt like the woman in that old movie, where Joseph Cotten is trying to drive her insane so he can steal her inheritance. Joseph Cotten, or George Sanders, one of those beautiful, ambiguous men who no longer seem to exist. And who was the actress? Joan Fontaine, I imagine. Joan Fontaine, or maybe Loretta Young. One of those beautiful, ambiguous women. 'What is it exactly that I'm supposed to have said?' I asked her, quietly now.

She didn't answer. For a moment, I thought she was crying. Then we passed through a pool of light and I could see that her face was set. We drove on in silence. I tried to think of something to say, to break the ice, but I couldn't. All I could think of was that film. I remember it was very good until just before the end, which is as much as anybody can hope for with those old movies.

My marriage to Amanda was already over by then, had I but known it. I should have done. By the time I left, she was so distant I sometimes felt like waving at her, as if through a cloud of fog, on the few occasions that I needed to attract her attention. There were times, during our few conversations, when I felt it would have been better to write things down so they were clear because, as soon as the conversation was over and we had agreed what we needed to agree, we both forgot it. We lived in a shared place, but we inhabited entirely separate spaces there, entirely separate dimensions. From time to time I would catch her looking at me, as if mildly curious, or bemused. There was nothing urgent about that look, nothing you could really call interest, just a passing curiosity, of the kind one might feel about a reclusive neighbour, or some odd-looking specimen at the zoo. The tapir, say. Still, I think it surprised her, at least to begin with, that not knowing who she was married to didn't cause her some huge existential crisis. I think it disappointed her too. But she drifted on, as I did, and we were married, more or less normal, no obvious trouble. No fights. No affairs — or not for a long time. No big dramas.

The thing about marriage is that it fades so slowly. Sometimes it fades in a fond way, like the warmth leaching from folded clothes in a linen cupboard, but it fades, and nobody seems to notice for the longest time. Sometimes it takes years to go then, all at once, there's nothing, just a faint watermark, or a figment of gilt edging, like the creased insignia on a useless bond tucked away in an old man's attic. Our marriage, Amanda's and mine, faded quickly, but it didn't occur to either of us to do anything to stop the rot. We just kept our heads down and lumbered on, trying to live the lives we now realised we really wanted — which, in her case as much as mine, I think, was the life we'd had before, when we were single. Thinking back, I'm surprised that she didn't act sooner than she did. Before I did my little Humbert Humbert routine, I was pretty difficult to be around: a sardonic, selfish man who knew exactly how selfish he was being, yet pretended that everything was fine — the cat's pyjamas, hunky dory, *comme il faut.*

The other thing about marriage is that it is a story. You have to keep adding some new event from time to time, a line here, a paragraph there, whole chapters that both the protagonists, while they may not be on stage for the entire drama, should still be able to share, indirectly, when they are. I suppose I shouldn't be talking about marriage in the abstract like this, of course I shouldn't, but I suspect there are many more couples who are living, right now, as Amanda and I did for so long, and I suspect there are all too many who achieve the sad little miracle of going all the way to the end without noticing how little they actually have. Maybe that was all my parents were doing, towards the end. They wouldn't have been alone in that — and surely they managed something far more civilised, far more nourishing, than Mrs K's tedious, and probably fairly ugly, ménage with Alec, or Moira's brutal *coniunctio* with Tom Birnie. I had to wonder why anybody got married, when they had the evidence of their parents' lives right there in front of them. And when they did tie the knot, what did they expect would happen? What did they hope for? I suspect that my difficulty, which I think Amanda shared, was that I was one of those idealists of marriage, one of the dewy-eyed clan who want the story to be intricate and, at the same time, open, a lattice of shared knowledge and possibilities, a true romance. The thing about marriage, though — the real thing — is that there is a moment when a husband begins to suspect his wife, or a wife her husband, of having another story altogether, a separate, private story, that remains, and perhaps will always remain, untold. This has nothing to do with the past, or with jealousy, or the everyday vices that familiarity exposes. It has nothing to do with loving or not loving. No: this is a story — no grand drama, probably, but something important on the local level, something that cannot be set aside — a story that is told silently, again and again, in the small hours, while the other sleeps, or on long, wet afternoons with the radio murmuring in the background and the whisper of rain at the window, the quiet, slow whisper of rain that sounds like a narrative in itself, a story that is being told elsewhere but has come into being here, for an hour or so, like the past relived, or a future perfectly foreseen. This is the story that sits at the centre of all the others, the one true thing, the defining moment that must be kept hidden, kept private, if it is to be kept intact. But the worst of it is, that story is also a choice: an invention, even. It didn't happen by chance, not at the point of origin, and not later, when it was purified, kept holy and enshrined in a memory so hidden that even the storyteller himself barely knows it is there. It sounds odd, but it happens: it is a choice, this private story, a choice that continues to be made, consciously or otherwise, while the outer narrative unfolds — and the time comes when the surface only unfolds to protect this one thing, this exclusive memory, to set it apart and keep it holy. This is the story that exists in spite of all the others, in its own separate space, in that private inner chamber where a man's only neighbour is the wind. No matter how innocent it might seem, if it could be told aloud, it is the one guilty secret, the one real lie in that surface existence, just as it is the one true fact in his own soul.

★   ★   ★

It was breakfast time. A Saturday morning, so Amanda wasn't in the usual rush. I preferred weekdays, when she scrambled through a cup of coffee and a slice of toast and was gone before I'd even begun to eat, leaving only the smell of molten butter in her wake. On the weekend, we ate breakfast together.

'Who's Katie?' she said, suddenly.

For a minute, everything stopped, then I turned and looked mildly puzzled, standing in the kitchen, clutching a cereal box.

'Katie?' I wasn't pretending. As far as I knew, I wasn't acquainted with anyone of that name.

'That's what you called me,' she said. 'Just

now. You called me Katie.'

I cranked the puzzlement up a notch — only now, though nothing had sprung to mind and I had no obvious guilty secret, it already had an element of fraud to it, a soupçon of deception. 'No, I didn't,' I said.

'Yes you did.' She was trying to be mild, merely curious, careful not to attach any great importance to the matter. It was all a question of preparation: if Katie existed, she wanted to be able to wriggle out, to know and not know, or perhaps simply save face. Or perhaps she was looking for a reason to begin her own private story, one that would, perhaps, contain a genuine affair, a riposte. 'Katie, you said. So — who's Katie?'

I found myself a bowl. I wasn't looking at her now, I was avoiding her eyes. 'Search me,' I said. I started pouring in the milk, trying to play it as cool as she was doing, but not quite managing. That was the annoying thing — more annoying than the fact that she was accusing me and not accusing me at the same time — and that was what stopped me from seeing the thing through, dispelling her suspicions, giving the matter its due and burying it. She was perfectly cool and I wasn't, and yet I had nothing to be guilty about. By that time, she really was suspicious, but she was doing fine, she was making light of it; if I could just have matched her in that, everything would have been fine. But I was never any good at those games.

She waited.

'I don't know anyone called Katie,' I said, trying for an air of long-suffering finality — but, of course, she didn't believe me. But she didn't say so. She just smiled grimly and went back to her coffee.

'Suit yourself,' she said, opening the paper. She had succeeded in making everything and nothing out of the moment. I knew it would pass, it did pass, and it *was* nothing. Still, I remember it now, and I see that it was the beginning of the end, for her, and then for me — though I didn't know about the affair until long after it began. I begin to see, looking back, with what may well be the requisite mixture of shame and compassion, that what bothered her most was the fact that I didn't even take the trouble to know.

★   ★   ★

Now, when I consider those last few months before I ran away, I remember a strange and, at times, terrifying sensation that time was about to stop. I just couldn't escape the idea that, at any minute, the world might come to a complete stand-still. With the benefit of hindsight, I can see that I was grieving for my father and for a dream I'd had and squandered, but I also see that there was something wilful in the way I spent whole weeks, entire months, doing nothing. Of course, I had a cover for this descent into inactivity: I wasn't just lying around on the sofa, watching daytime television. No. Every day I woke up and I took great pains to fill my life with pointless tasks and perverse hobbies, pieces of nonsense that appeared to keep me occupied while the days ticked by. I suppose, at some level, I knew what was going on; I had been to see Dr Gerard, the old family GP who had attended my father in his final illness and, after some beating around the bush — me trying to say nothing was wrong, even as I sat there looking for help, he talking around the problem, making it into a kind of story so I wouldn't lose face — I went home with a prescription for an anti-anxiety drug. This, I understood, would even out the days and give me a sense of calm. What the doctor meant, of course, was that it would — might — stave off the growing sense of imminent disaster, the permanent low-level dread that filled my days. Even now, I'm not sure what it was that I dreaded.

I have to admit that I didn't expect the

drugs to make a difference — or not, at least, to the extent that they did, within a matter of days. I had been told it might take some time, weeks, perhaps even months, but within a few days I was already adrift, muffled in a strange, rather pleasant indifference to almost everything, or at least, everything of consequence. Now, the events of my own life — my failing marriage, my lack of purpose, my anger at and for and about my parents — faded into the background, while everything minor, everything trivial, gained huge importance. It turned out, once I started taking the pills, that I was more or less contented with my life. I took real delight in sitting on the upper landing, listening to the starlings in the roof-space. I became even more attached to my daily walk, becoming irritable, even slightly hysterical, when something occurred to delay my departure. No matter what the weather, I went out and I always took the same route, at the same pace, thinking almost the same thoughts and noticing the same things at exactly the same places every morning. Yet, at the same time, I didn't think of myself as having *changed*, particularly. I just felt lulled, calm and, for a while, I even forgot my anxiety about time. I had a perfect routine, which included doing things about the house and taking care of the finances

— which had begun to slip — as well as more intimate activities, like my walks, or the evenings I spent reading the papers in the little room off the upstairs landing. Amanda went to work — she liked her job and insisted on going every day, full time, even though we didn't need the money — and in the evenings she watched television or sat downstairs in the sitting room making phone calls to 'the girls'. I imagine she was lonely at times; though not, I suspect, for me. Still, she had her friends and they had a regular evening out in some restaurant, just along the coast in Sandhaven, where she had gone to school and where most of her friends still lived. I can't imagine she missed my company, not then. We had quickly passed the stage in a marriage when being together counts for much and, besides, we didn't really like the same things. What she wanted from me was stability, a sense of order, the assurance that I was more or less contented or, if I wasn't, that things would never get so bad that I would become depressing or unpredictable. Looking back, I can't say that I blame her for that. On the contrary, it seems an entirely realistic, and not very demanding, basis for a marriage. After all, she never brought her troubles to me. Assuming there were troubles.

So it was that, with a little help from Dr

Gerard, things were going swimmingly for all concerned. It might have continued like that for years — I imagine it would — if I hadn't picked up that particular paper that Saturday, and read that particular story. I suspect it sounds incredible that reading a mere newspaper item could change the direction of a man's life, but that was what happened to me. Looking back, I'm glad it did. An ill wind, and all that. And isn't there also something terrible, something terrifying in the fact that, when I remember the deaths and the image of the burnt-out car, what I think of first, above everything else, is how these things eventually saved me from a daily routine of mild anxiety and ordinary deception? During that first consultation with Dr Gerard, I remember him saying that I was still recovering from my father's death and that I had to find something that mattered to me, something to care about. Presumably he was advising me to take up golf, or painting in water-colour. I can't imagine that he wanted me to run off with a fourteen-year-old girl and go wandering the countryside, trying to figure out what to do next.

The Dark End of the Fair

Mrs Collings died at the end of the year, when the town was busy with Christmas. She died alone, just as she had wished, but — and this is the last of my secrets — she didn't lie dead in her cottage, undiscovered, for as long as everyone thought she did. I had resolved not to be a bother to her any more, after it became evident that she was troubled by the Malcolm Kennedy affair, but my resolve had broken on the first day of the Christmas holidays and I had climbed the hill, one last time, just to see that she was all right and to take her a little gift, a knick-knack of no particular value, and of fairly dubious taste, that I had bought in town. I didn't intend to detain her long; I just wanted to sit with her a while, over a cup of tea and a piece of cake, not saying much, just letting a few minutes pass before I took my leave, once and for all. I was kidding myself in that, though, and I suspect I knew it. No matter what I pretended, I secretly *knew* that I was giving in to a much more serious temptation — the temptation to confess — when I made my way to Ceres cottage that morning. I'd promised myself I never would, but I didn't want her to die without offering some kind of explanation — so I suppose, looking back, that I was lucky she died when she did. I suppose we both were. Had I been in my right mind, and not softened up by all the Christmas sentiment, I imagine I wouldn't even have considered letting the cat out of the bag. And maybe that's wishful thinking too.

It was a bitterly cold morning, with snow on the way. We rarely get snow on this stretch of coastline, but when it does come, it comes thick and fast and it lies a long time. I was wrapped up well, my mother had seen to that when I told her I was going out — but I didn't tell her where I was going. I didn't show her my little Christmas present either — a mauve-coloured porcelain rose with faded-looking greenish leaves — because it was already wrapped and tucked away in my pocket, along with the card I'd made myself, a tiny, brightly coloured drawing of a Christmas tree covered in red and blue baubles, in an old, slightly battered envelope. These were my offerings. I didn't want to make too much of my visit, because that would have emphasised the finality of it all and I didn't want it to seem final, or in any way momentous. I just wanted to drop by and then take my leave, as if it were the most ordinary thing in the world. I wanted no sense of occasion. Or so I told myself — though all the while, an explanation was forming in my mind, a more or less true story, with some facts emphasised and some glossed over, the story of an everyday mistake. A story I never got to tell.

Even as I was knocking at her door, I knew something was wrong. A light was burning in the front room, though it was almost noon by the time I got there and I knew how finicky Mrs Collings was about electric lights. It wasn't a matter of mere thrift, it had to do with daylight. She didn't like artificial light and, even when it was getting dark, she would sit a long time in the last grey of twilight, waiting as long as she could before switching on the little lamp by the fireplace. So that day, even though it was overcast and threatening snow, I knew she wouldn't have had the light on unless there was some very good reason. I knocked again. There was no answer. I waited: if she wasn't expecting anyone, she might not be answering the door; she did that sometimes, when she was in the mood. I thought about knocking again but, instead, I went to the window and peered in. She was there, in the usual place, sitting in her chair by the fire, but she wasn't really there at all. I knew it as soon as I saw her. She was wearing her best dress and a thick, cable-knit, navy blue cardigan that she had knitted herself. A book lay face down on her lap. It looked like an old almanac, and it was just at the point of slipping to the floor, as if she had been reading it the previous evening and then, feeling tired, had set it down to rub her eyes, or to look up at the clock to see the time. She would have thought about going to bed but had fallen asleep in the chair, too tired to get up the stairs. Only she wasn't asleep at all. I could see that.

What I should have done then was run home and get my mother to call the authorities. An ambulance would have come out, a police car, a coroner. Whatever they did in these circumstances. Eventually, some of the townspeople would find reasons for walking or driving by, to see what they could see. Somebody, somewhere, would offer to do the house clearance at a knock-down price, in the hope of finding something valuable. And, of course, there would be gossip. All the old stories would be told again, in suitably embellished form. The story of the baby with two heads. The story of the drowned girl. The stories about the bad husband and what she must have done to make him go off the rails. Since I was the one who had raised the alarm, there would be speculation about my friendship with her and, no doubt, the circumstances would be made to look suspicious. Worst of all, somebody — somebody, no matter who — would touch her, somebody would handle her, lifting her frail, empty body out of the chair, laying it out on a stretcher or a slab at the morgue, examining her, sizing her up, preparing her for burial. This somebody would be a stranger, of course. I knew there was no way to prevent that from happening, but I at least had the opportunity to postpone it. It didn't have to be *me* who called the strangers in. I was still her friend, and I was in a position to protect her, for a while at least; I could let her sleep on in her chair and, if there was a spirit in that house still trying to make its peace with the world, I could give it more time. I stood looking in for a few minutes longer, taking my last sight of her, taking in the room I would never see again, all the things she had gathered over a lifetime, the knick-knacks and mementoes and the sparse, careful furnishings, and I made my goodbye. No confession; no explanation. It was almost Christmas, and that was all I wished her ghost, as I laid the cheap porcelain rose on the windowsill, where she could find it if she wanted: *Happy Christmas*. I didn't say it out loud, but I thought it in such a way that she could eavesdrop, if she wanted to. I didn't leave the card. She was beyond words and Christmas cards and, besides, I wanted it to be silent now between us. Walking back down the hill, I remembered her as she had been when she was still alive, then I did what I could to put her out of my mind. *He who remembers, forgets*, my father used to say. It was a Chinese proverb hc'd heard somewhere, and it made sense to me, right at that moment. I didn't want to remember her as such, I wanted her to fade, to become part of the story my body was telling itself as it made its way in the world. I wanted her to be there, unseen, in everything I did, so that my secret mistake would not go for nothing.

I have a photograph of her now, taken when she was still a young woman. She let me have it one day, not long before we parted. It seems impossible to me now that she was dying all that time, very slowly, and I didn't let myself see it. Not quite. I kept it from myself so that I didn't have to face it, but I knew; her face looked so dark, like those white crayon drawings on black paper that children make, the darkness always showing through. Yet in the photograph, she was totally different. I'll not say she was beautiful, or even pretty, because there is no denying she was a plain woman, but I am always

178

struck by how luminous people look in these old pictures. There's a quality in the light, and in the faces, that makes them look like saints in Victorian lithographs, or the witnesses in early miracle paintings, not entirely involved, but struck by the sheer immediacy of the events at which they are present. Even though the photograph was small, there was the sense of a garden behind her, a sense of space. She must have been in her twenties — it was taken, she had told me, before she married — which would have made it the Fifties, a decade of shadows and warm lamplight, or perhaps a little later, in the first years of the Sixties, when it still felt as if nothing would ever change. She isn't smiling in the picture, but she isn't unhappy; she just wasn't the kind of person who smiled much. She wasn't pretty, or matronly, or the kind of woman you just know is somebody's favourite aunt. All she had was a warm, yet relentless perseverance and that big mannish laugh of hers. I missed her.

I missed her because I needed someone to talk to about Hazel Birnie, and she was the only one who could have filled that role. I'm not sure what she would have said, but she might have broken the stalemate that had developed in my thinking. Because, even as I grew more and more obsessed with Hazel, I couldn't bring myself to do anything about it. I suppose, to begin with, it didn't occur to me that anything could be done: I had no rights; I had no jurisdiction in Hazel's life; I couldn't even be certain that I had any real connection to her. All I knew about her was what I had read in the papers and a few snippets of gossip, stories and scenes taken completely out of the context of her day to day existence. If she was being mistreated at home, it was up to the powers that be to do something about it. The police. Social Services. School. I kept telling myself the same thing, again and again: it wasn't my business. It was none of my business. And yet — it *was* my business, because, surely, I was connected to her, if not by blood, then by circumstance. My life was entwined with hers, one way or another. If I wasn't her father, that was only a matter of chance, and I was certainly connected to her mother, and to the killing of her brothers — one of whom was named Malcolm, after all — because, even if there had been other reasons for Moira's descent into madness, surely the horrible death of her brother, caused by me, had been the starting point, or a contributory factor, at least. Even if it had all been a terrible misunderstanding, an accident, I had killed the uncle Hazel never got to meet and, no matter how indirectly, I had helped drive her mother to the point where she was capable of burning her own children alive. Everything is connected. That could be a reason for doing nothing, or it could be a cause for acting, decisively, knowing that, whatever you do, you cannot foretell the consequences. I had not acted decisively, not once, in the twenty years since the day I lured Malcolm Kennedy to his death in the limeroom. I had not made a single decision of my own, not even about house furnishings. Now I was being presented with an opportunity to do something. Not only an opportunity, but a duty — because, wasn't it my *duty* to intervene, no matter how reckless or unjustified it might seem to others? Looking back, I can say — I can tell myself and everyone else — that I was suffering from a form of temporary insanity, but if that is so, if I really was mad for the few weeks that I spent wandering the roads that winter, with and without Hazel, it was an elective insanity.

★ ★ ★

The first time I saw her she was with three other girls, outside the school. It was a warm afternoon in early October, just a few months after the killings. I felt odd, even a little

181

ashamed, to begin with, watching her from the car park across the road; if I were to be discovered, there would be some very awkward questions. But then, I knew how to be discreet. I remembered my days of observing Malcolm Kennedy. I thought of my father, whose entire success had once rested upon an extreme form of candid photography, in which people in terrible predicaments, the imprisoned, the sick, the dying, infants, war casualties, were photographed without their knowledge, or before they could object. He had called himself a soul thief one day, when I had asked him about it, and I truly believed that, when he retired from news photography, he had wanted to turn his back on that part of his career — but the fact remained that his livelihood and the well-being of his family depended on money he had obtained, and in some cases was still obtaining, from the souls he had stolen. True, he had made more of his money from his landscape and wildlife work, but he'd already won his place in the photographic community by then. Besides, would it not be fair to say that, because of one terrible error, he had sacrificed a career that had helped change the course of events in one or two situations, in spite of the soul thefts and the disgust he sometimes felt with his subjects and with himself? Had I not, in observing Malcolm Kennedy, saved myself from a vicious bully? I thought about all this, but it was little more than rationalisation, a justification for doing the only thing I knew how to do. Though I might well be capable of nothing else, I was capable of being an observer — and no one could say for sure that my observations would have no worthwhile consequences. If I could find out more about Hazel Birnie, I might understand why her mother and brothers had died, and why she had kept on walking that day, out by Balcormo. If she was being abused, then my observations might help bring her abuser to justice. I knew what she looked like. I knew where she lived and where she went to school. I told myself that I was committing no crime. I would be discreet and, if nothing out of the ordinary happened, I would withdraw. End of story.

The four girls were standing on the pavement, talking about something serious. One of the group, a short, dark-haired girl with a soft, bluish mole on her right cheek, seemed to be particularly animated, doing most of the talking while the others listened and chipped in from time to time: it was very obviously one of those, *So I goes . . . and she goes . . . she didn't . . . yeah! . . . and I goes back to her . . .* type conversations, and they were all listening avidly, trainee gossips, future Mrs Ks.

At first sight, Hazel looked much taller than the other girls. Later, I saw that this was an illusion, an effect she was deliberately trying to create. She seemed tall because she was slender, and because she held herself very erect, unlike the three around her, who seemed on the point of crumpling into a heap. The effect was heightened by the adaptations she had made to her uniform — the skirt very straight and narrow, the blazer just an inch or so longer than it ought to have been — and by the way she wore her hair pulled back into a short ponytail, an affectation that also made her look older than the others. So she was a girl who wanted to be taller and older, a grown-up, moving on to other things. Here, with her friends, with school finished for the day, she looked relaxed and, though there was no reason to think she was happy, as such, there was no obvious sign of the recent tragedy that she had suffered, or of the trauma of having been abandoned in the countryside, miles from home. No sign, either, that she was downtrodden or abused. If anything, she looked pleasantly bored, listening to the others but not joining in much, just nodding from to time to show she was listening. They stood for fifteen minutes, then a car arrived and the other girls got in. Everyone called goodbye and waved, then the car drove off, and Hazel was left alone on the kerb. She lingered a moment, looking up and down the road as if she was expecting somebody, then she started to walk. I followed at a discreet distance.

I was reminded of something. Or perhaps I was experiencing a form of *déjà vu*, one of those moments when you feel, not just that a single incident has happened before, but that everything — all history — is repeating itself, again and again, always the same, or with only the subtlest, near-imperceptible variations. The tree on the corner, the shop windows, the lights, that woman crossing the road with a dog on a leash, they had all been there before, on a day exactly like this. A bus had passed, and a man and a boy had descended to the pavement then turned to wave as the bus pulled away. Somebody — a girl on her way home from school — had called out to a friend at exactly the same moment and the little boy, a blond-haired, clear-skinned child of four, had turned to look. It had happened before, just like this — and I had been there, too, walking on Sandhaven Road in the afternoon light.

Up ahead, Hazel Birnie had crossed the road to look at something in a shop window. I kept walking till I came to the corner, then I stopped too, and crossed a little further down. I didn't want her to think she was being followed, which was easy enough while she was on the move, but — as every spy film ever made demonstrates — it's harder to remain inconspicuous when the subject keeps stopping and starting, when they break off from the routine of the walk and do something unexpected, or suddenly turn and look about them with a slightly surprised air, as if they have just realised that they should be somewhere else entirely, having coffee with a friend, or attending a job interview. Hazel Birnie was that type of subject. She had no particular place to go; or she did, but she was delaying the inevitable arrival; or she had already arrived more or less where she was supposed to be and was waiting for someone to show. Then, quietly, without my noticing until it was almost too late, something shifted in her mood and she stopped. We were almost at the harbour by now, just at the end of Shore Street, by the chip shop. At first, I thought she was waiting there for someone, then I realised I was mistaken. She was being watched, and she knew it.

She didn't spot me, not as such. She only knew that someone was watching her — but it was somebody else, not me because, as she looked around — discreetly, not giving herself away — she looked at, and straight through me, then turned away. I wasn't the one, that was obvious from her face; which meant, of course, that the person she thought was following her was somebody she already knew. At first I was relieved. I was not suspected, I was still invisible. Then it came to me and, as obvious as it was, it took a good minute or so to filter through, that there really might be another observer, a second pair of eyes which by that time, I finally realised, would also be watching me. Now it was my turn to look around, but I resisted the temptation and went into the little florist's shop that, once upon a time, had been Mrs Collings' pride and joy.

The shop was empty of customers, but full of scent and colour. It looked different from how I remembered it, but then I hadn't been inside the place in years, not since my parents had died. The woman behind the counter was sitting on a high stool, making up a wreath; I had never seen her before, yet she looked familiar, as if I *ought* to know her. It was *déjà vu* time again. I looked around for something to buy. The flowers stood in rows on either side of the shop, red roses, yellow roses, chrysanthemums, carnations, freesias, miraculous arrays of pure colour set out in those tall metallic vases that only florists use. I had forgotten this: the intoxication of colour and humidity, and that combined scent, a scent that, no matter what flowers are in stock, is always more or less the same, an event in itself, an effect much greater than the sum of its parts. I remembered Mrs Collings, and how weak she had become in her last few months. Then I looked at the woman. She had finished what she was doing and was coming forward, around the counter, to stand next to me.

'I'm sorry to keep you,' she said. 'One of those fussy little things you just have to finish.' She smiled. 'Can I help you with something?'

'I don't know,' I said. 'I haven't decided. Things look different — '

She gave a big laugh that I knew from somewhere. 'Yes,' she said. 'I've just bought the shop. Thought I'd make a few changes.'

I nodded. 'It looks — better,' I said.

'Thank you.'

I looked at her. 'Are you from Coldhaven?' I asked. 'It's just that — '

'No, I'm not,' she put in. 'I've no real connection with the place, except that my aunt used to own this shop, oh, years ago.'

'Your aunt?'

'Oh, you probably wouldn't know her. She

died some years back. She'd given up the shop by then. Mrs Collings?'

I nodded. 'Yes,' I said. 'I knew her. A little. I was just a boy — '

'Yes,' she said. 'It was twenty years ago now. But when the place came up, I had to go for it. I used to visit sometimes, before she got ill and moved out, and this was my favourite place in the whole world.'

I gave her a surprised look. 'What, Coldhaven?' I asked.

She laughed out loud then. 'Oh, no,' she said. 'The shop. I just loved the scent of the flowers, and the way it was set out. That's what I'm doing now, really, restoring it to how it was back then. Anyway, I shan't keep you all day. Take your time, have a look around. Let me know when you're ready.'

When I emerged from the florist's clutching a bunch of yellow roses, Hazel Birnie was gone. I wasn't surprised, but I was curious about the sensation I'd had earlier, the distinct sensation that she had a sense of herself being watched, and by someone else, presumably someone she knew. Her father, perhaps? An unwanted boyfriend? She had probably attracted all manner of attention after the killings, some of it sympathetic, some curious, but there was always the kind of freak out there whose fascination went

189

beyond curiosity. But then, where did that leave me? The sums I had done in my head — the same piece of arithmetic, over and over — suggested at least the possibility that Hazel Birnie might be my daughter, but it had all been so long ago, and I knew that nothing could be solved by mere arithmetic. Which meant, did it not? that I was one of those freaks. Was, might be, was trying not to be, or was trying to convince myself, at least, that I wasn't. But what else could I do? I could hardly go to Tom Birnie and suggest that we had blood tests to determine the paternity of the girl he'd considered his daughter for fourteen years. All I could do was go home, put my roses in water and resume my surveillance — a more cautious surveillance, of course — the next day. If nothing else, I might discover the identity of Hazel's stalker.

The next day, however, she didn't show up at school. Or the next. It was Friday before I saw her again; when I did she looked different, less severe, less grown up. She wasn't at school that day either; in fact, I only came upon her by chance, as I walked home from the shops through the little park just above the promenade. She was sitting on a bench, alone, in a white summer dress and see-through plastic sandals, the kind kids wear to the beach; it looked as if she was waiting for someone. It was an odd, strangely touching picture: the clothes she was wearing weren't right for the kind of day it was, a little damp now, and a wind off the sea, and she was obviously cold. I didn't know if she had noticed me the last time I had followed her, but I didn't want to take any chances, so I kept my distance, waiting to see if anyone would turn up to meet her. It struck me, though, that I would have to become visible sooner or later, that there was no point in just watching her. Eventually, I would have to talk to her. First, though, I needed to observe, to find out more. Who she was waiting for, and why, for starters. Maybe it was a boy, an assignation. Why else would she be sitting out there in the cold? I couldn't say, but whoever it was, they didn't turn up and, after half an hour or so, she got up and turned for home.

★ ★ ★

It's a mistake to look too hard for the point at which things started. Things begin deep below the surface; by the time they are visible, they have a life and direction of their own. We don't see that, so we call it destiny, or fate, or chance, when something unexpected happens; yet we were preparing ourselves all along, in secret, to participate in the moment that, on the surface, we thought so surprising. I didn't decide what I was going to do until far into October, but I can't help thinking that it was something I witnessed two weeks or so before that started the wheels turning in my mind.

It was one of those duty things, a dinner with Amanda's boss and her husband; I had shaved and changed into a jacket and tie, but she wasn't ready yet, so I fixed myself a long, cool drink and went out into the garden. The evening was warm, the warmth an almost palpable pressure on my face and hands and, as I sat there, sipping at my lemonade, I felt something rise to the surface of my skin, something old, a forgotten sensation of fear, or if not fear exactly, then apprehension, an apprehension that somehow predated my human existence, a sluggish, almost reptilian apprehension, rising from deep in the bone and gristle, detached from my usual human concerns, but receptive to everything I normally missed — a shiver on the air, or a branch shaken on a tree at the edge of the garden that sent tremors through this deeper, simpler body. All at once, I was aware of a chill, animal pleasure, a continuity between my own flesh and the shadows in the bushes; yet the fear, the apprehension, was still there, and I realised that these two sensations were inseparable, fear and pleasure, apprehension and the tentative joy of being there, alive. At the same time, I became aware of something — it would be too much to say that I glimpsed something out of the corner of my eye, and there was no sound, as I recall, but I felt something was there, slipping away from me towards the long grass of the orchard. It only lasted a moment, but the sensation I had of having given rise to something was overwhelming. I felt an odd, strangely quiet panic, a sense that I was on the point of losing something before I had even grasped what it was, and I wanted desperately not to let it go, for a moment at least. I wanted to see it, to hold on to it and give it a name.

Amanda appeared at the French windows. 'Coming?'

I looked at her.

'What's wrong?' she said. 'You look like you've seen a ghost.'

I shook my head. 'It's nothing,' I said. 'I was just thinking.'

She did that thing she does, where she purses her lips and turns away as if there's something she could say but can't be bothered to repeat, yet again, for the hundredth time. 'Come on,' she said. 'We'll be late.' She was already putting on her coat.

'And tonight, try at least to look as if you're enjoying yourself.'

★ ★ ★

The days passed. Amanda went to work; I searched for Hazel Birnie: found her, lost her, found her again. Sometimes she had very regular, more or less normal days: school, friends, walk home; other times, she just wandered, bunking off so she could sit around on the seafront or in the park, apparently unconcerned about being caught. I imagine she knew that nobody would be very hard on her, after what had happened. She was just drifting, though, and I thought somebody ought to have done something to help her. Who knew what was in her mind?

Meanwhile; Amanda began to wander a little too. After work, she would stick around, going off for a glass of wine with one of the girls or some colleague or other. She always called — I was usually out or away from the phone — and she would leave a brief, non-committal message, which I didn't think about much. Did I suspect her of anything? An affair? A whole string of lovers? I have to confess that I didn't. I didn't think about it, to be honest. Sometimes she got home late and a little drunk, and she would try to start

194

an argument. I didn't have much time for it all. One Friday night she came home at one in the morning. I was in my father's old study, reading a book, when she appeared in the doorway.

'Hello,' she said. 'Been busy?'

I nodded. 'Hello,' I said.

She smiled. 'Don't you want to know where I've been?' she asked.

'Not particularly,' I said.

'Don't you want to know if I had a good time?'

'If you hadn't, you'd have come back earlier, I imagine.'

'You're just not interested, are you?'

I looked at her. She looked pretty, drunk. 'I'm glad you had a good time,' I said.

She snorted. 'Yeah, sure,' she said. 'Fat lot you care.'

I glanced at my book as if to remind myself of what I'd been doing before she arrived. 'I've been reading about the peat bogs in western France,' I said.

'Good for you.'

'Very interesting,' I said. 'I'd like to go visit one day.'

She fell silent, then. A little dizziness, perhaps. A touch of sadness. 'What am I doing here?' she said. 'I deserve better than this.' She leaned against the door frame.

'Don't I deserve better than this?' she asked, addressing herself mostly.

I looked at her. What a pity, I thought. She was so pretty, and so unlike me. 'You do,' I said. 'You deserve better than this.' I snapped the book shut, and she gave a startled little jump. I hadn't meant to scare her. 'Go to bed,' I said. 'You're tired.'

She looked at me and shook her head. 'Is that all you have to say?' she said. I shook my head. She sighed. 'Well what, then?'

'I'm glad you had a good time,' I said.

She looked at me for a long minute, more in sadness than in anger, then she went to bed.

★ ★ ★

'I've been watching you watching me.'

I thought about pretending I hadn't heard, that I'd thought she was talking to somebody else, but what was the point? She was only a few feet away and she had caught me out, fair and square. I looked up. She was wearing her school uniform, blue sweater, blue pleated skirt, white blouse, red and blue tie. She had her hair in short pigtails, with little ribbons at the ends. I was about to be arrested as a child molester.

'I'm sorry?' I said.

She laughed.

'So you should be,' she said. 'You're old enough to be my father.'

I shook my head. 'It's not like that,' I said.

'Like what?'

'You know.'

'How would I? I'm young enough to be your daughter.'

'It's not that,' I said. 'I was just — 'What? I was just trying to work out if she was being abused at home? I was just trying to see if I could find some family trait that might answer the question the arithmetic posed? I was just — what?

'So,' she said. 'What is it you want?'

'Nothing,' I said. 'I don't want anything.'

She shook her head. 'Everybody wants something,' she said. She smiled again, and turned away. I watched her go. I ought not to have done — I should have turned away myself, in case anybody saw — but I watched her go and I noticed — I couldn't help noticing, it was entirely, *entirely* involuntary — that she had bare legs, in spite of the chill, and her legs were pale, smooth and beautifully, terrifyingly slender.

I was confused. Had it been a tease? A pick-up? An invitation? She'd seen me watching her and, instead of running to the nearest policeman, she'd come over for a friendly chat. What did she think I wanted? And if everybody really did want something, what was it *she* wanted? And why had I noticed her legs? Why had I noticed how she looked in her school uniform, disconcerting and attractive and, oh it was all too clear, provocative in her pigtails and pleated skirt? I hadn't intended to notice that, ever; it wasn't what I was about. Was it? Did I know myself so little? Was all this some elaborate ruse to distract myself from some deep, secret, utterly horrific perversion that I'd been nurturing for years? I didn't want her to think what she had implied. I didn't want her to think I was some dirty old man. But what could I say to put the idea out of her head? I decided that, for a while at least, the best thing was to keep my head down. Pull back, stop being so obvious. I realised what I had done, of course: I'd wanted to move things forward, I'd wanted to talk to her, and I'd made myself obvious. With very little effort, she had wrong-footed me. Now I was out in the open. Now I was visible.

I did think about giving it all up. I thought about it often. I had terrifying nightmares, sometimes, where I was lying in bed and, suddenly, I realised someone else was there, lying on top of the duvet, on top of me. I couldn't see who it was, but I knew it was a woman, or a girl. Sometimes, when I woke, I thought it was Hazel; at other times, I was sure it was her mother. Almost every night I found myself grasping at a shadow as I woke, crying out and struggling, fighting to be free of the weight of the stranger and, at the same time, trying to catch hold of her to see who she was. One day, I fell asleep in the garden, and Amanda must have come out just as I was startled awake by the dream. I wasn't altogether aware of what was going on, or where I was, when I felt her leaning over me, talking, asking me what the matter was. Her voice was surprisingly kind, very gentle, like somebody talking to a child. I should have realised, then, that she had found another lover, the way she was so considerate with me.

'What is it? Who are you talking to?'

I sat up. I didn't know why I was so scared, but I was terrified. Someone had been there, a girl, or a woman, with white, flaking hands, trying to touch my face. The hands were poisoned or damaged, I knew that — it was like very bad eczema — but in the dream it had frightened me that I might come into contact with that white, flaking skin.

'What is it?' Amanda asked.

I looked around. 'There's somebody here,' I said. 'Somebody's in the garden.'

She looked at me. 'No,' she said. 'There's nobody. You were dreaming.'

'No,' I said. 'She was here.'

'Who?' She gave me a long questioning look; then she laid her hand on my forehead. 'You have a fever,' she said. 'You should go to bed, instead of sleeping out here in the garden.'

Moment by moment, I was coming out of it, and I knew she was right. I had fallen asleep on a warm day; I was tired; I was starting to lose my mind. I should go to bed, take a pill. Have a hot toddy. Be sensible. But I couldn't quite let it go; it was too real. I looked out across the garden — and there, just at the edge of the lawn, I saw something — nothing more than flicker, a trick of the light, perhaps, but *something* disappeared into the shrubbery. I shuddered. Maybe I *was* losing my mind.

Amanda straightened up, shook her head. 'Go to bed,' she said. 'You spend too much time up here on your own, brooding. You need to get out of yourself.'

I nodded. I tried to stand up, but I couldn't. 'I'm all right,' I said. 'I just need to sit for a bit.'

She nodded, then she went into the kitchen. 'I'll get you something to drink,' she said. 'Then you go to bed. You're making yourself ill.'

* * *

What I didn't know, during those final days, was that my life and Amanda's were running on parallel lines. Our problems weren't exactly the same but, for different reasons, we were asking ourselves the same question. Over the next week or two I gradually got to know Hazel Birnie, first through observation, then in a strange, drawn-out cat and mouse game that she initiated that first time she spoke to me, through odd, fleeting conversations, half-told stories and insinuations, something that could seem, on a good day, like a mild flirtation, and on a bad one, a tiny step from the most bitter mockery. I say got to know, but that is too strong, or perhaps too kind a term. I made her acquaintance. I skirted around her, trying to find a way in that was both innocent, in my own eyes, and casual, in hers. I don't think that ever really worked. I think she saw right through me from the first. She was curious, that was all — at least to begin with. Later, she may have had other motives for making my acquaintance, and those motives may not have been entirely her own, but to begin with it was curiosity and perhaps a sense of her own power, that she could conduct this game with me, and that she could control it, even while she was flattered by the attentions of a grown man with money and a car.

Meanwhile, Amanda was enjoying another kind of attention. I had no reason not to know it — she'd practically confessed it to me in her own roundabout way — but I don't think I ever realised how difficult she made it, for herself and for her — what shall I call him? Lover? Seducer? Boyfriend? He was young and smart and going places in the company she worked for, and he should have been irresistible to someone who'd had to live with me for so long, but I'll give Amanda her due, she agonised rather impressively before giving in. Even then, she couldn't bring herself to leave. I didn't find any of this out till much later, but it seems Amanda was ready to stay, to keep trying, for far longer than could reasonably have been expected. She believed in the vows she had made, and she had tried to live by them. For my part, I couldn't rightly remember what they were. When I look back now, I am ashamed of how badly I treated her; yet all that time, she would have been prepared to try again. It was only after I ran off, in decidedly questionable circumstances, that she chose to leave. The man's name was Robert. I think she didn't sleep with him until after I left, though I can't be sure of that. It's something that I really ought to consult Mrs K about. I'm sure she knows all the details.

The turning point, for me and, by extension, for Amanda, came one Wednesday afternoon. It was getting dark earlier, and the late afternoons were grey and soft as ash. Often it was wet, or misty, and people went about their business in too much of a hurry to notice what their neighbours were up to. I had arranged to meet Hazel in a little alleyway not far from her school: not because I had anything to hide, but because our friendship, our acquaintance, wasn't something I could have explained. I didn't want it getting back to Amanda that I was meeting a schoolgirl in back lanes and driving her out into the country, where we would sit in my car and stare at the wet fields, engaging in something that could scarcely be called polite conversation. I sometimes wondered, then, if she was curious about me, not as a lover, or a dirty old man, or whatever else I might have seemed to her, but as a possible father. She must have noticed her physical unlikeness to Tom Birnie; perhaps Moira had said something on that last day, before she abandoned her on the Balcormo road. If that was so, she didn't show it. Mostly, our conversations were random, discursive, occasionally vaguely flirtatious. Sometimes she told me jokes. They were childish, and silly, and oddly endearing — though, looking back, that may have been a calculation on her part. She probably knew how cute she was, when she softened up and told the kind of joke a seven-year-old might like.

'A man goes to the doctor,' she would begin. I'd look expectant, waiting. I never interrupted. 'And he says: 'Doc, it hurts when I press *here*' ' — she pressed her index finger to her forehead, ' 'and when I press *here*' ' — she pressed her finger against her chin — ' 'but it also hurts when I press *here*' ' — she put her finger to her stomach and pressed, hard. ' 'What do you think is wrong with me?' And the doctor says, 'Well, I think you've broken your finger'.'

When the punch-line came, I would always laugh, no matter how lame the joke was. Which she also found amusing. Far more amusing than the joke. And it was odd, because I always felt as though she was testing me. This business with the jokes, and her various moods, and the little flashes of dirty talk — it was all a test. It was a test when she agreed to meet me, and it was a test when she refused. It was a test when she was half an hour late and it was a test when she got to the rendezvous too early and had to wait for me. Everything was a test — and I had no idea if I was passing or failing.

That day, she didn't show — and that was probably a test, as well. I waited a while; then I got out of the car, left it in the side alley and walked back through the next wynd to the school gates. Most of the kids had dispersed by then, but Hazel was there, and she was talking to someone. At first, I thought it must be a teacher; then I saw that it was Tom Birnie. He looked more like his picture in the papers than Hazel had done, but he was still much changed from the tough, swaggering rather handsome boy I remembered from school. His face was dark, hard, a little crumpled, as if he were trying to hide himself and, at the same time, defy everyone and everything that had happened to him. He was obviously angry with Hazel and he was a big man, a dangerous man, but she wasn't cowed. It was clear, from the way she stood up to him, facing him directly, not giving any ground, that any respect she'd ever had for him had broken down some time before. Perhaps after the killings, perhaps long before that. She had fought this battle before too, that was obvious, and she wouldn't be browbeaten. The trouble was, she had chosen the wrong day to fight. Tom Birnie was in a black mood, his hands balled into fists, his body tensed. I was certain he was just about

205

to hit her, when I distracted them both, emerging from the wynd facing them, and started across the road. I had no particular intentions — I think all I wanted was to be a presence there, someone that Tom Birnie would think was a teacher, say — but my appearance changed everything. Birnie stopped talking and stepped away, turning his back on his daughter and fishing in his pocket for some cigarettes. I imagine he already saw himself as a man under suspicion of domestic abuse, or perhaps worse and, if I was a teacher, he didn't want to draw too much attention to himself. He couldn't be sure of course, but it was best to play safe. Whatever he had been saying could wait.

Hazel didn't look at me. Perhaps she didn't want her father to know what had been going on — though it was hard to say what, if anything, we had done, other than meet and talk, drive around, sit in silence, talk. It was the kind of quaint courtship I could imagine a man of my age conducting with a girl *young enough to be his daughter*, but it wasn't what I had intended, and I still hoped she didn't see me in that light. I hoped she saw me as — something undefined, I suppose. Something indefinable. I hadn't suggested a blood test, or that we run away together. I hadn't ever made any direct physical contact with her, not a touch, not a hug, not a glancing caress. We were — I was — innocent. Maybe that was what puzzled her most.

I passed them without comment, heading for the main door of the school. For appearances, I could be a teacher come back at the end of the day to pick up something he had forgotten. I had guessed that a direct confrontation with Tom Birnie would only make things worse — but then I had an idea. I turned back.

'Hazel?'

She looked at me, startled. Tom Birnie turned too, the lit cigarette cradled in his hand. He regarded me with only passing interest. I took a few steps towards them.

'I was wondering how that essay was coming along,' I said. 'It's due in on Friday, you know.'

She cottoned on right away. 'It's coming on fine,' she said.

'You don't need more time?' I asked, shooting a glance at her father. 'Under the circumstances?'

It was the kind of crude remark I could imagine myself making had I been her teacher, but it had a perfect effect on her father. He gave me an odd, almost frightened look, then he turned to Hazel, mumbled something that I couldn't make out and walked away, tossing the cigarette into the gutter as he went. Hazel waited until he was out of earshot, then she turned to me. 'What was that about?' she said.

'I thought — '

'He's going to ask me who you are. Later. He's going to want to know what the hell you were talking about.' She stepped closer. 'What essay?'

'I thought he was going to hit you — '

'Well? What's that to you?'

'I don't think — '

'Are you going to protect me, is that it? Are you going to save me from him?'

'It's not like that — '

'Well, you've seen what he's like. So what are you going to do about it?'

'You don't have to stay with him,' I said. I couldn't understand it. She was angry with *me*.

'And where else can I go?' She was speaking quietly, just above a whisper, really. She had a keener sense than I had of the risk we were taking, standing there, right outside her school, arguing. 'To a home?'

I didn't answer her.

'How about foster care? That would be fun.'

'There are other possibilities — '

She laughed. 'Oh, yes? And what would

they be?' She leaned in close, almost touching me. 'Maybe you could take me away from all this.' She waited, though she wasn't expecting an answer.

'Maybe I could,' I said, before she could say anything more.

She didn't laugh. I'll give her that. She didn't laugh. She knew that, even if the idea hadn't fully occurred to me until that moment, I was serious. She looked at my eyes; then she looked at my mouth. For a moment I thought she was going to hit me, but she just shook her head and turned away. 'I have to go,' she said. 'I've got an essay to finish.'

I didn't call after her. She hadn't laughed and she hadn't hit me, though I do believe she thought about it for a moment. She needed time to think, which meant she was serious too. The only problem was, I didn't know what she was serious about.

I didn't see her for three days. Then she called me at home, in the middle of the day, when Amanda was at work. I hadn't given her my number, and I was surprised when I picked up the phone and heard her voice.

'All right then,' she said.

'What?'

'I said all right then. Take me away from all this.'

For a moment, I didn't know what to say. I had been serious, I was still serious, but I think I also knew that I was going insane. A temporary, elective, perverse form of insanity, but insanity, nevertheless. I only hesitated for a moment, but I know, looking back, that what was running through my mind, in that split second — running through like some underground stream, invisible, barely heard — was a question. I couldn't have put that question into words then, but I can now. The question was in three parts. First, it occurred to me that things had happened, things had been said and done that I was not aware of. Signs had been passed, secrets had been revealed, without my even knowing. I was insane, really, in the ordinary, defeatist way that Peter is insane when he denies Jesus, in the way that Joseph is insane when the angel appears to him in a dream — *and he believes what he has seen.* When the angel appears, we are supposed to shrug and move on. When we are accused, we are meant, not to deny, but to equivocate, to dodge the bullet, to hedge our bets. We crack jokes. We create a diversion. Only the insane listen when the angel speaks, only the insane make wild-eyed denials and so confirm their guilt. I was insane, and I had been listening to angels, without even knowing. That was fine but, if I was insane,

210

what was she? I didn't think she was insane. So: did I think she was desperate? So desperate for help that she was prepared to run off with a near stranger? Did I think she was in love? Or did I realise, even then, that she had read in me some signal, some series of giveaways, that expressed, not desire, or romantic longing, but the insanity I was hardly aware of, a perverse insanity that would allow her to take me for a fool? Was I a fool? That was the question I should have asked myself — but even if the answer had been yes, I'm not sure that it would have made any difference.

'That would be kidnapping,' I said.

'Ah.'

'No. I mean. Really. It would be — '

'It's all right,' she said. 'You changed your mind. Can't say I blame you — '

'I'm not changing my mind,' I said. 'I'm just saying.'

'We'd have to get caught first,' she said.

'I'd get caught,' I said. '*You* would be rescued.'

'Change your mind then.'

'No.'

There was a silence, then she spoke, very softly, conspiratorially. 'All right,' she said. I felt a ridiculous shiver of excitement and — yes, romance. Was there a moment, there, when I had become infatuated with her? Perhaps; but I didn't *want* her, not as I'd once wanted her mother or, in another lifetime, Amanda. It wasn't sex, it was romance. We were two people who wanted to run away. That was all I thought. 'I'll be waiting at nine o'clock tomorrow morning,' she said. 'Just after school goes in. If you're serious and you haven't changed your mind, I'll see you then. All right?'

'All right,' I said. I was assuming she meant in the usual place, in the alley opposite the school, but I didn't want to make assumptions. I wanted to be sure. I didn't want her to think I'd not turned up because of some stupid misunderstanding — but before I could say anything else, before I could do that old movie routine of running through the plan one more time and synchronising our watches, she hung up. The line hummed for a moment; then it went quiet. I put the receiver down. Outside, it was a perfectly calm autumn day, the kind of day that makes for a good funeral: falling leaves, no wind, the occasional bird flitting through great swathes of stillness. The world seemed suddenly small and intimate. There was no doubt in my mind that I would get caught.

★　★　★

The rest of the day was slow and heavy. I tried to keep myself busy, to pick out things I should take on the coming excursion — in my mind, I see-sawed back and forth between full recognition of the enormity of the step I was about to take, and this sense I had that, really, all we were doing was setting out on a kind of holiday, an ordinary, perfectly normal excursion. I didn't really know what I was planning to do, or where we would go, so I didn't know what to pack; in the end, I just dumped two suitcases on the bed and crammed them full of shirts, jeans, T-shirts, sweaters, underwear. I took off the clothes I was wearing, had a shower and got dressed in warm, chunky, smart-casual autumn clothes. I put on the wristwatch I hardly ever wore and a pair of Bannister walking shoes. They were my favourites, lightweight yet warm, watertight, very comfortable. When I was ready, I put the suitcases in the boot of the car and sat down to wait for Amanda. I had every intention, in those first few hours, of telling her what I was doing: that I was going away, but I didn't know where; that we would come to some arrangement about property in due course but, in the meantime, she should stay in the house for as long as she wanted; that I would get in touch later, when I was settled. I wouldn't mention Hazel, of course.

There would be elements of truth and elements of fiction to my account but, for the most part, it would be the truth.

Maybe it was just bad luck that Amanda had decided to stay out that evening and, for the first time, forgot to call to say she would be late. Maybe it was fate, or chance. Maybe she didn't forget to call, she just got caught up in something else and couldn't get away. Maybe, by then, she couldn't be bothered. Whatever happened, I grew tired of waiting for her, and decided I would just go. I would telephone when I got the chance. I'd been full of good intentions, but I should have known that, presented with even the shortest delay, the least excuse, the smallest loophole, I would take the easy road. I did sit down before I left, to write her a letter, but it all seemed so absurd, so full of speculation and unknown variables that I gave up after my third attempt. I tore the unfinished letters into tiny shreds and threw them in the bin. Then I fetched my raincoat, picked up the car keys on the hall table, and left. It was grey now, almost dark. The garden was eerily still. I stopped for a moment at the gate, as a thread of wind off the point ghosted across my face; then I drove away. I had nowhere to go, and I could as easily have left it till morning. I could have picked Hazel up after

Amanda had gone to work. That would have been more logical, and more comfortable, too; but once I'd made my decision, I had to get out of there. I had to be gone. Maybe I was afraid that, if I stayed, I might change my mind. Maybe I thought if I didn't go right away, some spell would be broken and the world would just revert to normality. I was temporarily insane, but it was, as I said, an elective insanity, and I had to keep the momentum going. Otherwise, the effort would have been too great and I would have collapsed into some dark burrow of myself, gone into hiding, giving up for good.

★   ★   ★

I drove around for hours. I still hadn't really made up my mind to go through with it, or maybe I had, but I wasn't sure if it really was the right thing to do. I don't know; it's a little hard to remember it all in sequence now. I think driving around created the illusion that I was about to do something, but there was still room for manoeuvre, I was on my way, but I hadn't committed myself, I hadn't done anything *criminal* yet. An odd idea for anybody to have, that he is about to do something criminal. A man goes out to rob a bank, or kill somebody, or cash a stolen cheque, and he is doing exactly that thing, he doesn't think he is going out to commit a crime. The crime part of it is by the by. I had it back to front, really: I was thinking about the crime, rather than about what I was actually doing, which probably meant that I was innocent of any crime, because —

This was how my mind was turning, running around in circles while I drove around in circles, a man in a car he hardly ever used, wandering about in the dark. For a while I followed the coast road, looking for the moon, but the sky was flat and empty, no moon, no stars, just the faint shadows of scudding clouds and the inky spaces between. It was hours before our rendezvous and there was no need to be out there, driving around, getting exhausted, but I simply couldn't go back home, now that I had finally made the decision to leave. At last, after hours of pointless wandering, I pulled into a lay-by facing the water, and decided to get some sleep. It was late now, and cold. I fetched a blanket from the boot of the car and huddled down in the back seat. For about ten minutes I lay there, certain that I wouldn't sleep a wink. Then I woke and I saw that it was early morning, that time before dawn when the night could end, or it could just slip back and start all over again. I looked at the clock on the dashboard. It was a quarter past five.

I thought of going back to the house to freshen up, but decided against it. I drove around some more; then I went for a walk on the beach. It was cold, still, and windy; I was alone on the beach for a while, then a man arrived in one of those big, ugly four-wheel-drive vehicles, equipped, as such people always are, with a mobile phone and two immense Rottweilers. I left quickly and drove towards Seahouses. There was a greasy spoon there where I could get some breakfast, drink some tea. It's one of the great pleasures of a quiet life, being out in the wind for a while, then going indoors and drinking tea. Eating sausages and crispy bacon, poached eggs, fried bread, beans. Sitting vacantly, in the benign presence of truly unhealthy food. Drinking tea from a big off-white or beige mug with a chip out of the base. Strong, hot tea, with plenty of milk. Tomato ketchup. The eggs evenly powdered with fine white pepper. I took my time over that breakfast, the way a condemned man might savour his last meal.

When I drew into the alleyway, Hazel was already there. It was still early and a little cold, but she was dressed in the usual lightweight clothes, her face tired, a small, almost toylike valise at her feet. She didn't smile when I pulled up, she didn't seem pleased to see me. Maybe she was insane, too. Maybe she was just tired. She probably wasn't what Amanda called *a morning person.*

'You came,' she said, as I pushed open the passenger side door.

'Yes,' I said. 'Did you think I wouldn't?'

She got in and put the little valise down by her feet. 'I had no idea,' she said. 'It feels a bit — ' She cast around for the right word, then shook her head.

'Crazy?'

She nodded. I had put the car into reverse and was manoeuvring back along the alleyway. Neither of us spoke, as I swung the car round and headed out on to the Sandhaven road, the school behind us. 'So where are we going?' she said, finally, as we passed the last of Coldhaven's humourless grey houses.

'I don't know,' I said. I was suddenly aware of the fact that, though I'd had all night to think about it, I had no plan, no destination, nothing but good intentions. Hazel had expected something else: maps, fake passports, counterfeit money, movie stuff. Or maybe she just expected me to have some idea where I was going. I was the driver. I remembered a poem I'd read once, something about the surrounding darkness and a big car and somebody called John, whose name wasn't really John — and I felt suddenly happy, suddenly free. 'Let's just follow the road,' I said. 'See where it takes us.'

She gave me an odd, dissatisfied look. 'Let's just follow the road?' she said.

I laughed. 'Yes,' I said. 'What's wrong with that?'

She thought for a moment, then she gave me a faint, grudging half-smile. 'Nothing, I suppose,' she said. She thought some more, then, easing a little, looking almost satisfied, she nodded. 'You're the driver,' she said.

★　★　★

We drove south, then west. We didn't talk much: that morning, it was all about the road, and the land around us. I kept to back roads and long winding trails through the hill land and we sat apart with our own thoughts, me driving into the light and Hazel gazing out at the world passing by, her faced turned away, so all I saw, when I shot her the odd glance, was her hair, her hands folded in her lap, the absurd little valise at her feet. I didn't know what to make of her: one minute she looked and acted like a little girl, the next she was smart, sharp, mature, mocking. I suppose she'd had to grow up pretty quickly, with all she had been through — but then, there were teenage children who would have been crushed by it all. She had something special, I could see that. I didn't really know what it was, but I knew, even on that first day, that it could be dangerous for me.

Finally, after we'd been driving like that for the entire morning, she turned and looked at me. She hadn't spoken for almost an hour by then. 'I'm getting hungry,' she said.

'Me too.' I looked at her. 'What do you want to eat?'

'Don't mind,' she said. 'Food.'

'How about a Big Mac?'

'Are you kidding?' She gave me a roll of the eyes type look then pretended to gag.

'All right,' I said. 'Something else, then?'

'Definitely,' she said. 'Something else. And soon.'

★   ★   ★

After lunch — a salad and a baked potato covered in something unidentifiable at a nondescript off-motorway services — we drove on, heading south now. I still had no real plan. I thought the best thing to do was get as far as we could from Coldhaven, get some sleep in some anonymous hotel where we wouldn't draw attention to ourselves, then decide what to do from there. I didn't think anyone would have noticed Hazel was missing, not yet. She was in the habit of taking days off school, so her teachers wouldn't miss her, and Tom Birnie wouldn't notice anything till he didn't get his tea that evening. After that, it was hard to know what would happen. Amanda would already have realised that I was gone, but I doubted she would call the police. She would wait a day or two before doing that, or she might not call them at all. Meanwhile, unless we were really unlucky — unless someone had seen us together, in the car, or talking outside the school — nobody would make any connection between Hazel and me. Maybe Mrs K would work it out, but I was pretty sure she wouldn't say anything. We had a few days, maybe a week, before the abduction scenario came into play, as opposed to an ordinary teenage crisis. There was also the elopement theory, of course. When — if — a connection was finally made between us, there was a remote possibility that people would think we were in love and had run off together. There would be speculation all around the village about it. *He was always odd, that one. Aye, he was that. Like all thae Gardiners. That puir wee girl. The innocent wee lamb. After all she's been through.* Some of them would

221

be sorry for Tom Birnie, though I imagine many would think the worst. Meanwhile, there would be sightings from John O'Groats to Land's End. People would see us canoodling in the car. A shift worker would catch a glimpse of a suspicious-looking man on a back road, with a sack and a mud-caked shovel. A schoolboy would see someone fitting my description bundle a girl into a car and drive away. The car would be blue. Or grey. Or maybe black. An Audi. A Mondeo. Some kind of Volkswagen.

I drove all afternoon with this going through my head, until I realised I was too tired to drive any more. I glanced over at Hazel. She had fallen asleep in the passenger seat after her lunch; now she was waking up slowly, drifting upwards from the dark, gold chamber of a dream and coming to, with the land slipping by. 'I'm exhausted,' I said.

'Me too.'

'You've only just woken up.'

'Yeah, well. I didn't get much sleep last night.'

'All right. Let's stop for today. We can get some rest, think about tomorrow. OK?'

She nodded but she didn't say anything. Maybe she was starting to think about the practicalities. She couldn't have much in her little valise. I'd have to take her out, buy her some things. I was fine, for the moment. I kept driving till I came to the next town, where I pulled into the car park of a bland, pinkish-looking hotel called the Carlton. 'We'll stay here tonight,' I said. 'OK?'

She gave me an odd look, but she didn't say anything.

'What?'

'Nothing.'

'You don't like it?'

'It's fine.'

'What then?'

I waited for her to say something, maybe to say she wanted to stay somewhere swankier, maybe to ask about sleeping arrangements or what she would wear, but she just nodded, a little too gravely perhaps, and kept her thoughts to herself. It occurred to me that, for her, this was a kind of adventure, like that episode in *L'Ascenseur pour l'échafaud* where the Pretty Florist runs off with the Boyfriend in the hero's stolen car. There's a scene where they stay in a hotel, off the motorway somewhere, incognito. It was nothing special, after all, not for the Pretty Florist; she hadn't done anything wrong, so why not go along with it all? Even later, when the Boyfriend murders a German couple and steals *their* car, the audience knows she'll not suffer too much. Maybe a little fright, nothing more. The Pretty Florist is too young, too innocent and, possibly, too inconsequential for Louis Malle to make her suffer. Besides, there's something about her we like. The Boyfriend is just a guy, not much more than a leather jacket, but he's just a kid. Nothing special.

But then, Hazel wasn't the Pretty Florist. It was truc that she could sparkle, it was true that she was a child, but more often than not she had the air of someone almost too serious, with a hard, slightly forced gravity in the way she held herself, or in the way she listened to what I was saying then weighed it up, silently. Then, a moment later, she would hardly be there at all, a ghost of a person, disengaged, perhaps bored. When we'd first set out, and again, when we pulled into this, our first hotel, she would smile to herself, a smile that was entirely private, even if she didn't do anything to hide it. She knew I couldn't read her mind. She wasn't even sure if I knew my own. Now, when I think about her — and I do think about her, though not very often — I remember her as that ghostly, smiling child, and by a single phrase she must have repeated ten, or a dozen times. 'What do you want?' she would ask. 'What is it that you want?' Naturally, I had no answer.

The receptionist seemed annoyed when we

walked in, as if we had strayed accidentally into a private, very large but rather seedy house, whose sole occupant — a chubby, freckled girl in a white blouse and pink blazer — had been enjoying an evening of rare solitude. She seemed so put out by our arrival, in fact, that I almost turned around and walked straight back out the door. It's always a bad sign, in hotels and hospitals, this hostile reception: usually, it's an omen of worse to come, of rust-stained baths, bad odours, ancient and mysterious stains on the bedsheets. Had I been alone, I probably *would* have gone — but Hazel had already set her little valise down by the desk and was smiling sweetly at the receptionist, whose name, according to her lapel-tag, was Donna.

'We'd like a twin room, please,' she said. 'Do you have any twin rooms free for tonight?'

The girl nodded stupidly then pretended to consult a large, grubby register on the desk. 'Just the one?' she asked, almost *sotto voce*, with only the slightest hint of malice to increase the effect. Here was a woman who enjoyed sitcoms.

Hazel paused just long enough to force Donna to look up; then she smiled again, even more ingratiatingly than before. 'Yes, please,' she said. 'With a sea view, if you have it.'

* ★ ★

Up in the room, she lay down on the bed furthest from the window. I felt awkward now, like a boy on a first real date. The way I had felt, once, with her mother. 'Do you want to go out and get something to eat?' I asked her. 'Or we could get room service.'

She studied me idly. 'No hurry,' she said. 'Why don't you sit down. Relax for a bit. Watch TV or something.'

'I'm not much for television,' I said. I sat down on a chair near the bathroom door.

'Come on,' she said. 'Lighten up, why don't you?' She picked up the remote control from its cradle between the two beds — which were perilously close together. How old did she look to a complete stranger? Sixteen? More? Was I about to be arrested? 'I wonder if they get Sky,' she said. She flicked on the TV and ran through the channels. BBC1, BBC2, ITV, Channel 4, then radio. Not even Channel 5. 'That's awful,' she said and switched to standby. She turned back to me, mock-eagerly. 'Looks like you're going to have to entertain me,' she said.

'I'm not sure I'd be much good at that,' I said.

'No?'

'I can't imagine.'

226

'Well, what are you good for, then?' she said, with a curious look.

'We should talk about our plans,' I said. 'Where we're going. How we get there. What happens when — '

'We can talk about that later,' she said. 'Right now, I'd rather talk about you.'

'Me?'

She looked around. 'You talking to me,' she said, in a fairly accurate Robert de Niro voice. 'You talking to me?'

'OK,' I said. 'What about me?'

'Well. First question, for ten. Why are you here?'

'Here?'

'Here. In this hotel room. With me.'

'You were the one who asked for a twin room. I was going — '

'Answer the question! No conferring!'

I looked at her helplessly. I had no idea why I was there. Or maybe I did, but I didn't want to think about it.

'Is it because you fancy me?'

I shook my head.

'You don't fancy me?' She seemed shocked.

I didn't answer, then I shook my head again.

She thought for a moment. 'Are you having a midlife crisis? Something like that?'

'I'm too young for a midlife crisis,' I said.

'Is that so?' Apparently unconvinced, she thought some more. It was stage thinking, all puzzled expression and furrowed brow. 'Well, do you think we're connected in some way? Is that it?'

'How do you mean connected?'

'I don't know,' she said. 'I'm asking you.'

'Maybe.'

'How?'

'I don't know.'

'You know something. You know more than you're saying. Or else you wouldn't be here.'

'I think we should just order room service and get some rest. We've got a long day tomorrow.'

'Why? What are we doing?'

'I didn't mean . . . ' I looked at her, sitting there on the bed, fiddling with the remote. 'I meant — '

'Maybe you do fancy me,' she said. 'Only you don't want to admit it.'

'Maybe,' I said.

'I'd like a steak,' she said.

'What?'

'Room service. I'd like a steak. French fries. Side salad.'

'Well, if they have it — '

She found a room service menu and opened it. 'They always have steak in these places,' she said. 'It's what room service is all about. Steak, fries, club sandwiches, Thai-style fishcakes. What else could you want, in a place like this?'

★   ★   ★

Looking back, I can see that it wasn't much of an adventure. She must have got fed up with it all in fairly short order. Looking back, I know *I* did. I'd wanted to talk to her, to try to explain something, though I had no idea, really, what it was that I wanted to explain. Now that we were together, alone in a strange room, I couldn't work out how I was supposed to start a real conversation with her. Not that I would have had much of an opportunity: after we ate, she turned the TV back on and lay across her bed, watching, her bare legs kicking in the air, while I piled all the dirty dishes on to the tray and set it outside the door. I was trying to ignore the TV; I don't much like television, unless there's a movie on. I like movies. Old Hollywood, French cinema, films by Kuro-sawa and Kiéslowski. Franju. Wajda. Godard. Hazel's tastes were somewhat different — or maybe she didn't have any particular tastes, maybe she was just happy to watch whatever came on. For a while, she sat smirking and giggling at some sitcom that I'd never even heard of; then she spent half an hour surfing all four of the available channels, flicking to and fro between some kind of drama and a documentary about sharks, till she eventually settled on an American-made hospital series. I kept trying to engage her, to distract her from the melodrama, but she had gone into a trance, only half aware that I was in the room at all, her eyes fixed on the screen. In between the operations and the love scenes, she watched the adverts.

'God,' I said finally. 'Do you always watch television like this?'

She nodded. 'Absolutely,' she said.

I glanced at the screen. A man in green scrubs was arguing with a woman in a white coat. They both seemed overly clean and far too well groomed to be emergency room workers. 'So what's the attraction?' I asked.

'Hmm?'

'I said: what's the attraction? Don't you know what's going to happen in the end? More or less?'

She nodded again. 'Absolutely,' she said.

'Well,' I said. 'If you'll just turn it off for a moment, we can talk about what we need to do — '

'Shhh!' She looked at me. 'Sorry,' she said, quickly. 'But this is a good bit.'

I looked back to the screen. It was the same two people, arguing. 'How do you know?' I asked.

She didn't answer. She sat transfixed, watching the argument as if it were something that mattered to her, on a personal level, and I was fairly sure I wouldn't get anything sensible out of her that night. I still wasn't sure what I wanted to say to her, anyway. I was beginning to wonder why I was there, why I had committed this absurd crime. If I took her back, right then, right at that moment, would the authorities turn a blind eye? If I took her back and explained why I had done it, would they give me the help I so obviously needed? I doubted that. It didn't matter, anyway. I was tired, and I couldn't have driven another mile. I lay down on the bed and tried to rest, my mind buzzing with the dialogue from the TV show.

It can't have been long before I fell asleep, because the next thing I remember is waking up in the dark, still fully dressed. The curtains were open and the room was bathed in a silvery glow from the lamps in the hotel car park. A few feet away, in the other bed, Hazel lay sleeping. She had taken off her clothes and piled them on the chair by the bathroom door, a neat little pile of thin, inappropriate clothes, nicely folded, just the way she

231

probably did them when she was at home. I looked at her. The bedclothes were up around her chin and she was smiling to herself; only her face and hair were visible, and one shoulder, which was bare, slender, white in the glow from outside. I felt a sudden shock, then, when it came to me that she was naked, or almost naked, under the covers. She hadn't brought pyjamas or a nightdress, and now she was lying there, a sleeping nude, fourteen years old, smiling softly at some dream she was having. I looked away quickly. I thought about getting off the bed, about going over to her and pulling the bedsheets up so they covered that bare, white shoulder, but I didn't move. I couldn't. I turned to face the window and tried to go back to sleep, but I couldn't do that either. I couldn't do anything. I was temporarily insane — I even knew that I was — yet still, without a doubt, I was lost.

★ ★ ★

The next few days followed the same pattern. We drove, we stopped to eat, we found shelter for the night. While we drove, Hazel mocked me, teased me, tested me. Or she got earnest and asked me serious questions, though she always changed the subject before I could figure out an answer. What do you want? Why

232

are you here? Do you *really* not fancy me? So it went on. On the fourth day, we stopped at a hotel that, at first sight, seemed identical to the Carlton. For a moment, I even thought we'd driven in a circle and ended up where we'd started. We hadn't, though. This place was called the Maybury, and it was brown and white, not pink. Inside, the food and the bedrooms and the staff would be the same as they were everywhere else; there would be a little bar opposite reception with a row of the usual optics, high stools in a neat row and little bowls of peanuts set out here and there on the tables. It would be empty, of course. When we walked in, the receptionist would be doing the crossword puzzle, or a Sudoku, or she would be on the phone, talking to her sister about shoes or wedding arrangements, and she would barely notice us as we checked in. It made me think of a scene in *Lolita*, where Humbert and Lola are together in a hotel, though I couldn't remember if it was in the book or the film, or both. I seemed to recall James Mason painting Sue Lyon's toenails, so I imagine it was the movie. They were sharing a room, though it was so obvious that *this* man wasn't *this* girl's father — and I'd always found it hard to believe that nobody challenged them. But here we were, going from hotel to hotel, paying the bills in cash, sleeping together in the same room — and nobody challenged us, either. That was even harder to believe. Not that our behaviour was in any way out of the ordinary: if anything, we were rather a dull pair of guests, wherever we ended up. We drove around; we ate; we slept. I kept trying to start a conversation, and she kept stalling me. Or she would challenge me and, in spite of my best intentions, I would be lost for words. I had no idea, now, what we were doing — and our little adventure was turning out to be fairly boring stuff. Of course, I could tell myself that this didn't bother me, because I was still thinking, still trying to work out what I was going to do; but I also knew it couldn't have been any fun for Hazel — which meant that I felt guilty. Guilty, because I was the responsible adult here. Guilty, because I found myself watching her in a certain way, when she was preoccupied with television or eating. Guilty for a hundred reasons, and more than a little worried, too. Maybe she would just lose interest and wander off, the way she was about to wander off on the day her mother abandoned her. Maybe she would turn me in and say it had all been my fault. Maybe she would tell me some night, when the adverts were on, that she was tired of all this. I didn't want her to think I was just plain boring. I wanted her to be — happy. I wanted her to have fun. I suppose that was why I agreed to the fair. I didn't have any reason to mistrust her; I had no idea that she was in cahoots with anybody else. I didn't think she was setting a trap for me. I just thought she'd like to get out for a while, to take her mind off things.

She was the one who saw it, in the local paper. She'd picked the thing up in the hotel foyer, and she'd been flicking through idly, looking at the ads. I knew she was fed up with the routine we were falling into, and I'd decided already to do something about it. Maybe go to the cinema. Or we could go out for a meal together. That way, we could sit down and have a proper conversation. When we were in the car, or in a hotel room, it was impossible to talk. In the car, she just kept changing the subject; in the room, I felt awkward and unsettled, too close to her, too private. I had to find some kind of neutral ground.

'There's a fair on at the common,' she said, all of a sudden. It was as if she'd read my mind.

'Really?'

'I'd like to go,' she said. She gave me a big-eyed, mocking, please-daddy look.

'It's a bit dangerous,' I said. 'Somebody might see us — '

'Nobody's going to see us,' she said. 'Come on. It'll be fun.'

I went over and looked at the paper. A fair, sure enough, that very evening. Surely it would be all right. We wouldn't look out of place: a man and his daughter, going from stall to stall, eating candy floss. We were hardly likely to stand out from the crowd. 'OK,' I said. 'And maybe we can get something to eat, afterwards.'

'You mean, not room service?'

'I mean not room service.'

'Wow!' She smiled. 'So what are we waiting for?'

★   ★   ★

We got to the fair early. It was the usual set-up: rides, shooting galleries, hot dogs, drinks. It hadn't really started yet, but people were going round, smiling happily, families mostly, the kids excited, the grown-ups trying to seem blasé. To begin with, I felt a little wary, seeing policemen and spies everywhere, but it wasn't long before I started enjoying myself. It was infectious, that sense of the coming night, and red and blue and yellow stalls lit up around the field, though it was

236

still daylight: just the beginning of the evening and the sense of something about to happen, maybe some miraculous event, like turning a corner and finding the whole world unimaginably altered. Hazel felt it too — or so I thought, as we walked from stall to stall, peering into the dark rides, lingering by the plastic ducks floating in tanks of bright, greeny water, ready to be hooked out and exchanged for goldfish or big, good-humoured teddy bears. We weren't doing anything yet, though, we were saving it all for later, unwilling to give up on the pleasure of anticipation, aware of the fact that the anticipation was most of what the place had to offer. When I looked at her — quick, searching glances that I knew she found a little embarrassing — she smiled, or pressed her lips together as if to say, look at this, isn't it silly? and I thought she was happy. Maybe it was foolish of me, but I thought she was with me then, really with me, listening to what I said, talking to me and to nobody else and, once, even reaching out to touch my arm when she wanted me to look at something. It was a terrible moment, I see that now, but at the time I couldn't help myself, I just submitted to that passing gesture, which no doubt meant nothing at all to her. I submitted, I gave myself up to that moment of what was, for me, indelible contact.

And then, in a matter of moments, before I even had time to register what was happening, it was over. Hazel was still there, but she had slipped back into her old, preoccupied mood, and for a minute or so I thought I had done something to upset her. Perhaps something had registered in the muscles of my face, some signal of immodest pleasure or some possessive fantasy, betrayed in my mouth and eyes, or in the way I turned my head. At some point, she had turned to me in the half-light, and I had given myself away. I had shown her my true colours, somehow, even though I had no idea what my true colours were. I had betrayed my true feelings, my unconscious designs. I had given myself away — but as what? The dirty old man she'd thought I was to begin with? A sentimentalist, dreaming of love and family and human warmth? A soppy date? I was none of those things, and I wanted to tell her so, but I couldn't. Even if I could have explained, I knew she would only ask me, with that cool, puzzled look of hers, what I really wanted, or thought I wanted, if I was none of these things — and the truth was, I didn't know. I was a man. A more or less middle-aged man at a funfair with a pretty teenaged girl who probably wasn't, after all, the daughter she is young enough to be. A man: dirty, old, clean, young, what difference did it make? Just a man; which was to say: a set of wants, a collection of impulses, a huddle of needs, only half of them visible to his own sorry gaze. If I had said anything at all, she would only have asked me, again, what I wanted — and in truth, I had no idea. I hadn't the least clue what I wanted from her, or from myself, or from the night.

Now the mood of anticipation was broken. The sky had begun to get dark; the lights seemed brighter and, at the same time, less innocent; the rides were noisier. We were standing by one of the attractions, a ride that would have been called the Octopus in my day. I looked at her. She was staring off into the gloaming between two stalls. 'Do you want to try it?' I asked.

She give a brittle laugh and shook her head. 'No thanks,' she said.

'OK, how about the dodgems then — '

She returned for a moment from her reverie. 'Why don't you go over to that stall there and win me one of those big bears?' she said, pointing to a row of huge silver teddy bears on a shooting gallery up ahead.

I smiled, trying to get things back to how they had been. I knew there was no chance of actually winning one of those particular bears, they were just for show, but maybe if I slipped the guy some money, he'd let me pretend. 'All right,' I said. 'Let's go — '

She drew back. 'You go,' she said. 'I'll wait here. Then you can surprise me.'

★ ★ ★

When I got back from the shooting range, Hazel had company. It was obvious, even at first glance, that they were people she already knew. They were boys a little older than she was, and there were three of them. Two were nondescript, just fairground lads: punkish, but dressed in the usual anonymous, vaguely *sportif* clothes, cheap track suits and expensive trainers, ear-rings, chains: white boys trying to be gangsters. On his own, neither one of them would have said boo to a goose; they were pack animals, dog-boys. The other was different, though. He was the one the police always describe as *the ringleader*, not necessarily because he was the strongest or smartest, but because he didn't care about anything. He was a *tough*: self-sufficient, with that well-rehearsed fuck-you look to him that the others no doubt admired and copied. They were copying it now, in fact, or trying to — but in them it just looked silly. He was

240

dressed in a different style, a slicked-up icon from a golden age, with pencil-thin jeans and a black leather jacket left halfway open to reveal a red and black plaid shirt. His face was thin, long; his eyes were dangerous — and he had that classic leather jacket, like the boyfriend *type* in the Louis Malle film. He'd no doubt got the look from watching old movies on TV, just like the Boyfriend, but he had another, less contrived quality about him, a hard confidence based on the conviction that he was safe, because he was the one everybody had to watch out for. He was the dangerous one — and he was in charge. Most of all, he didn't care, and the others, who were only pretending, knew he didn't care. That was why they were with him, because they thought his indifference was contagious.

As I approached, he was standing next to Hazel, nonchalant, untouchable, but there was no mistaking his sense of proprietorship. He had claimed her; she was his. In other circumstances it might have been touching, or sociological, perhaps. He was utterly still; a pose, yes, but it worked, it gave him the necessary potential, it made of him the perfect cliché: *like a cat, poised for action.* Like a gunslinger. It was all the young toughs from every film he'd ever seen, all rolled into one. Elvis, in *Roustabout*; one of the chicken-run kids from *Rebel without a Cause*; who knows, even Zbygniew Cybulski in *Ashes and Diamonds*, or Alain Delon and Jean-Paul Belmondo in — No. It was pure Hollywood, with the slicked-back hair and the lit cigarette hanging from his lips. This boy wanted to be an actor, or a rock star. Yet the really odd thing was that he got away with it. He got away with looking like this when anyone else would have been laughed off the fairground, because he was the real thing, he wasn't pretending. He really didn't give a damn.

And yet. It was all very successful, this Fifties existentialist tough boy indifference, but there was something else, in his stillness, in his eyes, that only became apparent at close quarters. From a distance, he was impressive, he carried it off; closer up I saw — and it came as a real shock to me — that he was ugly. It wasn't the ugliness of the mutant or the ill-formed; nothing so obvious. It was ugliness of intent, ugliness of expectation. At some point this boy had been beaten down, and he had decided that, from here on in, he was going to be the one giving the beatings. I looked at Hazel.

'I think we ought to be going,' I said. 'It's late — '

242

'Where you going, mister?' One of the minions spat off to one side as he spoke, not looking at me because I wasn't worth the trouble.

I looked at Hazel. I wanted to keep my eyes on her, but it was a distraction, the way the ringleader held himself so still and said nothing, just watching me with a half-amused look. 'Hazel?' I said.

'You go,' she said. 'I want to stay here for a bit.' She gave me what she must have thought was a reassuring look. 'I'll see you later.'

'It would be better to go now,' I said. There was no hope of making her go and I knew it. Not because of these boys, or not just because of them, but because of her. She was going to do exactly what she wanted — and now, seeing her with the Boyfriend, having something to compare her against, I saw that she was just like him, that she didn't care, either. She didn't care, and she never had. She was just as indifferent, just as remote, as he was. And of course, it was obvious — and it struck me suddenly how ridiculous it was that I hadn't suspected a thing — it was so *obvious* that this moment was what she had been waiting for all along. It was all planned. I almost laughed out loud; then I felt sick to my stomach.

The ringleader didn't say a word. But then,

he wouldn't; not unless he had to. Still, I knew that, if he did speak, I would have to act, or back off fast. Maybe the better strategy was to relent a little, and hope that Hazel would see sense. I could get her away the next morning, I told myself, but not now. I was in a weak position, after all. *I think you had better come down to the station with us, Mr Humbert. It looks like you've got some explaining of your own to do, sir.* I nodded, still keeping my eyes on Hazel. 'Not too late, then, OK?' One of the boys sniggered and the ringleader gave him a warning glance.

'See you later,' Hazel said.

I nodded. 'All right,' I said. 'I'll see you.'

She gave me an odd smile — at once forgiving and curious, as if she had thought of some terrible thing I had done, long ago and, all at once, in that moment, had forgiven me for it. 'What happened to the bear?' she asked.

I shook my head. The ringleader was watching me curiously too now, a pained, almost saddened look in his eyes. 'No bear,' I said. 'Not this time.'

Hazel shrugged. 'Never mind,' she said; then she turned away and started off across the fairground, vanishing into the crowd and the lights.

★ ★ ★

All the way back to the hotel, I wondered why I'd let her go so easily. It wasn't just that I was avoiding unnecessary trouble. No: I think I had begun to see already what a mistake I had made. Hazel might have been my daughter, but she probably wasn't — and I wasn't sure I wanted her to be. I didn't like her, to be frank. She was a bit of a brat, and now it seemed obvious that she had been playing me for a fool all along. I didn't need her, anyway. I had used her as an excuse to leave Amanda, but I didn't need an excuse. Amanda wasn't really my wife; I had never really been her husband. We'd been playing at house, pretending to be what we were supposed to be, that was all.

By the time I got back to the hotel, I was all used up. I couldn't think any more and I didn't want to. I found the bar, had a large whisky, then another. Then I went to the room. I wasn't used to spirits and, as I wandered down the furry-looking corridors past identical door after identical door, I couldn't decide whether I felt sick or asleep on my feet. When I saw the bed, I opted for the latter. Not expecting to see Hazel for some time, and possibly never again, I emptied the contents of my pockets — wallet, keys, loose change — on to the dresser, stripped off quickly, then got under the covers and fell asleep almost immediately.

I was swimming. It was a place I used to go to when I was a student, a private swimming club on the river that I broke into sometimes, on summer nights. Somebody else owned it, but I had the best of it, pulling off my shirt in the moonlight and slipping into the inky water, feeling the cold seep down to the bone. As I kicked away from the side to hang in the current, feeling the riverweed brush against my skin, I felt an odd satisfaction, a kind of pride, that while they could fence off that piece of land and river, there was something else that nobody could enclose, something they probably didn't even know was there. To know it, they would have had to steal it. As I glided through the water, across to the far bank and back into the pool of moonlight at the river's centre, I felt transformed: it was as if I had slipped free of my usual self to become a spirit, a graceful, primeval creature, deft and newly sensitised, communicating with something else through the water, something that was almost, but not altogether there, like a character in a story that someone is telling as he goes along, making it up, endlessly inventing, making it true.

★   ★   ★

I woke suddenly. It took a long moment to remember where I was and what had happened. It was still dark, but I could have sworn that, a moment before, I'd heard an ice-cream van just outside the window. An ice-cream van, like the one that used to roll around Coldhaven on Sunday afternoons, coming to an unexpected stop in the hotel car park, waiting a while for customers, then moving off into the dark. Its music box jingle was still running in my head and for a long moment I had the impression that it was this — this tinkling, banal melody — that had woken me. It was a tune I knew from somewhere, a song from a film, I thought, a plaintive, wind-in-the-summer-grass kind of thing, not quite right for selling ice-cream, even if it had its own particular effect of creating nostalgia for a time, and a place, that had never existed outside Hollywood and, by implication, nostalgia for a past self who should be considered, at best, highly improbable.

Lara's Theme. That was it. Music from a love story, wind in the summer grass. Or was it new snow on a shawl, coming home from a dance? It hardly mattered, I had imagined it anyway. Why would anybody be out selling ice-cream in the middle of the night, in near winter, and in the car park of a second-rate chain hotel at that? I had dreamed it, of course I had, and I found myself wondering what else I had dreamed, the way a man does, sometimes, when he wakes and, even if he isn't sure of where he was a moment before, cannot quite shake off the feeling that, whatever it was, the dream was more real than the furniture he now sees around him. Or maybe not more real, just *better* — because something is wrong and, all the while, without knowing it, he has been registering the signs of a catastrophe: a clue here, something absent there, something else where it should not have been.

That was when I realised, finally, that Hazel wasn't in the room. The bed next to mine was empty and still made up. I looked at the bathroom door: no light. I looked at the curtained windows: no doubt about it, it was early morning, far too late for her to be at the fair, and far too early for her to be at breakfast. She wasn't there, that was obvious. Yet I still hadn't really understood, I still hadn't fully registered. I didn't think something was wrong; I thought I had made a mistake. It wasn't that she was gone, it was only that she was absent from that particular hotel room at that particular moment, possibly for good reason. Though that isn't quite right either because, at the same time, at the very same moment that I was explaining away her absence, I knew that she was gone. I had known it from the first moment I woke to the ice-cream jingle, and this *trompe l'esprit* had just been a temporary measure, to keep the knowledge at a distance. I had suspected it would happen before it happened: the night before, when I'd got back from the fair, I had fallen asleep thinking that, if I didn't abandon her first, Hazel would abandon me, if not that very night, then soon. I had known it all along. I had even guessed it on the first day. Even before the incident at the fair, I had seen that this, our shared experiment in the random, was doomed. Not that it had ever been a shared thing, not really. We had wanted different outcomes all along, even if neither of us seemed to know what it was we expected to happen.

I got out of bed. The air was cool, not the close, overheated air that normally breeds in hotel rooms, and I was surprised by that. Then I realised that this enclosed hotel air was moving slightly, as if in a draught. I took the few steps to the window and drew back the curtain: the window was open. The car park was illuminated by a garish silver light, a half-acre of tarmac surrounded by clipped cypress hedges and ground cover, a car park like any other hotel car park — no ice-cream van, no music, no movement. Just a hotel car park in the wee small hours of the morning. It looked so ordinarily dismal that it was a good minute before I saw that my car was no longer parked where I had left it, just a few yards from the window where I now stood, alone, betrayed in the most ridiculous of ways. No car and, when I turned to look at the dresser, no wallet, no car keys. Instead: a piece of paper, folded neatly in two. A note, printed in large, angular letters on a sheet of hotel notepaper.

I'M SORRY I HAD TO TAKE THIS STUFF BUT WE NEED IT. YOU'LL BE ALL RIGHT. WE BORROWED THE CAR TOO, BUT WE'LL BE CAREFUL WITH IT. YOU'LL GET IT BACK. AND DON'T WORRY YOU'RE NOT MY DAD IF THAT'S WHAT YOU WERE THINKING. I LET YOU THINK THAT BECAUSE I NEEDED TO GET AWAY. I WAS DESPERATE.

THIS MIGHT SOUND FUNNY BUT THANKS FOR HELPING ME. NOW I CAN BE HAPPY DOING WHAT I WANT AND I HOPE YOU WILL BE HAPPY TOO HAZEL X

I stood holding the note — it was evidence, a confession, in fact. I thought about keeping it, but after a moment I crumpled it up and tossed it into the bin. Then, a little panicky, I looked round for my clothes. For a moment, I thought that she — they — might have taken them, but everything was still there, piled on the chair by the bathroom door. She had left me my clothes; she had only taken what she and her friends could use. I was still amazed by the fact — by the fact that she had robbed me, though whether she had acted on her own initiative, or whether she'd been put up to it by her friends from the fair, I didn't know and, as shocked as I was, I didn't really care. I wasn't even surprised. I was alone, naked, broke, without transport. I had been tricked in the most ordinary way, and it was something I could have foreseen, but none of that bothered me as much as the echo of that phantom ice-cream van that was still running through my head. I tried to stop it, tried to focus, to work out what I was going to do, but it was pointless. I should have called reception immediately and reported the theft of my money and car; I should have called the credit card helpline to cancel my cards. I could at least have fantasised about some foul revenge I would inflict upon Hazel and the Boyfriend when I caught up with them. But all I really wanted was to go back to bed and finish the dream I had been having — and after a while, that is what I did.

Or rather, that is what I tried to do. I lay down; I closed my eyes; I tried to get comfortable — but I couldn't sleep. I was too exhausted, too empty. I lay on the bed for a while, staring at the ceiling. Suddenly, the room felt too small, claustrophobic, as if somebody had come in during the night and moved all the furniture closer together, and the walls had closed in a little tighter to fit the new layout. I sat up on the edge of the bed and thought about taking a shower, but even though I felt musty and dirty, my skin and face oddly smudged, my eyes cobwebbed, I didn't move and after a while I realised I was waiting for the ice-cream van to come back, the one I had heard when I first woke, a sound that had felt so real at the time, but had probably been something from a dream. What had the song been? I had remembered, before, and now I had forgotten again. It had sounded strange, a song that didn't really suit that music-box tinkle. I remembered the sound of it, but I couldn't remember what it was called, or the film it was from — *everything* is from a film — but I did think that the words had something to do with horses. Horses and time and friendship. Or maybe I was mistaken in that, too.

Finally, it turned seven-thirty and I went downstairs for an early breakfast. I think I still half expected to find Hazel there, sitting alone at a window table over orange juice and rice krispies. In reality, however, the dining room was empty, except for a thin, tired-looking girl in a red waistcoat, who wasn't pleased to see me. Nevertheless, she came forward. 'Table for one?' she enquired; according to the training manual, page 4, point number 3. I looked at the tag on her waistcoat: it informed me that her name was Zoë and that she was a trainee.

'For two,' I said; then regretted it immediately. I noticed that she was looking at me curiously, the way people do when they think they know you from somewhere, and it struck me that she knew something about what had happened the night before.

'Table for two,' she repeated, then she sighed softly. 'This way.'

I have always wondered, and never quite got up enough interest to ask why it is that, once she has established the kind of table you need or want, every self-respecting waitress in every type of establishment, from a tea house to a cordon bleu restaurant, then proceeds to lead you past five or six perfectly good tables — window tables, tables in their own pool of light or space, large, sunlit tables — to the dingiest, grubbiest, most cramped table in the house. It's a moment they relish, watching the wretched client slide into the dark, narrow space between a pillar and a wall, not far from the kitchen door or, worse, the toilets but, even though they know exactly what they are doing, they always look terribly hurt if you challenge them, as if all their skill and judgement in this, a fairly menial job with few perks and absolutely no pleasures, has been called into question. True to form, Zoë started off towards the far end of the room into strip-light and swing-door country. I watched her go, then took a seat by the window, a few yards from the door. From here, I could see Hazel, if she returned. I didn't have very high hopes of that, but I couldn't help going through the motions.

It was a moment before Zoë noticed I wasn't there and another, slightly theatrical moment for her to turn, register my absence and, this time uttering an audible sigh, proceed in an orderly fashion to the table I had selected. 'Coffee or tea?' she asked, in a weary, have it your own way, seen it all before voice.

'Coffee, please,' I said, feeling a little cheered by the thought. It was especially cheering, all of a sudden, to think that I couldn't pay for this breakfast.

'Full cooked English, continental or — ' she thought for a moment — 'kippers?'

'I'll have the full breakfast.'

'Toast?'

'Yes, thank you.'

'Brown or white?'

'Some of each, I think.'

She looked at me with something approaching pity, though with enough annoyance to make her even more annoyed with herself, as if she had conceded defeat or made a bad move in some absurd game. 'And your room number, please, sir?' she said, with an air of finality, a signal that she had done her duty and could now go off and attend to more important matters. I gave her the room number and, to my surprise, she smirked. It was only the faintest of smirks; but it was there and there was no doubting that it was there for a reason. She was so sure of her reason, in fact, that she *performed* that smirk: almost instinctively, she got it just right, enough to be shrugged off as an innocent smile, but enough, also, for me to know that *she* knew something about me that I would rather have kept concealed. She even had the sense not to linger, or to dwell on her victory; instead she gave me a curt, dismissive little nod and hurried off to the kitchen to place my order.

Alone again, I sat looking out of the window. The garden, a patch of chipped bark and ground cover, was a soft, damp grey, faintly powdery in the corners, like something freshly sifted. The sky was a mass of pearl-coloured clouds, slightly dark around the edges, but out at the far end of the garden, on a thin horizon, there was a hint of blue; barely a promise, but visible nevertheless. For the first time, I thought about what I was going to do — and by the time breakfast arrived, an idea had begun to form. It was a good idea and I was pleased with it, but it was also an idea that would keep, while I ate a hearty breakfast.

Until that moment, I hadn't actually felt hungry. I had just come down for something to do and to get out of my narrow room. I had needed a distraction to help me think. If anything, I would have been satisfied with a cup of coffee, maybe a slice of toast — but as soon as the food appeared. I realised I was ravenous. I had barely eaten the night before, and I had been awake for hours, going through everything that had happened and listening for a phantom ice-cream vendor, all the while hoping for something to slide into place, some explanation for what I had done that existed outside the limits of thought but might emerge, of its own accord, from my nerves, or my blood, or from thin air. And until that moment, when the smug girl crossed to me from the kitchen bearing a large plate of bacon and eggs, sausages, beans, black pudding, mushrooms — *everything* — until that moment, nothing had come. All I could think was that I had made a terrible mistake, a ridiculous error of judgement that I'd known I was making all along and had persisted in from sheer perversity, compounding it hour by hour and day by day, almost deliberately, as if to spite myself. Now, however, as Zoë set the plate before me, I felt a sudden rush of — not understanding, that wasn't what I needed — but a rush of affirmation, a dark, sweet rush of agreement with the world that had brought me to this place.

'Full English,' Zoë said, drawing herself up to her full five foot five inches and scowling at me happily. 'That'll keep your strength up . . .'

There was a touch of innuendo in this, of course, but it was too late. I really didn't care what they talked about in the kitchens, or in the little office behind reception. They had been wrong in their assumptions, even to the extent that they may have been right — what *had* I wanted, anyhow? I didn't know. All kinds of things. Nothing. It didn't matter. Whatever it was, it was nothing that Zoë could have imagined. I looked at the food, greasy and bright and wet here and there with the juice from plum tomatoes — though there were no tomatoes on the plate — and gathered up my cutlery. 'Good,' I said. 'I'm *famished.*'

★   ★   ★

Back in the room, I lay down across the bed and turned on the TV. It flickered into life; then a plump, hapless-looking man called Tony was in the middle of confessing to his wife that he had been visiting a prostitute for seven years. The wife had, presumably, been lured to the studio under false pretences, but she was doing a fair job of hiding her disgust, or humiliation, or loathing — whatever it was she was feeling. She was doing it so well, in fact, that she looked almost bored and the presenter, afraid that this clever stunt was about to fall flat on its face, started prompting her.

'What do you feel about that, Irene?' he asked, with exaggerated concern.

Irene looked at him blankly, then turned to study Tony. Something was beginning to dawn on her; she was just beginning to see that she genuinely wasn't going to be as surprised as everybody hoped. She was going to come through.

'What do you *feel*, Irene? Can you tell Tony what you feel?' The presenter was goading her now, but Irene had switched off. At the bottom of the screen, like a slogan from a soap advert, the legend

HAS JUST DISCOVERED HUSBAND CHEATS WITH PROSTITUTES

kept flashing on and off. I watched for another minute; then I hit the mute button. Looking at Tony, it didn't surprise me that he slept with prostitutes; the despicable thing was that he should choose to tell Irene about it on daytime television. This was what she couldn't bear, and this was why she was about to hire a divorce lawyer and take him for everything she could, because he was subjecting her to *this*. I watched his dry, slightly bulbous lips moving for a while longer — from his expression, it seemed he was offering some kind of explanation — then the camera turned to Irene, and I switched the thing off. As the screen went blank with an oddly old-fashioned little fizz of static, I lay back across the bed. Something was missing.

There was more to do, some piece left to fit into the puzzle. Then I remembered the minibar.

I have never understood why people confess their sins. It's as if the need to confess is the compelling factor, and the thought occurs to me, from to time, that most people sin in order to have something to tell. Though I don't really understand what sin is anyhow. A mistake, an error, *une bêtise*, an act of madness, a miscalculation; yes. Misadventure; *of course*. But sin; no. My folly, my mistake, my act of madness remains mine and though I may choose whether or not to take responsibility for it, it's still nobody else's business. But a sin is public, it has to be acknowledged and forgiven. 'My mistake,' I say, and I keep some part of myself, of my good faith, but my sin belongs to the world and the only way I can win it back is to obtain forgiveness. This was what was going through my head, this or something like it, when I returned to the idea I'd had in the dining room — and quickly, logically, reached the decision that, rather than seek help, I would *walk* what I had calculated was the hundred or so miles home. It was a decision I arrived at without emotion or melodrama, as I sat on the floor consuming the contents of the minibar — all those little jewel-like bottles and tins and crackling cellophane bags spread out before me. At first the idea struck me as absurd: I remember I laughed at myself for even thinking about it. After the second of the little green bottles, however, I began to understand the logic. It wasn't penance I had in mind, it wasn't some theatrical notion of self-abasement, like Raskolnikov in the public square, declaring his humanity. It was a purely personal matter, a secret I wanted to keep for myself. It was one possible finale to a series of events that had taken me as far as that hotel room floor, one of many, no doubt, but the one that, for the moment, struck me as the most authentic. As I washed down a diminutive Toblerone with the contents of a little yellow can, the idea developed. As I mixed the contents of the little clear bottles with cola in a chewy-looking plastic glass, it seemed inevitable. After the last of the little gold bottles and a handful of stale pistachios, I went into the bathroom and threw up. It was a surprise, how quickly it happened and I knelt there, fascinated, as the half-digested cheese straws and chocolate and the undigested remains of breakfast disappeared. Then I fell asleep on the bathroom floor and lay perfectly still till the chambermaid woke me, some time around noon.

I was violently sick for the next twelve

hours. I had never experienced such misery. I vomited, I gasped for air, I gagged; it was as if something was tearing in my gullet, some fine tissue that I didn't even have a name for. As if something were fighting its way out of my chest; something dark and thick forcing its way up through my throat. In the short, agonising, breathless spaces between the spasms, I lay listening, wondering how loud I had been, kneeling on the bathroom floor with the after-echo of that tile-and-ceramic acoustic ringing in my ears. I was afraid someone would hear and come to see what was going on. Not to help, but to accuse me of some obscure crime.

Then, around midnight, a chill stillness descended. My muscles and bones were steeped in pain; I thought I could even feel the hurt moving in my blood: a rare, self-generating poison working its way through from cell to cell, corpuscle to corpuscle. Still, at least I had stopped retching. I crawled off the bath-room floor. I was ice cold now; and at the same time, I was bathed in sweat. I got back to the bed on my hands and knees. The relief of lying down was indescribable. I must have slept again for an hour or so, but it was still dark when I woke. The hotel was silent. I stood up, went to the bathroom and stared at myself in the near-full-length mirror. I looked surprisingly normal. My hair was matted from the sweat, and my skin was ice white, but after I'd rinsed my face in warm water I looked perfectly acceptable. I had nothing to carry but the clothes on my back and the coat that, for some reason, I had carried in from the car the day before, so I placed my key-card on the edge of the sink and headed for the door.

Traffic From Paradise

I decided to walk day and night, at first just to keep moving and so stay warm but later because the darkness pleased me, especially out on the country roads, where there were no street lamps. There was a moon, so visibility was mostly good; when it got so dark that I couldn't see where I was going, I would stop, then make my way slowly, one step at a time, probing the blackness, guided by an inner sense of dark space that had begun to develop, a sense that made up its own rules as it went along, guided as it was by the cold or by something that resembled gravity, the mass and density of some object that blocked my path somehow written on the air for me to read. I made mistakes, but what did it matter if I tumbled off the verge now and then? What did it matter if I fell forwards and lay face down on the road, the scent of frosted tarmac on my lips? I didn't mind the odd bruise on my shins and forearms; I didn't think of the injuries I sustained as pain in the real sense. It was amusing, mostly. When I fell, I wanted to laugh out loud. What did it matter? This was the beginning of night vision, I decided. Who cared if I fell now and then, when it was like a child falling off a bike, or going under at the swimming baths, nose filling with chlorine? I was learning to walk in the dark, like a cat, or a fox. Or so I thought.

Mostly, the night felt large and peaceful. Large, quiet, safe; a form of concealment. It seems to go against instinct, to say that the night feels safe, but what I am thinking of isn't so much safety from physical harm, or from accident, or some ancestral terror of wild beasts; what I mean by safe is, safe from the noise and the mess and the sheer visibility of daytime, amongst people. What I mean is safe from the way things are when other people are present. Safe from the feeling that other people knew who I was, and where I lived. Safe from the fear of being found. Safe from the fear of being found out. Or maybe not safe *from*, but safe *in*. Safe *as*. I felt safe *in* the dark, *as* myself. I felt uninterrupted. As I walked, I started practising an idea: I would stop thinking all the time; I would shut off the voices in my head, the endless trivia, the inward dialogue of nonsense that goes on all the time. The needless error of all that inner rambling, which is not part of the real self, but something that has been incorporated, something learned. Does that make sense? If it doesn't, I don't know how else to say it. I don't know how to transplant that idea, because it belongs to that dark road, and to the sounds I made as I walked, the sound of my breathing, the sound of my feet, the odd stumble and scuff, the quiet when I stopped, the occasional call of a bird or an animal across the fields.

It was going to snow early that winter: the only question was when. From time to time the sky grew livid, the clouds tinged with a hard, iron gleam, only gradually resolving into a quick, inky rain that left the hedgerows and verges black and sodden. Closer to home, I might have kept walking no matter what, and I was unhappy every time the rain interrupted my progress. It seemed important, for some reason, to keep going, as if it was the momentum, not the return, that I needed. That early in the journey, however, there was no choice but to duck into whatever shelter I could find when the rain started beating down. The only trouble about stopping was that my mind would immediately start working overtime again, running through the usual rationalisations and conjectures, the mental wallpaper of a resolutely beige spirit. I kept thinking about penance, and what it meant to be making that walk, when all I should have been doing was going on, for no given reason — because, new as I was to the idea, I felt that penance, or whatever it was I intended, should be an everyday matter, a deliberate return from the glamour of sin. In other words, I didn't want to see myself walking, I didn't want to make too much of it. It mattered to me, for example that, had I been observed on that road, I would look like a man whose car had broken down, walking the two or three miles to the next garage. Even better, of course, not to be observed. I had to be invisible, even to myself, for as long as I walked. I had to disappear into the banal.

But then, if you walk for long enough, in the cold, or fast rain, or facing the wind, you become aware of another walker, out in the distance somewhere: an echo, an exact copy of yourself who is nevertheless a distinct animal, a different body. I was following the roads home, trying to avoid the towns, caught up in the strange discipline of being almost lost and, somewhere, that other animal was walking too, among dunes, or across a stretch of marshland. Alone, and yet companion to the birds and animals who go invisibly along with him, he lives on his wits. He lives on windfalls, on what he loses and what he finds, apples and water, mushrooms and charity. He is the one who is in danger of being lost for ever, the one who might at any moment turn into a pillar of salt. Most important of all, he is the one who has to carry the name of the devil in his memory, the bones of the devil in his bones, the blood of the devil in his veins — and, for the duration of that walk, he was my true companion: *mon semblable, mon frère.* This, of course, was delirium.

I was trying to take the country roads, but from time to time it was easier just to cut through a town quickly. Towns were a distraction, with the lights and the warmth that every bakery or bus station café offered; towns were also full of people, and I wanted to avoid people. I wanted the clean, hard discipline of a country road: birds, hedges, fields, quiet. When I reached Stonefield, however, I realised that preparations were already under way for Christmas and I lingered a while, just to look at the lights. I had arrived in the early evening, in a slow, fuzzy rain, but everything was already lit up, the wet streets glittering with splashes of red and blue and green under the lights. I saw no harm in taking my time to come through the little town — it wasn't terribly crowded, and the lights cheered me, tiny splashes of colour scattered about the pavements, reflected in the puddles and gutters. I was keeping my head down, trying to remain invisible, a ghost of a passer-by when, around ten yards away, standing by a pelican crossing, I saw Hazel, in her familiar little blue jacket and short red skirt more suited to the summer than a cold December night. It was definitely her outfit. The only thing that was different about her was that her black boots had been exchanged for a pair of thick-soled, clunky trainers. Her hair and face were wet, but she looked happy. Untroubled. As I stood watching, unable to move, unable to call out, a car approached, slowed to a near stop, and the passenger door opened. At the same time, she glanced back, not at me, not at anything in particular, just a girl looking around on a wet winter's night while someone stops to offer her a lift — and, as she slipped into the car, I felt a surge of grief, a wave of something approaching real pain, running through my body and, for the first time, I realised how utterly lost I was. Just because this girl — this beautiful, impossible girl who was not Hazel after all but another girl, just like her and utterly different — happened to turn and look at me through a fuzz of cold rain.

I must have stepped into the road at that point, involuntarily taking her lead, not knowing I had walked into the path of an oncoming van. It wasn't going very fast, but it hit me, just shunting me enough to push me over and I tumbled to the ground with an unceremonious splash, like a circus clown. This brought the traffic to a halt, as I struggled back to my feet and the driver, a big, puffy man with very thick, dark eyebrows, climbed out of the vehicle to see if I was hurt. A small crowd gathered, and other drivers slowed to watch as they passed by. I was undamaged, a little shocked, a little dizzy. I stood on the pavement, swaying a little, trying to work out my exit point among all those bodies.

'Hey, matey, are you all right?' the van driver said, putting his hand on my elbow.

I slipped free. 'I'm OK,' I said. 'I'm not hurt.'

Somebody among the crowd shuffled towards. 'You want to be more careful,' she said. It was a woman's voice, coarse and querulous, with just a hint of fishwife.

'I'm fine,' I said. I tried to step away through a gap in the crowd.

This seemed to annoy the van driver. 'All right,' he said. 'People are just trying to help. You gave us all a scare there, stepping into the road like that.'

'He wants to be more careful,' cried the fishwife. 'He ought to look where he's going instead of eyeing up some girl.'

I looked around in panic. What girl? Where

had the girl gone? Had she witnessed the entire scene? I turned to where I had seen her last, but she and the car were gone. I looked at the van driver. 'I'm sorry,' I said. 'I'm just tired.'

'No worries, mate,' the van driver said, relaxing. He didn't want trouble. 'As long as you're all right.' He patted me on the elbow and turned away. His van was causing an obstruction now.

'He wants to look where he's going,' the fishwife called, as she wandered off, dissatisfied. She'd been hoping for more, but it was coming up to Christmas, and people had better things to do.

★   ★   ★

After that little misadventure I avoided the towns entirely, even if it lengthened the walk. Till then, I had been following the main roads; at one point I had even walked along a stretch of motorway at night, following the line of the road but keeping to the verge, in the no man's land between the silver road lighting and the dark hinterland of willows and pastureland beyond. Now I began searching out footpaths and back roads through woods and farmland, and where I couldn't find any other way forward, I struck

271

out over fields and stretches of bog, picking my way through the mud and cowshit in the gloaming of nightfall or early morning. In the middle of the day I found whatever shelter I could: I wanted to be alone now and, most of the time, I managed to remain barely a step away from invisible. Now and then I would see people in the distance: a group of walkers, or a farmer out with his gun and a pair of dogs, even a gang of children, who ran off when they saw me coming. I suppose, by then, I looked odd to them, perhaps even frightening: the bad man their parents had told them to avoid. I didn't mind that, though. I reckoned that, the more forbidding I looked, the better chance I had of being left in peace.

After the first few days, I stopped feeling so hungry. It wasn't as bad as I would have imagined, once I got through the first pangs; what was worse, for me, was the uncertainty of shelter, the fact that, no matter where I went or what kind of cover I found, there was always the chance of being discovered. Because I was still doing most of my walking at night, to stay warm, I would find a sheltered spot halfway through the day and bunk down for a short spell, just an hour or so at a time. I got some sleep that way, but not much. It was cold still, even when it was bright. The main thing was to rest, to keep pacing myself; sleep was a bonus. Yet when I did sleep, it was deep and dark and dreamless. On the second-last day I found what could have been a perfect hiding place, a tiny, almost miniature church, right out in the middle of the country, away from any obvious habitation. It was set in its own small garden, all holly and yew and a handful of skewed headstones from the early 1900s and even from the outside it looked ornate, like the chapel in an Arthurian romance. I walked up to the door casually, a tourist out for an unseasonable walk, and tried the handle, expecting it to be locked. Immediately, with almost no effort on my part, the door swung open and I stepped inside.

'Hello?' My voice echoed slightly at the far end of the interior, just above the altar, but nobody replied. I ventured a few steps. It was dry, not in the least damp, yet it looked as if no one had been there for months. It had never been a parish church, from the look of it; maybe it was part of an old estate, or a folly erected to the memory of a lost wife by some long-dead aristocrat. Certainly, it had that air about it, the air of having once been prized, of having been a fond man's folly. It was decorated in what I would have called the Pre-Raphaelite style, with modest-scale but colourful frescoes around the altar. In spite of the fact that it was, or seemed to be, no longer in use, it was surprisingly clean and well maintained. Perhaps somebody drove here, once or twice a month, and tidied up. Perhaps there was a group of volunteers, some club dedicated to its preservation. It seemed likely, especially given the absence of damp. 'Is anybody here?' I called again.

Silence. I walked into the centre of the little space and sat down in one of the pews facing the altar. I had no intention of going to sleep, but I could rest a while and, if anybody came upon me, I would just be a rambler taking a break from the cold. Or I would be a foreign visitor, come all this way to see an architectural curiosity. It certainly was worth a visit, with its flat, austere altar painting of Christ resurrected, the man Mary mistook for a gardener walking in an avenue of dark shrubs and generic fruit trees in the gold of a Palestinian morning. It was utterly silent and I felt calmed, stilled, the fatigue in my body settling into a tight, manageable weight in the small of my back, like some calculated exaggeration of gravity. It was a moment I wanted to last, if not for ever, then at least for a little longer. Another fifteen minutes; another hour. This was what I had intended when I set out: this moment. Or rather, I probably hadn't intended anything: all I had known was that, once certain things have happened, certain other things have to happen in order for that part of the story to end. And yet still, somewhere, far at the back of my mind, I had been half expecting this. It wasn't comfort, and it wasn't absolution; nothing like that. It was just — being *present*, being stripped of all pretence. Being myself at last, empty handed, with nothing to defend.

I have no recollection of drifting off — I didn't fall asleep, as such, I just started to slide, drifting into a half-world of shadows and reverie — but I'm fairly sure it was no more than a minute or two before I heard a voice, off to the right, and I started awake; the settled mass of my fatigue shattered into hundreds of tiny shards of pain in my muscles and my bones. I looked around. At first, it seemed no one was there; then, like a mirage or a hallucination, a shape appeared, a dark, thin shape among the pews that gradually resolved itself into a woman.

'I'm sorry,' she said. She looked about forty-five, with a long, thin face and wispy, sand-coloured hair. 'I didn't mean to startle you.'

I shook my head. 'You didn't,' I said. I wanted to tell her that I hadn't been asleep, but I couldn't figure out how to say it in any way that would convince either of us.

'Are you all right?' she asked.

I stood up. 'I'm fine,' I said, a little too loudly. Then, to make up for my abruptness, I added, 'I'm the one who should be sorry. I didn't mean — '

'No, no,' she said. 'Don't worry. You were weary and He gave you rest.'

I looked at her. She was dressed in a quaint, old-fashioned twin-set; nearby, her tweedy-looking coat was draped over a pew, next to a bunch of twigs and flowers. She looked like a refugee from *Brief Encounter*. I decided she was one of those women who tend churches, dusting the pews, arranging flowers, tending the altar. A woman of goodwill and simple, slightly casual faith. Ten years before, maybe even five, she was still rather pretty, the kind of young middle-aged woman who wears *L'air du temps* and silk scarves and never quite looks her best in summer; now, she had become something finer, transformed by recent grief, or a hard-won joy, or perhaps even by some brush with the angel, into a late-flowering beauty.

'What church is this?' I asked her.

She smiled. I felt she was reading my thoughts, listening in to every observation, every detail I noticed about her, every judgement I made. 'It's not a church,' she said. 'Not officially.' She didn't say anything else and I stood watching her face, waiting; but she remained silent. By now, she had begun to see that I wasn't quite the tired country rambler she had first chosen to take me for and I think she was puzzled by me; she sensed there was trouble or a problem of some kind, and she wanted to help, but it would be impolite to presume. One had to wait to be asked. After a moment, she brightened and put her hand gently on my arm. 'You could do with a drink, I imagine,' she said. Before I could reply, she fetched a thermos from her coat and poured something steamy and bright into a little blue plastic cup that seemed to materialise from nowhere, like the crockery at a Wonderland party. 'Here you are,' she said. 'This will warm you up.'

I took the cup and drank from it. It wasn't tea, as I had expected, but orange juice. Orange juice with hot water, just the way my father used to make it for me when I was small and had a cold. I cradled the cup in my hands to feel the warmth and sat silent a moment, drinking. The woman watched. The thought crossed my mind that we might have stayed there for ever like that, like one of the murals around the altar. At the same time, however, there was an air of nothing more to say, an air of finality between us that was becoming almost palpable. I handed her the cup. 'Thank you,' I said.

She beamed desperately. 'Don't mention it,' she said.

We were silent for a moment. Still. A tableau. 'Well,' I said, finally. 'I suppose I had better be going.' I glanced at her makeshift winter bouquet. 'You have things to do.'

She didn't try to detain me. For a moment, I rather thought she would. Instead, she smiled again and held out her hand. 'It was nice to meet you,' she said. 'Don't be a stranger, should you pass this way again.'

I took her hand. It was very warm, or perhaps I was just very cold. I nodded. 'It was good to meet *you*,' I said. I wanted to say something else, but I couldn't think what. I made my way to the door, feeling awkward. There was something I wanted her to understand, but I didn't want to presume on her any more than she would have presumed on me. Or rather, I wanted to touch her in some tactful, innocent way and, at the same time, remain a total stranger. Finally, as I pulled the door ajar and felt the draught of cold air coming in, I turned. 'Have a nice Christmas,' I said. I wasn't certain of the date, but I knew Christmas wasn't far off.

She nodded. 'You too,' she said. Then she

turned to her work and I closed the door behind me, to keep in the warm.

★ ★ ★

As cold as it had been before, there had still been a softness, a kind of late autumnal quality to the air when I entered the little chapel. Not quite autumn, perhaps, but sweet, nevertheless, sweet and soft, almost transparent, like molten butter. Now, as I left, crossing the next field by way of a footpath that skirted the hedged, ploughed space, it was suddenly hard winter. It must have been late afternoon, but the horizon and the spaces between the trees and hedges were already beginning to darken; overhead, the flat, celadon sky was cloudless. I walked on quickly up the long gentle slope of the field that would take me, according to my best guess, to within ten miles of the coast and, as I went, I realised that the weather was going to get a good deal worse before morning. I had a straight decision to make: I could walk a little further and find a more discreet sheltering place than the chapel to spend the worst of the night, or I could keep going, moving to stay warm, and hope to cover the remaining ground before I started to shut down from the cold. It made more sense to find somewhere sheltered and hidden and build a fire there, but all at once I couldn't wait any longer, and I decided to walk on.

It was going to snow for sure. I could smell it, I could feel it in the air, an early snow was coming and it was going to be a real one. When I reached the brow of the ridge the wind hit me, a wind touched with murderous cold. All around, the fields and woods were slipping towards twilight but, not far off, at the end of the next field, a group of deer, a family I supposed, had come out to feed, standing in the open but staying close to the hedgeline, cautious, alert to everything, aware, even at that distance, that they were being watched. Their sudden presence made everything seem like a magic show, an elaborate but ultimately deceptive trick, like a game of Chinese whispers in which, the more the formula is repeated, the more it gets distorted. For a moment I even considered the possibility that they weren't real, that the woman in the chapel had not been real, that the aftertaste of warm orange on my tongue and the smell of snow on the air weren't in the least real, and I felt a rush of panic as I cast around, looking for something solid and incontrovertible to focus upon. At this the deer bolted, as if they had picked up my mood, or perhaps they had sensed something that I had not, some shadow, some scent, some rumour crossing the field towards them, or towards me, some rushing, predatory thing that, as I turned, seemed almost upon me, a swift, merciless presence sweeping into my face. For a moment I was lost; for a moment, I did what I had always wanted to do: I thought of nothing. I call it panic, now, at home, in the safety of my armchair, but panic is just a word, and this was something else. It was total abandonment. It was the finger of a god scraping the inside of my skull.

When I realised what I was doing, I was running. Running in the near-dark, stumbling on to the road, into the path of any traffic that might have been passing that way, at that time of the evening. A schoolteacher coming home late with a pile of marking on the passenger seat; a country doctor out on a call, her stethoscope stuffed into her coat pocket. Anyone could have come over the ridge at that moment and hit me as I ran, blind and reckless, into the middle of the carriageway. There was nothing. I ran like that for some time — minutes, longer, who knows — until I came to myself enough to see what I was doing. Then I threw myself on to the verge, as if to avoid a vehicle that was rushing at me straight out of the dark. It was a long time before I sat up, my chest heaving, a sob trapped in my lungs, unable to work free. It was longer still before I got to my feet, exhausted, empty, beyond even fear, and walked on into the night.

★   ★   ★

My father told me all about our neighbour troubles before he died, everything from the wet slurry of leaves and rain and dogshit that would appear on the doormat overnight at Cockburn Street to the muttered imprecations on the telephone in the wee small hours. He told me how Peter Tone had once threatened my mother and how, when they reported the incident to the police, no action was taken.

'I'd let it go, if I were you,' the desk sergeant had said. 'It'll just be the drink talking.'

My father had decided to take his advice. He knew there was more to it than that: it might have been the drink talking, in Peter Tone's case, but he had the backing of a large part of the community. He had approval, no matter how tacit.

'But why?' I asked him. I couldn't understand it. I was sure he and my mother must have done *something* to merit such venom. In spite of my experiences with Malcolm Kennedy, I couldn't believe that it had all happened — that my mother had died — just because they were outsiders.

'I don't know,' my father said. 'I never did understand.' He was sitting by the window, with his binoculars on his lap, not long before the end. He looked semi-transparent, a trick of the light. 'I suppose I prefer birds to people, in the main.'

I didn't say anything. I was wondering how many times he'd asked me to go out along the point with him, when I was a boy. Just to look at some birds. I felt as if I had deliberately denied him — but then he'd never shown that he minded. Not even for a moment.

'Anyhow,' he said. 'What happened, happened. It's all in the past now.' He looked out at the sea. 'I haven't got time to think too much about the past these days. And I've no particular reason to be thinking about the future.' He turned back to me and smiled. 'All that matters is the present, anyway,' he said. 'That's all that ever matters, because the present is all there is. The light. The sea. The wind. Whenever you stop to look, there's nothing but the present. The present goes on for ever.'

I shook my head. I didn't believe him. I

283

mean, I didn't believe that *he* believed what he was saying. Even though he was giving me a dying man's testimony, I thought he was just philosophising.

★ ★ ★

I came to the rise above Coldhaven in the early hours of the morning. It had been snowing again for some time by then, but I wasn't prepared for the scene that greeted me, as I paused atop the path that skirted the golf course and wound down into the west side of the town. It was unusual for snow to settle on that stretch of the coast: it could be an inch thick a mile inland but here, in any normal year, it dusted the roofs and the little wynds that ran down to the harbour with a fleeting silver before it melted away, almost as it fell, and left only an inky sheen on the tiles and windows. That morning, however, it was deep and still and utterly undisturbed, a Dutch landscape of a town in winter: the church spire, the town hall, even the harbourfront, buried in whiteness, and everything silent, everything lit from within, the whole coast, for as far as the eye could see, motionless and eternal. The town was asleep, as it had been on that night a hundred years before, when the devil came up from the sea and walked from street to street, leaving hard, black, feral marks in the snow. Only now it was me who was walking down the rise and in, past the Waterside, past the chemist's and the dry cleaner's, past the old library and down, along Shore Street, with the harbour to my right, the boats on the stocks, gloved in snow, the warning light at the end of the quay burning a cold cherry-red. I stopped for a minute, there, to take it all in: the empty firth, the lights over the harbour, the painted shop fronts, the boats moored by the jetty — a typical East Coast town in the week before Christmas, made perfect by snow and silence. It should all have been painfully familiar, but I was coming back to it, now, as a stranger — and I was seeing it all as if for the first time.

A few yards further along Shore Street, the florist's shop that had once belonged to Mrs Collings was full of poinsettias and Christmas wreaths, no different from the ones she had sold. The butcher's next door had closed down — now it was a hair salon — but there was another butcher around the corner, on Stills Wynd, and someone had opened a picture framing and giftware business further along, opposite the new marina. The fishing was almost gone now, but it had been replaced by pleasure craft, bright, clean boats with names like *Arcturus* and *Khayyam* and *Braveheart*. It made no difference. It was the same sea, the same shore. In summer the swallows worked the harbour walls for the flies that bred in the seaweed; now, even the gulls were absent, gone inland for shelter, like the curlews and sandpipers who drifted back and forth with the tides, coming to the beach when the water was out to harvest the worms and stranded shellfish, then heading inland when the tide came in, to feed on the newly ploughed fields or the stretches of pasture-land just above the town. There was a pattern to it all, and even if that pattern was disrupted, a new pattern would emerge, as if from nothing, insistent, neutral, self-governing. I knew this, and I think, for those few minutes at least, I rejoiced in it, but I couldn't help feeling, in exactly the same moment, an almost unbearable sense of regret for what had passed, for what was passing, for what was still to come and still to pass away.

Maybe it was that mix of sensations, that mingling of emotions that did it, but it felt, as I stood there on Shore Street in the early hours of the morning, as if something I had kept whole and concealed inside myself, some vial of gall and longing sealed in my throat, had broken suddenly, and a bitter, warm taste filled my mouth and chest. I look back now, and I see that I was exhausted. I had walked a hundred miles, maybe more, with almost nothing to eat, and only patchy sleep and yet, as I remember it, I felt good, I felt alive, aware of things to an almost painful degree, my body attuned to the cold and pared down to some essential state by fatigue and hunger, and I remember thinking — oh, yes, I was exhausted, and I was broken and emotional, but I remember, not thinking, but knowing, with no sense of being either comforted or disturbed by the notion — that I also belonged to those wide, eternal patterns, those laws that guided the birds and the tides and the weather that had brought me home: the pattern, the law, that kept everything in motion and the pattern that allowed it all to open a little, every hundred years or so, to let the devil in.

★ ★ ★

At first I didn't notice the marks. They must have been faint to begin with but after a time I could see, quite clearly, one dark print in the snow, then another, and another, quite far apart, then closer, too close for a man to have made them, so close and small, in fact, that I thought it must have been a child — a child of six or seven, walking on tiptoe for one of those serious games that children play when they are trying to deceive the whole world. I remember doing it myself, as a boy, trying to pull a fast one, trying to become something I wasn't. When I was nine, just before we moved to the Whitland house, I had a game of pretending to be dead, just lying on the bed with pennies on my eyes and a white sheet drawn up over my face — and this was the same kind of game, this clever deception by some kid who had heard the old story, a trick that was just minor and innocent enough to be almost convincing. Almost, but not quite. That wasn't what mattered: it's not the purpose of the game to replace one fixed reality with another, the idea is to suggest a variation, a possibility. Like telling a story. It's not meant to be true, but it has to be real, it has to *run*.

But how could it have been a child? The snow had only just begun to settle, and it was early, early enough for a paper boy, maybe, but then he'd have other things on his mind, like delivering his round as fast as he could and getting back into the warm. Besides, when I looked closely, I could see they weren't just random marks in the snow. There was detail to them, fine ridges, barely smudged in the new snow, like the tracks an animal leaves — a fox, or a cat, maybe. Yet they were too large for any animal that might pass this way, so close to the water; too large, probably, for any animal not in a zoo. I had slowed down, again, to study the prints; then I realised that whatever, or whoever, had made them had passed through only minutes before and, with that thought in my mind, with the notion that I might catch sight of this mystery creature, I quickened my pace and went on, following the tracks along the shore road and up, past the Baptist church, past the old bakery, and along Toll Wynd, where my usual walk broke away along the coast path and left the pavement behind.

★   ★   ★

This was the story I told myself for years: one night, while the people of Coldhaven slept, the devil walked out of the sea, up from the west shore, along Shore Road, passing the brae that led to my front door, heading away inland, to nobody knew where. Nobody knew where he was going, or why he chose that particular spot to make his presence visible. Nobody knew where he'd come from, either, but I suppose they imagined some other dimension, some dark place under the earth, and some fault line where the land meets the sea, a gap between this world and another kingdom, another realm, a separate world like the separate world where God dwells, forever in the present tense. But there wasn't a separate world, there was only this: the air, the sky, the snow, these strange marks, the water, the odd gust of wind finding me as I followed the tracks to where they stopped, all of a sudden, at exactly the point where my path diverged from the road. Now, there was no other world; perhaps there never had been. But how could the devil disappear? I had always thought that he — or she, or it — was an invention, a corruption of some older and finer presence, some god of the earth, some spirit that stitched everything together, stitched it with sap and blood and birdsong and made it whole. Before it became the devil, that spirit had been something else — an angel, Pan, the *genius cucullatus*, some wandering breath of wind or light that touched a man from time to time when he was working in the nether field, or steering his boat through the fishing grounds, far at sea. The people had known it once and they had respected it; then the priests came, and they'd made it into something else. They took that bright, dark spirit and called it Satan, Beelzebub, Baal. The Devil. They didn't *want* to be stitched together with rocks and stones and trees, they didn't want to share their world with animals and birds and sprites. They wanted to be alone and separate. They wanted to own the land and have their God be a man, like them, so he could grant them dominion over the beasts of the earth. I had told myself this story because it was easy, and there was even a grain of truth in it — but there was another story, a story that was exactly the same as the first, except for the fact that it took into account the possibility that those old-time priests and landowners had loved the earth, and that they had also been touched by the breath of the spirit, only it had touched them with a terror they couldn't overcome, and their love had turned to fear.

Now, in this new story, they woke in the night and they were aware of something in the room beside the bed, and they realised, to their horror, that this *thing* they met in the fields, or on the fishing grounds, could follow them home and sit, biding its time, under their own roofs. They had thought it only existed out there, an unquiet grave in the meadows where the old spirit lay buried. Now they saw that it *had* been buried, but it wasn't dead, it couldn't be dead, it could only be hidden. With no small effort and a willed blindness to the things that moved in the night, in the grass, in their own flesh, it could be concealed almost indefinitely — or so they had hoped. But it couldn't be hidden for ever, and soon it began to reveal itself in all manner of signs and gestures and sly, fleeting hints of a terrible beauty and a terrifying wildness. The devil they knew, and the devil they didn't know. And maybe there were times when they suspected the devil wasn't a devil at all, but something worse. Why did they see possession in so many of their neighbours? Why were they so keen to drown and burn harmless old women in their market squares and on their shorefronts? Because *they* were the ones who were afraid of being possessed, *they* were the ones who thought that the day might come when a decent citizen was going about his ordinary business, walking his fields or steering his boat through the harbour mouth, and the devil would come and touch him on the shoulder, singling him out and taking him aside so he could see and hear and smell his own true self. There must have been times, in the life of every one of those upright men and true, when he imagined letting go of everything that kept him steady and allowing himself to slip into the incandescent calm of the truly possessed. They must have known how close it was: they could smell the sulphur, they could feel the heat of the flames. They were the devil's own;

they were his chosen. They knew, in their hearts, that the simpletons and scapegoats they tried and burned were nothing but unholy innocents. They knew, because they tasted the devil on their own lips, smelt him on their own hands. They woke in the night and something from the fields had followed them into their inner chambers to await its moment. All they had to do was open their hearts.

★　★　★

I didn't have a key to the house. Hazel had it, along with my money and my car keys. I stood a moment on my own front step and thought about what to do: I believe I stood there a long time before I remembered that I had always left a key to the French windows under a plant pot on the patio. It was bitterly cold, and still dark, but I found the key, managed, on my third attempt, to open the French windows and — finally, with a sense of resuming a life that had been suspended for years — stepped inside. The house was cold — and as soon as I was in, I knew, not only that it was empty, but that it had been empty for some time. Amanda was gone. Not out for the night, or staying over with one of the girls, but *gone*. I walked through the kitchen into the sitting room, then into the hall. It was cold and still and silent. In the darkness, I found the controls for the central heating and turned everything on. Then I went back to the kitchen, switched on the light and filled the kettle.

It was only after I'd made the tea that I noticed the changes. Everything was neat and clean, as if Mrs K had been there just a few hours before, but I sensed that something was wrong. I walked through the rooms again, the sitting room, the hallway, the downstairs study that Amanda had insisted on calling the drawing room. And gradually, with something of an effort, really, I noticed that some of the things were missing. Furniture, a few pictures, ornaments. Amanda must have taken them with her when she'd left — which meant, presumably, that she was never coming back. I walked to the foot of the stairs and listened. I have no idea why I was being so careful; it was perfectly obvious that the house was empty. But I was excited and, at the same time, I was becoming superstitious: I really *was* resuming my own life, the life that had been set aside when Amanda moved in, the life my parents had gifted to me, and I didn't want anything to spoil it. I didn't want to presume. I started up the stairs. Somewhere outside, like a sound effect from an old

B movie, an owl called. It was up on the driveway, in amongst the trees that separated our house from the road, and I guessed it was a tawny owl, but I wasn't sure. Naturally, my father would have known.

Upstairs, the clearances had been even more extensive. My little box room was exactly as I had left it, but most of the things in the other rooms that weren't nailed to the floor or the wall had been taken away. In what Amanda always referred to as the master bedroom — presumably because, when we were first married, it had been the room where we both slept — every stick of furniture, every ornament, every picture had been carried away. Even the lampshades were gone. Not that it mattered very much to me. She had always thought of those things as hers and, to be fair, she had been the one who spent hours driving around the furniture stores on the big retail estates in Dundee and Edinburgh, picking out things that she liked and deciding which of them *went together*. It had always been a mystery to me, how it was decided that one thing went with another, beyond some basic rules of colour and style, but I hadn't much cared and I was quite happy to let her get on with it. The trouble was, as the new things started arriving, old things had been disposed of, one way or another, to give them room. My parents' old bed, for example, was gone now, consigned to an auction house in St Andrews — which meant I had nowhere to sleep. My own childhood bed, a narrow little single of a thing, was — presumably — in the attic, where I had stored it. Amanda had wanted to get rid of it but I couldn't quite bring myself to let it go. Just as well now, I thought.

I wasn't disappointed. I didn't feel let down. I had no one to blame for this situation but myself, and I certainly didn't want Amanda back. Still, I have to admit that I felt a moment's sadness, standing there in that empty room, staring at the rectangle of thick grey dust where the bed had been. I crossed over to the window and stood next to the smaller, but equally dense, square of dust that marked the former site of her dressing table and looked out. This was one of my favourite places in the house, high up on the third floor with a big bay window looking out over the point. How often had I stood here, gazing at the stars, or the lights of the night-fishing boats as they made their way out to the fishing grounds? I had stood here and listened to the wind on stormy nights when I couldn't sleep, and I had sat in the big chair by the window while Amanda slept, after we had spent half the night talking and making love in the first, almost happy days. Now, there was nothing — or rather, there was something at once worse and more beautiful than nothing because, in that corner, there was a faint, but unmistakable scent, the scent of Amanda in all her aspects, nearly eight years of her sitting at her mirror, applying perfume and discreet touches of make-up, eight years of fleeting conversation and silence and beautification perfectly mapped out on the floor. I studied the space where the dressing table had stood and I saw that it was nothing but dust — there were no spills of perfume, no stains of lipstick or eyeliner, no smears of rouge or mascara or the exotic powders that I couldn't even name — but that dust was saturated with the scent that this particular woman had possessed, a combination of skin and hair and lips, mingling with years of art and weather and accident. I looked; I smelt it all; I breathed it in — and yes, for a moment I was sad for our tiny local failure; and for the promises we had meant to keep, years before we learned not only that we had nothing in common, but that we had each intended something quite different by those promises than the other had understood.

★   ★   ★

Amanda had left me a note. For some reason, I hadn't noticed it when I'd come in, all powdered with snow, my face and hands numb with cold. I think I'd felt the change to the house from the first, the emptiness in the sitting room and the study, the bare, almost weightless sense of the rooms upstairs, and I'd been distracted. Now, in the kitchen, as I refilled the kettle — I was so glad she hadn't taken the kettle — I noticed the envelope on the table, so I opened it up, while I waited for the water to boil. It didn't say much. She had written it for herself, really, as a justification, or maybe as a dutiful last act. Not that she owed me anything, or needed to justify herself. Whatever had come about, I had brought it upon myself. The note was fairly long and I couldn't read it all the way through, but it started off well, and I was glad of that, for her sake. Still, I didn't read more than a few lines: whatever she had to say, it was of no real consequence to me. She had left, and that was all that mattered. I hoped she would find someone else, or even some other way of being happy, but, in truth, Amanda was already far in the past. What mattered now was tea, warmth, toast, butter, somewhere to sleep. Of course, there was no butter, and no bread; but there was tea in the cupboard, still in the old caddy my mother had used, and there was sugar, which would have to stand in for milk at this early hour before the shops opened. Not that I was going to the shops, of course. I was exhausted and, no matter how hungry I was, what mattered most was sleep.

Still, I couldn't help taking a look around the place once more before I turned in. It had been my parents' house, the house where I had grown up, then it had been my solitary refuge, a place apart that had never quite rejoined the world, even when Amanda had come up from the town and started buying all those curtains and pieces of furniture. It was my home, the only one I had and yet, for a while, I didn't really recognise it. I went from room to room, quietly taking stock of what had been taken away and what remained. Most of Amanda's decisions were choices I could have predicted: she had taken everything that she had picked out, over the years, and left whatever survived from my parents' time. Here and there, though, there were odd oversights and omissions: some of her clothes still hung in the wardrobe and, downstairs in the hall, the raincoat she had bought on a trip we'd made to Brussels was still on its usual peg. She had taken all but one of the personal pictures, but I couldn't see why she had left that single snapshot, sitting on a shelf in its beechwood frame, a picture of the two of us, along with some people I didn't recognise, in the kind of clothes people wear to special occasions. I had no memory that I could associate with that picture, nor even the vaguest idea of who was being baptised, or given the keys to the house, or engaged that day. I had no memory of the occasion itself, of where it had taken place, or the time of year. I couldn't remember who had invited us, or who else had been there. I didn't even recall ever having seen this photograph before, but what I noticed, now, was that, while I was gazing straight into the camera, Amanda was looking through the picture to thc person behind the lens, a person with whom, it was quite obvious, she shared a secret — and suddenly, in that moment' recognition, at the moment at which I realised, for the first time, that she had been betraying me all along, I felt a surprising rush of warmth, of fondness even, for the woman in the photograph. I had been married to her for close on nine years, and now, looking at her in this snapshot, she seemed little more than a passing acquaintance: familiar, yes; but not particularly vivid. I felt a surge of warmth, of what I suppose might be thought of as empathy. Then I went back upstairs, threw some duvets and covers down on the floor of the master bedroom, and went to sleep.

* * *

When I woke it was early morning, and I could tell the snow was still falling from that greyish, forty-watt-light-bulb effect on the walls. I lay awake for a while — a few minutes, half an hour, it was hard to know — then I got up and went to the window. I had a sudden, unwanted image of my father, living out his last weeks in this room, more or less alone, but happy, I think, with his situation. It seemed to me that, towards the end, he had chosen a different order, a different pattern from the one he'd known all his life. He'd known what the cost would be all along, but he'd had no choice. He might have regretted his isolation, but he had the pictures he was making and, even if nobody had ever seen them, or even if they saw what he had done and missed the point entirely, it didn't matter. He had no choice; that was the thing. Or rather, he had made the only choice he could: to withdraw from the lesser, more local patterns, in order to work through to something wider. It was the only choice he could make, not because he had lost his faith when Thomas Mallon died, or because, when he came to Coldhaven, his neighbours had disappointed him, but because what he had come to think of as his real work, his vocation, demanded a calculated withdrawal, an utterly unwitnessed solitude. It was a choice that could as easily have been accomplished in London, or New York; there had been no need to run away from anything. But he had needed the symbolism of the move, he had needed to find a place where nothing mattered to him, a place that had nothing to offer him, other than the light. That was why he had come, first to Coldhaven, then to Whitland: for the light. It was a choice he would have had to make even if he hadn't been a photographer. He had to close himself off in one direction, in order to be open in another.

That was what I was thinking, that morning, though thinking isn't really the right word. It was half-thought, half-dream, an in-between state where time doesn't operate in the usual way, a brief gap in the self-consciousness that gets in the way of understanding. I had never understood my father; I had never understood either of my parents, but it occurred to me that I had known them, and knowing them had been enough. I have no idea, now, whether they ever believed that they knew me. I don't think there was much to know, in truth, though I am sure they did their best. For myself, I couldn't help thinking that, for the first time, I knew where I was, and what I had come to, and I was convinced, suddenly, that it was what I had wanted all along. What I had never realised, at fifteen, or thirty, or two months before, was that I had always wished that I would come to where I was then: the dusk of a winter's morning on the streets and the houses, dusk on the point, the starlight above the firth a perfect echo to the night boats coming in, and someone watching it all from an upper room, a man who might as easily have been someone else but, as it happened, was me: a quiet, solitary man in a world lit by new snow, leaning towards the window and touching the dark, empty pane, to feel the cool of something other than the night, remembering his fingers through the glass.

★   ★   ★

I woke again, in what felt like the middle of the morning, in a pale, lemony glow that I thought at first was daylight. It was very warm and, with the strange light, it was like waking on a summer's morning: birds

303

singing, a sense of something green some-where, a taste on the air of new sap. For a minute or so I just lay there, floating; then I remembered where I was, and what had happened. I sat up. The yellow light was coming from the windows, but it wasn't daylight; someone had put up a pair of fine, almost transparent curtains and, on the floor by my makeshift bed, had left a vase of flowers — or not flowers so much as twigs and branches from the shrubs in the garden, mixed with a few tired-looking chrysan-themums and forced pinks. I was confused. I didn't remember those curtains — they certainly weren't Amanda's taste — and the vase was just as unfamiliar, though it was less unexpected, a large, almost classical glass piece of the type Amanda might have bought. More confusing was the realisation that someone had been there while I was asleep. Had Amanda come back? Why hadn't she wakened me? It wouldn't have been her style to let me sleep, so we could talk about things sensibly in the morning. But if it wasn't Amanda, then who was it?

I got up. I felt gritty and a little smudged, from the heat and from sleeping in my clothes. Normally there would have been a clock in the room, a radio alarm thing that Amanda used to get herself up for work in the morning. She had set it to Radio 1, because she liked Radio 1, or maybe because I didn't. Now it was gone: no great loss, but I had a sudden need to know what time it was, what was happening in the world, what the weather would be. I walked over to the window and drew the curtains. Maybe they had been there when I'd gone to bed, and I just hadn't noticed them. Maybe — but I didn't think so. I seemed to remember the night at the window, a hint of starlight, a suggestion of snow. Now, looking out, I saw that it had snowed heavily while I was sleeping. The garden had disappeared, all that remained of the shrubs and the lawn, even the trees, was a thick, unmarked blanket of soft new snow and, though there was a cool, orange and pearl light in the distance, it was evident that more snow was on the way. I was surprised, then, because it seemed that so much had happened in a few hours — and then, for the first time, it occurred to me that I might have been asleep longer than I had thought. At the same time, I heard a sound and I turned to face the door.

It was Mrs K. She was standing in the doorway with an apron hanging loose around her neck. 'I saw you were back,' she said, in her usual no-nonsense manner.

'What time is it?' I asked. I was oddly relieved — I had half expected it to be

Amanda or even, without the least trace of logic to the notion, Hazel.

Mrs K smiled — to herself, mostly — and shook her head. 'What day is it, would be more like,' she said.

'Sorry?'

'It's Thursday,' she said. 'You got home on Monday night, if I'm not mistaken.'

I stared at her. She looked different, I noticed, a little thinner, a little less severe. I did the arithmetic and shook my head. 'That can't be right,' I said.

'Trust me,' she said — and I could see that she was serious. 'You've lost a little chunk of your life,' she added. 'Still, when your body tells you to sleep, you have to sleep.' She considered me a moment, serious, cool, a little curious, then she finished tying her apron strings. 'Anyway, you'll be hungry,' she said. It wasn't a question. 'I'll make you some soup.' She turned to go. 'Have a shower,' she said. 'Everything was turned off when Mrs Gardiner left, but I see you've put the heating on, and there's plenty of hot water.' She started away down the stairs, back to her kitchen. 'It's good that you're home,' she called softly, talking as much to herself, it seemed, as to me.

The Curlew Sandpiper

Almost a year has passed since then. I haven't done much to the house — it felt better half-empty and, besides, I wouldn't have wanted to fill the gaps Amanda left with anything other than my parents' old furniture, which was, by now, long gone. Burned on bonfires at Hallowe'en, sold off to students in bedsits, or packing the furnished houses that the Gillespies and the Hutchisons rented out, it would have been unrecognisable, one way or another. It amazes me, now, that I agreed to get rid of so many of my father's things, in particular; but then, I must have been attached, in some way, to Amanda, and I was — I see it now, after all this time — I was, and still am, grieving. What I'd tried to do was abolish my grief by starting a new way of life, inventing a new house, becoming a new man — as if grief could be abolished, as if a house could be made new, as if a man could become anything other than a truer version of himself. I was an idiot, and I chose a strange way of realising it. I could have sat up here in this room above the point, with my face to the window, and worked things out for myself. All I had to do was learn to stop thinking about it.

As far as I know, Hazel has disappeared. Nobody ever found out about our brief adventure — it was just assumed that she had run off with the Boyfriend. There was a big fuss about the car and my lost credit cards, about why I hadn't reported them missing sooner, and where I had been when they went missing. For a while, I even thought I was under suspicion, not for abducting Hazel, but for fraud. It went on for some time, and I had some awkward moments: I didn't want to get into trouble, but I didn't want to say or do anything that might connect me to Hazel and her friends. I just wanted to get back home and be alone. As it happened, my little chats with Dr Gerard helped: the authorities eventually took the view that I had been suffering from depression when I lost the car and my wallet and, later, when the car was found abandoned in the middle of a roundabout — it had been trashed, of course, but then Hazel couldn't have known that was what those boys would do — the insurance people took a remarkably soft stance. My premiums went up, and I had various other items of business to attend to. But I didn't care. It takes a while for some things to be over, even when they are done with. There are always two endings to everything, an inner and an outer. The world takes a while to catch up, that's just the way of things, but when the inner and the outer got back in step, I was alone, and nothing else mattered.

Mrs K comes up the rise from time to time, but not to clean. Not now. We have a pot of tea and some Digestives and she gives me all the latest gossip. She looks warmed-up, somehow, a little happier and, though it's hard to say how, a little prettier. She looks more like herself, I suppose; one day, perhaps, she will tell me what has changed to make this so. What I can say is that I never see the ghost of Ingrid Bergman in her face these days. She's just Mrs K.

After my long walk home, everything seemed to begin again, from scratch. I was ill for a while, which probably had something to do with it, but even after I was well I was like a baby, learning what it likes and doesn't like: foods I had eaten before had no appeal, other things, things I had never even thought to eat, became staples of my new regime. Music sounded different. Everything tasted and smelt and felt different. After that first night, I took to sleeping on the floor. I rearranged the furniture that remained to make it more like it was in the first place. Everything is mine now. I live here.

Out along the coast, the wading birds gather. Sandpipers, curlews, turnstones, oystercatchers feeding in the shallows. My walk takes me out that way, these days. I try not to disturb the birds, to creep up on them and not frighten them off, so I can begin to learn what I never bothered to learn, in all these years of living on the coast. The colours of their different plumage. The size and call of each bird. The way one differs from another. The food they eat. Their mating habits. I have my father's binoculars and field guides to help me. I suppose I'm making something up to him by doing this, but it's not just that. I really do want to know those names and shapes and songs. I want to know what he meant when he said his favourite bird was the curlew sandpiper. I want to know what he felt, out in the wind of a morning, watching the birds, breathing the same air they breathed.

I rarely go into Coldhaven now. Sometimes, in winter, when the wind off the sea is hard and icy, I wander through the little wynds and out along the shorefront, past the shops, past the Baptist church, past the old library. When it snows, I go out early, following the usual route, but not really looking for signs. Sometimes I see Tom Birnie out in the early morning cold, his face haggard from illness and dismay. It turns out he wasn't the devil after all; he was just a man. Maybe he goes out early because he needs space to think, to work out what happened to his life. Maybe he is trying to figure out some kind of penance or explanation, or perhaps some excuse. I feel sorry for him, I suppose. I never speak to him, or give out any signal that I know who he is, but there are times when I want to take him out to the point and show him the birds.